Allergic to Death

Peg Cochran

BERKLEY PRIME CRIME, NEW YORK

THE BERKLEY PUBLISHING GROUP
Published by the Penguin Group
Penguin Group (USA) Inc.
375 Hudson Street, New York, New York 10014, USA

Penguin Group (Canada), 90 Eglinton Avenue East, Suite 700, Toronto, Ontario M4P 2Y3, Canada (a division of Pearson Penguin Canada Inc.) • Penguin Books Ltd., 80 Strand, London WC2R 0RL, England • Penguin Group Ireland, 25 St. Stephen's Green, Dublin 2, Ireland (a division of Penguin Books Ltd.) • Penguin Group (Australia), 250 Camberwell Road, Camberwell, Victoria 3124, Australia (a division of Pearson Australia Group Pty. Ltd.) • Penguin Books India Pvt. Ltd., 11 Community Centre, Panchsheel Park, New Delhi—110 017, India • Penguin Group (NZ), 67 Apollo Drive, Rosedale, Auckland 0632, New Zealand (a division of Pearson New Zealand Ltd.) • Penguin Books (South Africa) (Pty.) Ltd., 24 Sturdee Avenue, Rosebank, Johannesburg 2196, South Africa

Penguin Books Ltd., Registered Offices: 80 Strand, London WC2R 0RL, England

This is a work of fiction. Names, characters, places, and incidents either are the product of the author's imagination or are used fictitiously, and any resemblance to actual persons, living or dead, business establishments, events, or locales is entirely coincidental. The publisher does not have any control over and does not assume any responsibility for author or third-party websites or their content.

PUBLISHER'S NOTE: The recipes contained in this book are to be followed exactly as written. The publisher is not responsible for your specific health or allergy needs that may require medical supervision. The publisher is not responsible for any adverse reactions to the recipes contained in this book.

ALLERGIC TO DEATH

A Berkley Prime Crime Book / published by arrangement with the author

PUBLISHING HISTORY
Berkley Prime Crime mass-market edition / August 2012

Copyright © 2012 by Peg Cochran.
Cover illustration by Teresa Fasolino.
Cover design by Sarah Oberrender.

ISBN: 978-0-425-25146-1

BERKLEY® PRIME CRIME
Berkley Prime Crime Books are published by The Berkley Publishing Group,
a division of Penguin Group (USA) Inc.,
375 Hudson Street, New York, New York 10014.
BERKLEY®PRIME CRIME and the PRIME CRIME logo are trademarks of
Penguin Group (USA) Inc.

PRINTED IN THE UNITED STATES OF AMERICA

10 9 8 7 6 5 4 3 2 1

ALWAYS LEARNING   PEARSON

To Krista Davis,
without whose help, mentoring,
encouragement, brainstorming and door-opening,
my dream would not have come true!

Acknowledgments

First, my mother who nurtured my love of reading and with whom I share a love for words.

My husband, Fletcher, who shares my excitement as if it were his own.

My two beautiful daughters, Francesca and Annabelle, who always encouraged me to go for my dream.

My sister, Chris Knoer, who created the pork tenderloin with spinach and feta recipe and allowed me to share it in this book and who is just possibly even *more* excited than I am to see this book in print.

The Guppies—a wonderfully supportive Internet writing group.

My Plothatcher buddies who were always there with a suggestion, encouragement and sympathy—Avery Aames, Laura Alden, Janet Bolin, Krista Davis, Kaye George, and Marilyn Levinson.

My agent, Jessica Faust, and editor, Faith Black, who helped make the book as good as it could be.

Various other friends and family who have been supportive over the years—Esther Benz, Mary Loudon, Cathy Sciarappa and Olive Bragazzi.

Chapter 1

"I'm not a cheater."

"I didn't say you were, Mrs. Nagel." Giovanna "Gigi" Fitzgerald sandwiched the phone between her ear and shoulder and pulled a sheet of golden brown, homemade melba toast rounds from the hot oven.

"It's just that your diet isn't working for me."

Gigi remembered the last time she'd delivered a meal to Mrs. Nagel—there had been a waterfall of cookie crumbs cascading down her ample front, even though she insisted she never ate anything except the gourmet diet food Gigi delivered three times a day.

"Unless I see some results soon, I'm going to have to demand my money back."

Gigi glanced at the plaque over her sink—*I have an Irish temper and an Italian attitude*. Right now, she was trying to display neither. But it wasn't easy. Patience didn't generally go hand in hand with red hair.

She made some sympathetic noises, encouraged Mrs. Nagel to try again and finally hung up. She had very little time to finish lunch preparations and get the food delivered.

With a fine brush, she glazed each melba toast round with a whisper of extra virgin olive oil, then followed with a scant teaspoon of finely chopped fresh tomato and basil marinated in balsamic vinegar. Finally—the pièce de résistance—a shiny, black Kalamata olive placed dead center on each.

Gigi tucked an unruly curl of dark auburn hair behind one ear, pulled her calculator from the drawer and plugged in the calories for all the assembled items. She frowned at the total, worrying her lower lip between her teeth, and made some calculations on a sheet of white scratch paper. Finally, she plucked the olives from each round, cut them precisely in half and placed just one half on each piece of melba toast. She plugged the revised numbers into the calculator. Bingo. Just the right amount. Her customers, all eager for immediate and spectacular results, expected her to keep their daily calorie allotment to a meager but delicious number.

It was difficult, but not impossible. Gigi's diet theories were simple—only eat real food, watch your portion sizes and don't waste calories on junk. Unless the junk happened to be strawberry Twizzlers, in which case all bets were off.

Gigi swept up the discarded olive halves and, one by one, popped them into her mouth. She grinned. She was always willing to take a caloric hit for her customers even though she continued to struggle with the unwanted five pounds that had ushered in her first birthday after the big three-five.

She packed two of the toast rounds into each of a dozen cardboard containers festooned with *Gigi's Gourmet De-Lite* in silver script. Her eye caught sight of the day's crossword puzzle folded open on the table. *Four across: To get by (with out)*. That was easy. She paused briefly and penciled in *eke*. Eking out was the story of her life at the moment. Although things were bound to pick up now that she'd snared Martha Bernhardt as a client. She was the restaurant reviewer for the *Woodstone Times*, Woodstone, Connecticut's local paper. She could really give Gigi's business a boost. As long as nothing went wrong. Gigi stuck out her index and little fingers in the time-honored gesture meant to ward off the evil eye of the jealous.

Her red MINI Cooper was waiting in the driveway of her cottage. She'd traded in the overly extravagant engagement ring her miserable, no-good, cheating ex-husband had given her and used the money to buy the car. So far it had been a most satisfying trade. The car was far more reliable than Ted had ever been.

Gigi pushed open the screen door with her hip, the first stack of boxes balanced in her arms, her chin tucked on top to keep them steady. She loaded them carefully into the backseat of the car and returned to the kitchen for the next batch.

With the last load of containers stowed in the car, she paused to look up at the sky. Dark clouds swirled overhead, and the previously warm May breeze had a frigid edge. Gigi slid behind the wheel just as plump drops of rain splattered across the windshield and a jagged bolt of lightning rent the darkening sky.

People were running for cover along High Street, Woodstone's main street, by the time Gigi got there. The wind swirled a sheet of newspaper down the gutter like a mini tornado, and a woman struggled with an inverted umbrella, her bright red skirt a blurry drop of color through Gigi's rain-washed windshield. Gigi idled at the light and watched as the woman yanked open the door to Bon Appétit, the town's gourmet and cookery shop, and disappeared inside.

The light changed, and Gigi slowly stepped on the gas. She passed the Book Nook, where she imagined she could see the vague outline of her friend and the owner, Sienna Paisley, through the rain-streaked window. Right next door was the Silver Lining, a jewelry store specializing in hand-crafted pieces that tourists from Manhattan snapped up despite the stratospheric price tags. Gigi crested the hill that led away from town and toward rolling, green hills and open meadows. Right at the top of the hill stood the Woodstone Theater, a converted barn that was home to Woodstone's amateur theater group.

Gigi pulled into the gravel parking lot and maneuvered as close to the front door as possible. Several of her clients would be there, busy rehearsing for the opening of *Truth or Dare* the first weekend in June, when tourists would swarm like unwelcome ants over the quaint and charming town of Woodstone.

Gigi stacked up containers for Barbie Bernhardt, Alice Slocum and the star of the upcoming play, Adora Sands. She was grateful that for lunch, at least, so many of her clients were grouped together. A short run down the other side of the hill and she would be able to deliver Martha's four-hundred-calorie repast as well. It saved gas and wear and tear on the MINI. Gigi craned her neck. Although, maybe the extra trip wouldn't be necessary. Wasn't that Martha's dark blue Honda Element in the back row next to the idling black Mercedes?

Gigi risked freeing one hand to pull open the front door to the theater. She held it wedged with her knee and crooked elbow as she slipped past and into the darkened foyer. Even though it was gloomy outside, the contrast still made her stop for a moment and blink. One of the inner doors was propped partially open, and a chink of light spilled across the foyer floor. Somewhere to the left she could hear hammering and someone humming, and from the theater itself she heard raised voices.

Gigi edged through the inner door and paused for a moment. The actors were assembled on stage, a man facing them. Gigi recognized him as Hunter Pierce, the play's director. Although the theater was hot and stuffy, he was wearing a worn tweed jacket with patches at the elbow. His black hair was combed straight back, bits of scalp gleaming between the greasy strands.

He gestured toward the telephone that squatted on one of the tables onstage. "We must reset the phone." He pointed a long, imperious index finger at a young stagehand in baggy overalls. "Move it to that table over there. It's just not working where it is." He waved at the other corner of the stage and stood back, watching as the young man repositioned the offending instrument.

Pierce clapped his hands. "Okay, costume call, everyone. Let's go," he lisped in his slightly effeminate voice.

A low grumbling rose from the stage.

"We're hungry," came a plaintive wail from upstage.

"And tired," another voice added.

"And hot," someone else contributed from downstage.

Pierce clapped his hands again, more briskly this time. "Costume call, please. We must act like professionals if we are going to give our audience a professional performance."

"If we were professionals, we'd have Actors' Equity to protect us, and we'd get breaks every hour and two hours for meals," someone shouted from downstage.

Pierce pursed his lips in displeasure and craned his neck to see who had spoken.

"Gigi's here with our lunch." A woman—Gigi thought it was Alice Slocum—approached the edge of the stage and peered into the audience, a hand over her eyes to shade them from the stage lights.

"This will only take a minute." Pierce snapped his fingers.

The cast reluctantly got in line and came and stood at the front of the stage while Pierce made notes on a clipboard, occasionally exchanging remarks with a mousy woman in a black dress who had appeared from backstage. She had pins in her mouth and bits and pieces of different-colored threads stuck to her bodice.

Alice stepped forward and turned slowly in a circle.

"Where's the sweater?" Pierce flipped through several pages of notes. "The little blue cardigan?" He sketched an outline with his hands.

Alice stuck out her lower lip and blew a puff of air that flopped her frizzy gray bangs up and down. "It's too hot." She folded her arms across her chest and glared at Pierce over the footlights.

"I want to see the sweater," Pierce lisped petulantly. "Don't you understand? It positively defines your character."

Alice raised an eyebrow.

Pierce sighed. "Sylvia is a cautious woman. And a modest one. She hides behind her clothes. The sweater gives her a feeling of being protected. You can't really get a feel for Sylvia as a character without the sweater."

Alice spun on her heel and exited the stage, a mulish look on her face.

"Next," Pierce demanded.

Finally, the entire line had trooped dutifully past, including Alice, who had the blue cardigan draped over her shoulders.

"Adora? Where is Adora?" Pierce demanded, looking around. "Where has she gotten to? And Emilio?" He stalked up and down the stage muttering, "Very unprofessional," under his breath.

Someone tapped Gigi on the shoulder, and she spun around with a stifled cry.

"I'm starving. Where's my lunch?" a young man demanded.

Gigi began to stammer. The fellow wasn't one of her clients. Did he think she'd brought food for everyone? He was wearing a T-shirt, shorts and heavy work boots and had cropped blond hair.

Gigi squinted at him. Could she possibly have forgotten a client?

"Adora. There you are." Pierce leaned over the edge of the stage, wagging his finger. "Now where's Emilio?"

Gigi squinted at the young man again and realized it was Adora Sands in costume for the part she was playing in *Truth or Dare.*

The androgynous outfit did little to hide Adora's ample curves, which strained her thin cotton T-shirt and shorts as well as her credibility as the boyish Tina. The shorts were still way too tight. Adora had insisted on having them a size smaller in anticipation of losing weight. If she stuck with the twelve hundred calories of food Gigi delivered daily, she would certainly lose, but on more than one occasion, Gigi had noticed grease from chips on her fingers or a dab of chocolate at the corner of her mouth. Gigi sighed.

Adora took the container with her name neatly printed in the corner, whipped it open and stared at the contents. She'd pulled off the short wig, and her own blond tresses cascaded to her shoulders. "I could eat three of these," she moaned, gesturing at the meal Gigi had delivered. "Pierce has been working us hard all morning. We've burned millions of calories, I'm sure."

"Well, you can't have mine," said Barbie Bernhardt, clutching her container of food to her chest. She was pretty in a cotton candy kind of way and already had a figure to die for. But as the "trophy" second wife of rich investor Winston Bernhardt, she had to stay on her toes. Someone even younger, more attractive and with a better figure, might come along and snatch him away at any moment.

Which is exactly what Barbie herself had done, or so Gigi had heard—stealing Winston right out from under Martha Bernhardt's nose. Barbie and Martha were icily polite with each other whenever their paths crossed, with Martha's mouth set in a permanently bitter line and Barbie looking as smug as a cat that had discovered crème fraîche.

Adora took out a piece of melba toast and downed it in one bite. She closed her eyes. "Mmmmm, you do manage to make things taste delicious." She ran the tip of her tongue languidly across her lips.

"I don't know about you all, but I'm going outside for a breath of air." Barbie tossed her blond ponytail over her shoulder. "It's beastly in here."

"Don't bother, *cara mia*, it's raining." A man appeared from the shadowy depths of the theater, his shirt darkened with splotches of rain. He shook out his umbrella before placing it across one of the seats.

Pierce scowled at him over the footlights. "Emilio. You're late."

"I am so sorry."

"Well, I'm going outside anyway. Winston's here," Barbie replied sulkily. "We'll sit in the car, I guess."

Emilio shrugged. "Bon appétit."

"Where's Alice?" Gigi looked around, holding the last of her Gourmet De-Lite lunches.

"Here I am," a voice sang out from the darkness, and Alice made her way toward them, her gray hair frizzed out around her like a halo. She took her lunch and sighed, weighing it in her hand. "Not enough here to keep a bird alive," she grumbled.

"Now, Alice, you know if you want to lose enough weight in time for your daughter's wedding, you have to make some sacrifices," Adora purred.

Alice shot her a look. "Please. You don't have to remind me. I have to look good for my daughter in front of that . . . that woman."

"The future mother-in-law?" Emilio reached toward Alice's open container, and she playfully slapped his hand away.

"This is mine, and I'm not sharing. I can't. I need every bite Gigi allows me." She took out one of the melba toast rounds and delicately bit it in half. "Mmmm, delicious, as always." She licked the tips of her fingers. "Yes, you could say we're having in-law problems already. Or, at least I am." Alice sighed. "She's a perfect size six, and she's bought the perfect dress for this perfect wedding for the perfect couple," Alice mimicked in a chirping falsetto. "And I perfectly despise her! Look at me." She gestured toward herself. "I'm a perfect whale!"

"You're going to be beautiful," Gigi reassured her.

"It's just that we were in high school together," Alice mumbled around another bite of melba toast. "And she always thought she was better than me. She stole the first boyfriend I ever had. Just once I'd like to get the better of her."

"You will. You've lost weight already, and you'll lose even more before the wedding."

Alice raised her chin slightly. "You're right. I can't let her get me down. Besides, it's going to be my Stacy's special day, and that's all that matters."

Gigi glanced at her watch. "I've got to get the rest of my meals delivered." She looked around the darkened theater. "I thought I saw Martha Bernhardt's car in the parking lot."

Alice gestured toward the back wall with her chin. "She's in the office, I think. I heard her on the phone when I went back to get Pierce's stupid sweater. Sounded really furious with someone."

Gigi found her way to the corridor that ran behind the stage. The bare lightbulb hanging from the ceiling didn't even begin to penetrate the gloom. Suddenly, one of the doors opened, and a woman brushed past her, jostling her elbow.

"What a waste of time," the woman muttered under her breath. "People just aren't reliable anymore."

"Pardon me?" Gigi swiveled around and realized it was Martha Bernhardt who had bumped into her.

Martha turned toward Gigi. "I'm sorry. I didn't mean you." She peered at Gigi more closely. "Oh, it's you. Have you brought my lunch?"

"It's in my car just outside."

"Well," Martha sniffed loudly. "At least the morning won't have been a complete waste, then."

Martha's cheeks were flushed, and her pointed nose quivered with indignation. Her black hair was swept off her high forehead and teased and sprayed into a bouffant, chin-length flip. She might have been called attractive, but with her features set into rigid and bitter lines, she was merely forbidding.

She followed Gigi out to the parking lot, her black cape swirling around her legs.

It was raining heavily. Gigi could see Barbie and Winston huddled together in the front seat of his Mercedes. Martha noticed, too, and scowled at the car as she stomped toward Gigi's MINI.

"Why don't you hop in, and I'll drive you over to your car?" Gigi dashed around to the front door and pulled it open. The rain was heavier, and cold drops slid down the back of her shirt.

Martha got in beside her, her cape tucked under her. It made the interior of the car reek of wet wool, and Gigi wrinkled her nose as she turned the key and put the car in gear.

"I'm very grateful, Miss Fitzgerald," Martha said when they pulled up in front of her Element. She accepted her Gourmet De-Lite container and opened the door. Gigi watched as she dashed toward her car, pulled open the door and stuck her head inside.

Gigi was about to pull away when Martha began backing out of the driver's seat of her Element, her broad backside aimed in Gigi's direction. She turned toward Gigi and gestured wildly, her mouth moving furiously. Gigi buzzed down her window.

"Someone's stolen my purse. It was right here on the front seat. And now it's gone."

"Did you lock your door?"

"No, of course not. This is Woodstone, not New York or Detroit or someplace like that."

"I have my cell. We can call the police." Gigi twisted around and pulled her bag from the backseat.

Martha shook her head. Rain dripped off the end of her sharp nose and her hair was slowly deflating in the humid-

ity. "Never mind. The police station is just down the road.
I'll drive over and make a report. Not that it's going to make
any difference. They're unlikely to ever find the thief. I don't
know what this town is coming to—"

"If you're sure . . ."

Martha nodded and slid into the front seat of her Element,
rolling down the window. "It's going to be dreadfully annoying, canceling all the credit cards and all, but fortunately I
rarely carry much cash. If memory serves, I had around five
dollars and eighty-nine cents in my wallet." She pursed her
lips thoughtfully. "Well, I'll just have a tiny bite of my lunch
first." She opened her Gourmet De-Lite container and
extracted one of the melba toast rounds. "Heavenly! Absolutely heavenly."

She crammed the rest of the piece of toast into her mouth,
nodded at Gigi, rolled up the window, put the car in gear
and drove slowly out of the parking lot.

Gigi followed behind her. They passed the Knit Knack
Shop on the right, and then Folio next to it. Gigi made a
mental note to call to see if her new stationery was ready.
They were passing the Take the Cake Bakery when Martha
began driving erratically, weaving back and forth along the
narrow lane and nearly bumping the curb at one point. Several pedestrians drew back from the road and into the shadows along the storefronts.

What on earth was Martha doing, Gigi wondered? Was
something wrong?

Gigi watched helplessly as Martha swerved across the
center yellow line. The Element jumped the cobblestone
curb in front of Bon Appétit and headed straight for one of
the massive oak trees that lined the sidewalk.

Chapter 2

"*Mama mia*, you look terrible, *cara*. What happened?" Emilio Franchi rushed forward, wiping his wet hands on the apron tied around his substantial waist.

"There's been an accident." Sienna urged Gigi forward into the sheltering depths of Al Forno.

The restaurant was empty. The lunch crowd had finished their meal, and the after-work crowd hadn't yet arrived. A waitress was replacing burned-out candles on the tables, while a busboy whistled tunelessly to himself as he bundled up dirty tablecloths. Carlo Franchi had his back to them, writing specials on the blackboard that hung over the bar. Today they were offering osso buco Milanese and chicken francese. Tantalizing aromas drifted from the kitchen, infusing the air with the scent of garlic, lemon and thyme.

"Carlo," Emilio called, snapping his fingers.

Carlo whirled around, chalk in hand.

Emilio motioned toward Gigi. "Get our friend a drink, quick."

Carlo turned back toward the bar, his hand hovering over several bottles.

"A whiskey," Emilio called to him after another look at Gigi's face.

Carlo selected a bottle, twisted off the cap and poured a generous splash into a tumbler. He slid the glass of amber-colored liquid across the counter toward Gigi. "Drink," he commanded, his brown eyes dark with concern.

Gigi's hand shook as she picked up the glass. She took a sip and sputtered as liquid heat slid down her throat. Slowly the shivery feeling in the pit of her stomach was replaced with spreading warmth. She put the glass down with slightly steadier hands.

"Tell us what happened?" Carlo looked from Gigi to Sienna and back again.

Sienna perched on the stool next to Gigi, her long cotton skirt tucked around her legs. Carlo held up the bottle of whiskey, but she shook her head.

"Just some water, please."

Carlo grabbed a large fluted glass, dug ice out of the freezer and filled it to the top with water. He set it on the counter in front of Sienna, then looked at Gigi. "You're not hurt, are you? You said there's been an accident?"

Gigi nodded. The scene had been playing over and over in her mind like a tape, only in long, drawn-out slow motion—Martha's car gliding across the center line, into the other lane, over the curb and finally straight into an oak tree whose limbs were bursting forth with spring greenery. A sickening *thud*, leaves and small branches swirling down, people dashing forward, voices raised and yelling. She shuddered.

The police and an ambulance from Woodstone General had arrived almost immediately, their sirens tearing through the quiet of the weekday afternoon. Gigi had waited, pacing, as emergency crews spent an hour extricating Martha from the crushed Element.

They were loading her onto a gurney when Sienna came running out of the Book Nook, pausing only long enough to lock the front door. She took Gigi gently by the arm and urged her down the street and into the safety of Al Forno.

Emilio slid behind the bar, chose a wine glass from the shelf and filled it with merlot. "Tell us what happened, *cara*." He took Gigi's empty whiskey glass and pushed the wine toward her.

"I don't know." Gigi twirled the wine glass between her fingers. "Martha was driving just in front of me. All of a sudden she started weaving all over the road." Gigi made a wavy motion with her hand. "Her car went up over the curb and hit the tree in front of Bon Appétit."

Sienna pushed a hand through her long mane of curly, honey-colored hair. "I wonder what happened. Did one of her tires blow?"

"I don't think so." Gigi glanced at her friend. "I didn't hear anything, and I would have, wouldn't I?"

Emilio *thunk*ed his chest with his fist. "It was probably a heart attack."

"You might be right." Gigi had another sip of her wine. She was starting to feel better—less cold and shivery. "Her purse was stolen while she was at the theater. She was furious. Maybe that caused a heart attack?" She looked from Carlo to Emilio.

"Hooligans," Emilio shook his dish towel in the air. "Carlo? Remember old Mr. DeSapio?"

Carlo nodded. "Certainly, Uncle. I was just a little boy.

Before we came to this country. Poor Antonio." He glanced at Gigi and Sienna. "He had a heart attack."

"He was driving?"

"Yes. Followed by an accident. Same thing, he hit a tree."

"There was only one difference," Emilio chuckled.

"That's right," Carlo began to laugh, too. "He was riding a bicycle."

They both burst out laughing then, and Gigi and Sienna joined in.

"If you could have seen him." Carlo wiped tears from his eyes with the edge of his apron. "Wobbling like crazy, then, *bam*"—he punched his fist into his palm—"right into the tree."

"I'll never forget it." Emilio opened the oven and slid a pizza from its wood-fired depths. He cut it deftly into eighths, the pizza wheel biting easily through the thin, blistered crust.

"I do hope Martha will be okay," Gigi said as Emilio slid the pizza onto the counter and handed out plates and small paper napkins.

"Me, too." Sienna swirled the ice around in her glass. "Wasn't she going to do a whole write-up about your gourmet diet business?"

Gigi nodded. Just her luck. She'd finally snagged a client who could help her publicize her business, and now look what had happened. Martha had had a whole series planned for the newspaper—complete with recipes and before and after pictures. Gigi mentally shook herself. Poor Martha was possibly fighting for her life in the hospital at this very minute, and here she was moaning about her lost opportunity.

The bell over the front door tinkled, and Alice Slocum burst through it and into the restaurant. Her hair was even more disheveled than usual, with drops of rain glittering on the ends of the curling, gray strands.

"Have you heard?" Her voice was breathless. She bustled over to the bar, where she eyed the pizza longingly.

"About Martha's accident?" they chorused.

"Gigi"—Carlo put a hand lightly on her shoulder—"actually saw it." Gigi could feel the warmth of his palm through her blouse and felt herself beginning to blush.

"You know she's dead?" Alice's eyes nearly bugged out from beneath their shaggy brows.

"No!" Gigi half rose from her seat.

Alice nodded and absentmindedly grabbed a piece of pizza and took a huge bite. "I heard the guys talking about it when they got back to the station." Alice worked part-time as a secretary for the Woodstone Police Department. "It's hard to believe. I just saw her at the theater this morning, and now . . ."

"Was it a heart attack?" Gigi asked while simultaneously raising an eyebrow at the piece of pizza in Alice's hand.

Alice put the slice down abruptly. "I don't know. No one does. The docs still have to do the autopsy. But what else could it have been?" Alice shook her head.

The bell over the front door tinkled again, and everyone turned in that direction. Adora Sands strode in, snatching a scarf from her head and shaking off the raindrops. Her unnaturally bright blond hair tumbled in artfully created waves around her shoulders.

She was wearing a calf-length pencil skirt with an off-the-shoulder blouse and wide patent leather belt.

Sienna snorted when she saw her and leaned over to whisper in Gigi's ear. "Looks like Adora is channeling her inner Gina Lollobrigida."

Adora sidled up to Emilio and batted long, sooty eye-lashes at him. Emilio immediately reached for a glass and began to pour some wine. It sloshed over the side, and he apologized profusely, grabbing a rag from the bar and soaking up the small puddle.

"I've just heard the news, and it's all too dreadfully sad. Poor, poor Martha." Adora took her glass and perched on one of the empty bar stools. Emilio continued to fuss behind the bar, and Gigi noticed him glancing longingly at Adora.

"We weren't just neighbors, you know." Adora looked around the group, her eyelashes lowered demurely. "We were friends as well." She put a strong emphasis on the word *friends*.

"That why she came to see you this morning?" Alice asked with what looked to Gigi like a slight smirk.

"To see me?" Adora fiddled with her cocktail napkin. "She didn't come to see me. What ever gave you that idea?"

"What was she doing at the theater, then, I wonder?" Alice plucked an anchovy off the remaining piece of pizza and popped it into her mouth.

"I . . . I . . . don't know." Adora's hands fluttered to her face. "Something to do with repairing the air conditioner, I think." She gave a loud sniff. "I can't believe she's gone." She reached for a napkin on the bar and pressed it to her eyes. She gave a sob, and Emilio rushed over to pat her shoulder.

"Let's just hope she got the air conditioner fixed before she died." Alice rolled her eyes. "Especially if I have to wear that blasted sweater."

Adora gave another sob. "How can you say that when poor, dear Martha is dead?" She buried her face in her hands. Emilio patted her shoulder harder, looking distressed.

Alice rolled her eyes again.

"I just hate to think of how frightened Martha must have been." Adora leaned back against Emilio and glanced at him over her shoulder.

"It must have been a heart attack, no?" Carlo looked around the group, his eyebrows raised. "Maybe she went like *that*"—he snapped his fingers—"and never knew what happened."

Adora smiled at him. "I hope so. I certainly hope so."

"Gigi said her purse was stolen and she was very upset."

Gigi nodded at Carlo. "Yes, and she was upset already. When I ran into her in the hall, she said something about the morning having been a complete waste of time."

"I feel so terrible," Adora said, looking anything but. "I never even said good-bye."

"*Cara*, please, do not upset yourself." Emilio hastened to refill Adora's wine glass. "We never know, do we? Life can be snatched away like *that*." He snapped his fingers and looked around the table.

Sienna insisted on driving Gigi home and helping with preparations for that evening's Gourmet De-Lite dinner.

"These smell divine. What did you put in here?" Sienna sniffed the pan of marinating chicken kebobs that Gigi pulled from the refrigerator.

"Lime juice, tequila, some chopped jalapenos and a bit of olive oil."

"Anything I can do to help?"

"Sure." Gigi grabbed a bowl of cut-up peppers, cherry tomatoes and onion wedges. "These need to go on skewers, then I'll go heat the grill."

Sienna set to work. "How's this?" She held up a skewer of alternating peppers, tomatoes and onions.

"Perfect." Gigi added one last tomato to the end of her skewer.

"Did you notice Emilio and Adora this afternoon?" Sienna fished an onion wedge from the bowl.

Gigi shook her head. "Frankly, I was too shaken up to notice much of anything. What were they doing?"

"Let's just say that Emilio seems quite taken with Adora, and vice versa." Sienna stabbed the last piece of pepper and held the skewer up triumphantly. "There!"

"Thanks." Gigi took the skewers, placed them on a baking sheet and brushed them with the marinade. "Carlo said Emilio hasn't been interested in much of anything since his wife died two years ago. Maybe Adora will bring him out of his shell."

"If she doesn't break his heart instead." Sienna wiped her hands on some paper towels. "I didn't realize Martha and Adora were such good friends."

Gigi shrugged. "Neither did I. They certainly don't seem like they'd have much in common."

A horn tooted just outside, and Sienna looked up. "That must be Oliver. Anything else I can do?"

"Thanks, no. You've been a great help."

"Feeling better?" Sienna put a hand on Gigi's arm.

Gigi shook her head. "I'll be okay. I'm going to get these meals finished and delivered, and then I'm going to spend some quality time with the television." She grinned as she pulled open the front door to the cottage.

Sienna waved from the driveway before hopping into Oliver's station wagon.

Gigi stood on the steps for a moment, admiring the pots of geraniums that flanked her front door. She pulled a few dead leaves off one and poked at the soil to see if they needed water. She rubbed at a spot on the shiny brass door knocker, which she polished weekly.

She got a thrill every time she realized this house

was hers. In a manner of speaking, of course—she was renting it, but saving every penny she could toward its eventual purchase. Martha Bernhardt had been her landlord. Gigi felt a frisson of panic. With Martha dead, what would happen to the cottage? Would a son or daughter or long-forgotten sister sweep in from some far-off place and demand the keys? She shivered. She didn't want to think about that.

Sienna had been the one who'd talked her into giving Woodstone a try, and together they had brainstormed the idea for Gigi's business. Gigi had felt like a fish out of water at first, but now she complained as loudly as the rest of them over the annual summer and fall influx of tourists from the city who crowded their shops and sped down their country lanes in expensive sports cars.

Her Italian grandmother on her mother's side always said, "It's all for the best." Maybe she was right. It had all started with a forty-thousand-dollar Versace wedding gown—one that Gigi had lost track of during a photo shoot for *Wedding Spectacular* magazine. Some assistant to an assistant would probably be sporting it at her own wedding in Brooklyn any day now.

Gigi still couldn't believe she had been so careless! She'd always prided herself on her organization—her spices were alphabetized, her taxes done by the afternoon of January 1, her Christmas wrapping finished while the Thanksgiving turkeys were mere babes. How could she have let it happen?

It had all been Ted's fault. Gigi slammed the front door and felt the satisfying shudder the house gave. She had to stop blaming Ted for everything. But if he hadn't devastated her by leaving, she certainly never would have messed up so badly and lost her job as food and entertainment editor of *Wedding Spectacular.* Ironically, he had left her for an older woman—just when she'd begun to fret about another birthday and being on the wrong side of thirty-five.

But then if it hadn't all happened, she wouldn't be here now. Maybe she should thank Ted instead of blaming him. She loved her little cottage, her business was taking off and there was Carlo.

But she didn't want to admit that last bit even to herself.

Gigi was taking the chicken and vegetable kebobs off the grill when she heard a car pull up outside, followed by the faint *thump* of the door knocker echoing from the front hall. She brought the platter in and set it on the counter. The chicken, grilled to a golden brown, continued to sizzle slightly, the bright red cherry tomatoes looked ready to burst and the green peppers were blistered and shiny.

Gigi glanced at her watch as she hurried to the foyer. She could see the hazy outline of a man through the sheer curtains covering the windowpanes of the Dutch door. A salesman? she wondered. She didn't have much time. She had to pack up the dinners and be on the road shortly. Her clients were usually too hungry to be kept waiting.

"Yes?" Gigi opened the top half of the door and looked out.

"Ms. Fitzgerald?"

"Yes," Gigi repeated.

"Detective Bill Mertz. May I come in for a minute?"

Gigi unlatched the bottom half of the door and opened it. She supposed he had come to talk about Martha's accident. A policeman at the scene had taken down her name, phone number and address.

"Do you mind terribly if we go into the kitchen? I was right in the middle of something."

He was tall, ramrod straight and looked as if he'd been chipped out of stone. Sharp blue eyes, light brown hair cut short and precisely parted and thick, and straight brows gave him an air of authority that came off him in waves and nearly vibrated in the small space of Gigi's front hall.

She felt herself bristling and was tempted to click her heels as she turned and led him down the hall and into the kitchen at the back of the house.

He looked around without saying anything, legs slightly apart and hands clasped in front of him. Gigi moved to the tiny work island where she had Gourmet De-Lite containers lined up and ready. She grabbed the platter of kebobs, placed them on a wooden chopping block next to the open containers and added one skewer of grilled chicken and vegetables to each. She paused and entered a number on her calculator.

She could sense Mertz watching her, and she felt her face getting flushed. She stole a glance at him out of the corner of her eye. He really was quite good looking. She continued to ignore him as she exchanged the pan of kebobs for a pot of brown rice pilaf. Carefully, she measured half a cup into each container and then punched another number into her calculator.

Mertz cleared his throat. "Do you mind if I ask you a few questions?"

"Certainly, but I hope you don't mind if I continue with what I'm doing." Gigi knew she sounded waspish, but she couldn't help it. He was making her uncomfortable. He reminded her of the guards at Buckingham Palace who never responded to what was going on around them. What would it take to make Detective Mertz lose his cool?

"I believe you witnessed an accident this afternoon in front of Bone Appetit," he said, mangling the pronunciation like so many of the denizens of Woodstone.

Gigi nodded as she took a ripe, round cantaloupe from the counter and placed it on a clean cutting board.

Mertz reached into the inner pocket of his jacket and pulled out a pad and pen. He clicked the pen and held it poised over the paper. "Did you witness the entire thing?"

"Yes." Gigi shuddered and closed her eyes for a moment as the accident played through her mind. She wondered how long it would be before she stopped seeing it over and over again.

"Where were you standing?"

"I wasn't. I was in my car, right behind."

"Can you tell me, in your own words, what happened?"

Who else's words would she use? Gigi wondered. She selected a knife from her knife block—her biggest, sharpest chef's knife. She thought she noticed Mertz flinch slightly, and she smiled to herself as the knife sliced through the cantaloupe as if it were butter.

"I followed Martha out of the theater parking lot—"

"You were acquainted with the deceased?"

"Martha? Yes." Gigi held half the melon over the sink and scooped out the seeds. "Everything was fine, at first. We turned onto High Street and headed toward town. We were passing the bakery when Martha started driving strangely. She was weaving from one side of the road to the other, going back and forth across the yellow line. At one point she even hit the curb. I didn't know what to do. There wasn't anything I could do." She turned toward Mertz, palms up.

He nodded briskly. "Go on."

Gigi sighed. "That's it, really. She went up over the curb and hit that tree outside of Bon Appétit." Gigi shuddered. She scooped the seeds from the other half of the melon, then began to cut it up, putting a half moon slice in each of the containers.

"Did you speak to Ms. Bernhardt before leaving the parking lot?" Mertz looked up from his notepad.

"Yes. Yes, I did."

"Was she acting normally? Did she appear ill or agitated?"

Gigi took a container of blueberries from the refrigerator, where they had been macerating in a couple of tablespoons of orange juice and some artificial sweetener. She put a spoonful on top of each melon slice. "Not ill, no, but she was upset. Someone had stolen her purse."

Mertz jerked as if startled. "Her purse was stolen?" He scribbled some notes on his pad.

"Someone took it out of her car while she was in the theater. Apparently she'd left the doors unlocked."

"I wish the lovely people of Woodstone would realize it's not nineteen forty anymore. They can't go around leaving things unlocked." Mertz sighed and ran a hand through his cropped hair. "Did you happen to notice if she ate anything while she was at the theater?"

"As a matter of fact, yes." Gigi began closing up the containers. "I'd just delivered her lunch—"

"She was a client of yours?" Mertz's eyebrows rose slightly as he gestured toward the containers on Gigi's counter.

Gigi nodded.

"And she ate something you'd given her before getting in the car?"

Gigi nodded again. "One of the melba toast appetizers I'd prepared for this afternoon's lunch."

"Melba toast? Did you buy them—"

"Of course not. I made them."

"That's all they were? Just toast?"

"No." Gigi ran through the list of ingredients. She couldn't imagine what Mertz was getting at. What could the melba toast possibly have to do with Martha having a heart attack?

"Any peanuts?" Mertz asked.

"Absolutely not." Gigi said emphatically. "Martha was deathly allergic to peanuts. It's one of the first things I ask a new client."

"So you knew Ms. Bernhardt was allergic?"

"Yes." Gigi closed the last container and paused with one hand on the lid. "But she had a heart attack, didn't she?"

Mertz shook his head. "The autopsy hasn't been performed yet, but the doctor is fairly certain she was in anaphylactic shock when her car hit that tree. And her medical records indicate a severe allergy to peanuts."

Gigi's hand flew to her mouth.

"You're certain that you did not use any peanuts, peanut oil or any other product containing peanuts in the preparation of the meal you delivered to Martha Bernhardt this afternoon?" he asked, sounding as if they were already in court.

Gigi shook her head so vehemently, her hair lashed from side to side. "No. Absolutely not. I don't even keep peanuts in the house." She gestured toward the pantry as if inviting him to look for himself.

"Thank you." Mertz replaced his pen and pad in the inner pocket of his jacket.

Gigi led him to the foyer and opened the front door. She watched as he walked down the path toward his car.

She knew she hadn't used any peanuts at all in Martha's meal.

But why did she have the feeling that Detective Mertz didn't believe her?

Chapter 3

Gigi put the keys to the MINI on the hook she'd installed next to the wall phone in the kitchen specifically for that purpose. A place for everything, she thought as she surveyed the room. She'd just delivered a dozen Gourmet De-Lite lunches, and now it was time to clean up.

She snapped on some rubber gloves and sprayed down the counters with cleaner. She enjoyed tidying. She liked seeing order slowly emerge from the chaos. Today she was tired, though. She'd tossed and turned most of the night listening to the rain lashing the windows and seeing Martha's terrible accident play out in her mind over and over again.

Then there'd been that very unsettling conversation with Detective Mertz. She rinsed her sponge and squeezed it out over the sink. She had the distinct feeling that he thought she'd been careless and had caused Martha to have an allergic reaction. Mertz himself had unsettled her, too. On the one hand, he rubbed her the wrong way. On the other hand, she found him impossibly attractive.

She cleaned the tops of her flour and sugar canisters and pushed them back into position against the wall. Spices next. She carefully inserted the paprika into the empty space on the rack between the marjoram and the sage and the tin of thyme between the sage and the dark brown bottle of vanilla extract. Sienna sometimes laughed at her system, but it was the only way she could be efficient enough to prepare a dozen meals three times a day.

She was hanging up the dish towel when the phone rang. Gigi grabbed the receiver and held it propped by her chin as she sprinkled cleanser into the sink. "Hello?"

Gigi hung up the phone with trembling hands. She couldn't believe the conversation she'd just had. She had to tell Sienna about it. She grabbed her coat and ran out to her car. The drive seemed to take forever, but finally Gigi was shaking out her umbrella and pushing open the door to the Book Nook. Sienna was behind the counter making notations on a computer printout.

"You won't believe what just happened," Gigi burst out before even saying hello.

"What?" Sienna pushed the stack of papers aside and leaned her elbows on the front counter.

Gigi's fingers itched to organize the papers, not to mention the entire counter, and, what the heck, do a little dusting while she was at it.

Sienna gathered her long, strawberry blond hair into a knot at the back of her neck and secured it with a pencil. "Carlo has asked you out?"

Gigi laughed. "No. Of course not. Don't be silly." The

idea made her stomach do strange flip-flops, and she could feel her face getting as red as her hair.

Sienna sighed. "I thought Italians were supposed to be so good with women. What's wrong with that man? Anyone can see he's crazy about you."

"He's just a friend," Gigi protested.

Sienna snorted.

The bell over the front door jangled, and Gigi turned gratefully in that direction.

"It's just me." Alice came into the shop, her raincoat glistening with moisture. She pulled off her hat and shook it over the front mat. "Will this rain never end?" She began to unbutton her coat. "But just so it doesn't rain on my Stacy's wedding day, it can flood for all I care."

"Come on. Let's have a cup of coffee."

They followed Sienna into the area known as the "coffee corner." Two faded sofas sat at right angles to each other, along with a cracked brown leather arm chair and an orphaned red corduroy ottoman. Richly colored shawls were draped over the arms, and soft pillows were stuffed into every corner. Delicious-smelling coffee gurgled from a gleaming chrome machine. The result was warm and inviting. Patrons were known to spend whole afternoons in the coffee corner, reading and perusing books.

Sienna often complained that that didn't do much for the Book Nook's profits, but so far she was making a go of it, selling new books as well as used. Not that Sienna really had to worry about money. Gigi sometimes envied Sienna her husband, Oliver, who worked on Wall Street and made more in a week than the Book Nook took in all year. Sienna herself had given up a six-figure income as a publicist when they'd moved to Woodstone in hopes of having a family. So far it was still just the two of them, with Sienna pouring all her energy into her bookstore. If she was disappointed, she didn't let on.

"Help yourself." Sienna gestured toward the coffee machine, which was now humming quietly.

Gigi grabbed two cream-colored mugs with *The Book Nook* written on them. She held one up to Alice.

"Sure. No cream or sugar." She shot a grin at Gigi.

Gigi filled the mugs and handed one to Alice. "Let me tell you my news."

"What news?" Alice asked eagerly, taking a seat on the sofa.

"Okay, shoot." Sienna filled a mug with hot water and added a strangely colored tea bag.

"Do you know Branston Foods?"

"Sure. They're that big place outside of town, right?" Sienna cradled her mug in her hands. "I've been caught in traffic out there a few times when the plant let out. It added twenty minutes to my trip." She repositioned the pencil in her hair. "Why?"

"I had a call from them today. Right before I got here." Gigi paused dramatically. "They want to talk to me about producing a line of diet foods." Her cup shook slightly, and she set it down carefully on the table. "Called Gigi's Gourmet De-Lite." Her voice cracked. "And they're going to pay me for the name and for me to come up with the recipes and . . . everything!"

Sienna whistled.

"That's fantastic!" Alice hooted.

"This means I can save money to buy my cottage from Martha's estate." Gigi smiled at them, but then her face clouded over. "As long as nothing goes wrong. I won't really believe it until the papers are signed and . . . and . . . everything." She surreptitiously stuck out her pinky and index finger in case any jealous, evil spirits were hovering over Sienna's shop.

"What could go wrong?"

Gigi thought of Detective Mertz, and she could feel the hot coffee sloshing around in her stomach. It made her feel like being sick.

"What's the matter?" Sienna leaned forward and put a hand on Gigi's shoulder.

"I had a visit yesterday from a Detective Mertz from the Woodstone Police Department. Apparently Martha didn't have a heart attack like we thought. She was in anaphylactic shock when she hit that tree."

"Ana . . . what?" Alice blew on her coffee and took a sip.

"It's a kind of shock caused by an allergy. Like to a bee sting. Or, in Martha's case, peanuts."

"So Martha ate some peanuts and—"

Gigi shook her head. "She knew she was deathly allergic. She'd never knowingly eat peanuts or anything with peanuts in it. Unfortunately, according to Detective Mertz, the last thing she ate was some of my Gourmet De-Lite food."

"But you knew she was allergic, didn't you?" Sienna frowned.

"Yes. But Detective Mertz doesn't believe me. He thinks I'm responsible." Gigi fiddled with the fringe on one of Sienna's throw pillows.

"So she must have eaten something else." Alice took another sip of her coffee and gazed longingly at the jar of chocolate biscotti Sienna kept next to the coffeepot.

"She must have. But how can we prove it?"

Alice stroked her chin. "If she had eaten something else, maybe there's a trace of it in her car somewhere."

"Like a candy wrapper or something?" Sienna refilled

her mug with hot water and swished the tea bag around and around.

"Exactly." Alice gave a last glance at the biscotti and then resolutely turned her back on the display. "Most of the cars get towed to Moe's over on Broad Street. It shouldn't be too hard to sneak in and have a peek." She looked from Sienna to Gigi and back again.

Gigi grinned. "What are we waiting for, then?"

Moe's was on the wrong side of Woodstone, near the bus depot and the electric plant. The rain had stopped, and the sun peeked through the parting clouds, sending waves of moist heat shimmering off the cracked sidewalks.

Gigi slid out of her raincoat and draped it over her arm. She could feel her hair curling around her face, and she knew, without looking, that her nose was as shiny as a beacon. They'd all been praying for warmer, sunnier weather, and now it was making them miserable.

Moe's lot was surrounded by a rusting chain-link fence with a sign out front that read *Moe's Towing and Storage*. Clumps of weeds poked through the crumbling macadam, and next to the front gate a ramshackle, windowless shed leaned drunkenly to the right.

Gigi picked her way along the buckling sidewalk. A trickle of sweat slid down her back, and she shivered.

"It's probably best if Moe doesn't see us," Alice whispered, pointing toward the shed.

Gigi and Sienna nodded and followed Alice as she tiptoed past the open door under cover of the red tow truck parked out front.

She stopped when they were out of earshot of the shed and scratched her head, gazing at the cars, lined up row after row, in various stages of decay, the sun glancing off their metalwork. "For some reason I thought this was going to be easy," she whispered. "How are we going to find Martha's car among all these others?"

"What kind is it?" Sienna asked, craning her neck and looking in every direction.

"It's a dark blue Honda Element." Gigi's spirits sank at the sight of so many cars. It had sounded like a good idea while they were sitting in the Book Nook, but it now looked like an impossible task. If her whole life didn't depend on proving that Martha hadn't died from eating her food, she'd be tempted to give up and go home.

"Let's split up and take it row by row," Alice decided. "And stay low. We don't want Moe to see us."

Gigi started down her appointed row, rushing toward a dark blue car that just might be . . . she stopped short, disappointed. It was a Volvo station wagon with the front end pushed in and the bumper missing. Gigi continued down the aisle, her knees slightly bent so that her head was hopefully not visible above the car roofs. She'd rounded the corner of the next row when she heard a low growling sound. She stopped to listen for a moment, but all she could hear was her own heart thumping like a bass drum. She took a cautious step forward. *Grrrrowl.* There it came again. The hair on the back of her neck stood at attention. She stayed perfectly still and looked behind her and to the sides. A mangy, matted mutt slunk out from between two cars and stared at her, head lowered. Gigi smiled, inanely hoping the animal would sense she wanted to be friends. Well, not friends exactly, but hopefully not dinner, either.

She barely allowed herself to breathe, wondering if she should put a hand out in a gesture of goodwill. The animal gave another deep, rumbling growl, and Gigi thought better of it. Every fiber in her being was twitching, urging her to run until she couldn't run anymore. The animal looked away, its attention caught by a crow landing on the hood of a nearby car. Should she make a run for it? Gigi hesitated, but then the dog swiveled its head back in her direction again, its eyes narrowed to mere slits.

What should she do? The dog took a step closer. Its ears were back and its tail up. Gigi tried to remember whether that was good or bad. Was it friend or foe? Another guttural growl told her everything she needed to know. Gigi had heard dogs were supposed to be able to smell fear. Was fear like sweat? Would her deodorant protect her? She gave a surreptitious sniff but couldn't smell anything herself. She tried thinking of lavender and vanilla and ocean spray, hoping to exude the scent of inner calm instead of the heart-crushing terror that had her in its grip.

Someone gave a long, low whistle. The dog's ears perked up and its head swiveled in the direction of the sound. Another whistle, and it padded off, tail wagging. Gigi had barely let out her breath when Moe appeared around the end of the row of cars. His teeth slashed a white line between the dark of his beard and the dark of his moustache, and black, curly hair sprouted around the knit cap he had pulled down to his eyebrows. Gigi dove between a Pontiac that was twisted on its axle and a Cabriolet that looked more like an accordion than a car.

She inhaled as Moe's overall-clad legs swished past, inches from her nose, and didn't exhale until he had disappeared into the tow truck, the dog perched beside him in the cab.

"I think I've found it," Alice called under cover of the departing backfire of the truck's engine. Gigi straightened up and saw a floral print scarf beckoning in the breeze three rows away. She headed in that direction.

"Is this it?" Alice pointed toward a boxy, dark blue car sandwiched between two hulking SUVs.

"It's an Element." Sienna checked the insignia on the rear of the car. "And it's blue."

"It looks like Martha's car." Gigi put her hands up to the glass and peered in the driver's window. "Yes," she gestured to Alice and Sienna. "I remember she had that ticket hanging from her rearview mirror." She pointed at a white square with *Paid. Hartford City Parking Garage* centered on it in black lettering.

Alice tried the door handle. "It's unlocked." She pulled open the door, releasing a *whoosh* of hot, baked air.

Gigi closed her eyes and crossed her fingers behind her back. They had to find something in Martha's car—a Snickers wrapper, the cellophane from a package of cookies, a half-eaten granola bar—something, anything that might indicate Martha had come upon some peanuts in something other than Gigi's gourmet diet food.

The inside of Martha's car was neat and orderly, with a pack of tissues on the dashboard and a black umbrella on the package shelf. Alice opened the glove compartment and turned up a couple of neatly folded maps, a plastic rain slicker in a travel case and the car's maintenance log.

"I don't see my Gourmet De-Lite containers." Gigi glanced in the front seat, then the back.

"The boys will have taken those," Alice said as she swept a hand under the driver's seat. "Nothing here except some spare change." She held out a quarter and two pennies.

Gigi crouched in the backseat and poked a hand around the edges of the cushions and then wriggled an arm under the front passenger seat. "Ouch." She pulled her hand out and examined the inch-long scrape on the back of her arm.

"Anything?" Alice rummaged in her handbag and handed Gigi a crumpled tissue.

Gigi pressed it to the blob of blood that had appeared on her wrist. "No candy wrappers, fast food bags . . . nothing."

"Just because we haven't found anything doesn't mean she didn't eat something." Sienna said trying to console her. "Maybe she put the wrapper in her purse?"

Gigi sighed. "Someone stole her purse. As a matter of fact, she was on her way to report it when she had the accident." She shook her head. "I know I didn't put any peanuts in Martha's food. There's got to be some other explanation." She turned toward Alice and Sienna. "But how am I going to convince Detective Mertz of that?"

Chapter 4

The police station was a square, red brick building that once housed a small knitting factory. The Woodstone Garden Club had hauled some elaborate cement planters in front of it, and members took turns tending the colorful red and white geraniums that did little to disguise the squat ugliness of the building's exterior. Gigi pushed open the front door, resisting the urge to whip a tissue from her bag to clean the smeary fingerprints off the dirty glass.

She hoped Alice and her other clients would enjoy the lunch she'd prepared—a new recipe that combined canned tuna and cannellini beans in a lemony vinaigrette with plenty of chopped, fresh parsley.

She went up to the reception desk that was screened from the public by a thick piece of glass. It, too, was in desperate need of washing. Gigi wondered if it was bulletproof. She shuddered. Not that there were all that many shootings in Woodstone. The only one she knew about had happened more than thirty years ago when some longtime resident came home to find her husband in bed with her best friend. She'd tried to make her displeasure known via a shotgun but, fortunately, her aim was terrible, and she'd merely nicked his ear. The story might have died down long ago, except the participants themselves were particularly fond of telling it and had managed to keep it alive even as they approached their golden wedding anniversary.

Gigi peered through the smudged glass and into the small room beyond. An empty swivel chair was pushed back from the desk as if its occupant had gotten up in a hurry. There was no one else in sight. Gigi thought about tapping on the glass, but then someone came into view, edging sideways into the cubicle. She saw Gigi and leaned over toward the window, speaking into a microphone embedded in the glass.

"Help you?"

"Thanks. I have a delivery for Alice Slocum." Gigi brandished the Gourmet De-Lite container in front of the window.

The woman picked up the phone and stabbed several numbers. Gigi could see her mouth moving but couldn't hear what she was saying.

She heard the front door open and footsteps clatter across the tile floor. Gigi felt her breath catch in her throat. What if it was Detective Mertz? The thought of running into him made her feel queasy. She hoped Alice would come out soon and get her lunch.

Gigi peeked over her shoulder and gave a sigh of relief when she realized it wasn't Mertz. She heard a buzz, and a door opened.

Alice stuck her head around the open door and gestured to Gigi. "Come on back for a sec. I want to show you this adorable garter I found for Stacy. It plays the Wedding March when you push a button."

Gigi somewhat reluctantly followed Alice through the door and into the rabbit warren of corridors and hallways that made up the Woodstone Police Department. She just hoped Mertz was occupied outside somewhere. Or, better yet, was on vacation or something.

"My cube's right over there." Alice pointed to a tiny space under a high, multipaned window that was flecked with dirt. Several tottering stacks of paper were visible over the waist-high wall that ringed the desk.

"Alice?" A male voice came from somewhere behind them.

Gigi stopped and closed her eyes for a second. It sounded like Mertz. Please let it not be Mertz, she prayed silently.

She turned around.

It was Mertz.

"Can I speak to Miss Fitzgerald for a second?"

Alice shrugged and looked at Gigi, then at Mertz, and then back again.

Gigi had a feeling she knew what Alice was thinking. And she didn't like it. Why on earth did every person in the entire town of Woodstone feel it their duty to try to fix up unmarried women?

The look on Mertz's face made Gigi's mouth go dry.

Alice looked back and forth between them again and waved a hand. "Go on, don't let me stop you."

Gigi ran her tongue over her lips. "If I could get a glass of water?"

"No problem."

She followed Mertz down the corridor, trying to guess by his posture whether he had something good or bad to tell her, but it was useless. Mertz walked as if he were on parade—shoulders back, chest out, head high. He stopped at the water cooler, filled a paper cup and handed it to her.

Gigi was horrified to see that her hand was shaking. She took a quick sip to wet her mouth.

"We sent the food and the containers found in Ms. Bernhardt's car to the lab." He motioned toward the box in Gigi's hand, and Gigi realized she was still clutching Alice's lunch. "They appear to be the same as that one there."

"They are—were," Gigi stammered. What was he getting at? "I told you. I had just delivered them to Martha and my other clients at the theater."

"And you still maintain that you didn't use any peanuts in the preparation of Ms. Bernhardt's dinner?"

"No, I didn't." Gigi felt her face get hot. What did he want her to do, swear on the Bible or something?

Mertz nodded and regarded her gravely. "Can you explain, then, why the lab found peanut oil all over the food?"

Everything stood still, and Gigi heard a weird *whoosh*ing noise in her ears. Mertz's face swam hazily before her eyes, and her heart pounded against her ribs as if it wanted to get out. "What?" she demanded. Her life was ruined. She could see it passing in front of her eyes as if she were drowning.

Her right hand squeezed the paper cup convulsively, crushing it and sending a geyser of water down the front of her blouse.

Gigi thrust Alice's lunch at her and fled, leaving Alice open-mouthed and stammering. She delivered the rest of the lunches in a fog. Her hands shook on the steering wheel, and she could barely concentrate. At the corner of High Street and Cherry, she nearly went through a red light. She stopped just in time but not without her brakes screeching hideously. An older woman walking her dog gave her a strange look, and Gigi felt herself flush with embarrassment. She really shouldn't have been driving at all, but she had her meals to deliver if she hoped to keep Gigi's Gourmet De-Lite afloat.

Although that looked to become a losing battle. When people found out about Martha and the peanut oil, she'd be ruined. It wasn't her fault, but how would she convince everyone of that? She didn't know what she would do if her business failed. She'd have to leave Woodstone and maybe go back to the city. She couldn't bear it again—the noise, the smells, the traffic.

She had to talk to someone. Up ahead she could see the curly black lettering of the sign for Al Forno. She thought of Carlo. Why not? He was always so easy to talk to. She put on her blinker and made a left turn into the small parking lot carved out of the space between Al Forno and Gibson's Hardware next door.

At the back of Al Forno there was a flagstone terrace, just beyond which the ground sloped gently toward the small river that ran through Woodstone. Gigi noticed that today the tables were out with their bright red striped umbrellas fluttering in the brisk breeze. Several patrons sat outside enjoying their lunches, their water glasses sweating in the sun.

Gigi went through the door into the darkened interior. The air was redolent with the scent of garlic, olive oil and herbs. She felt her stomach rumble appreciatively. The lunchtime crowd had arrived, and the low hum of voices drifted toward her along with the melodic tinkle of cutlery and occasional clash of crockery. Carlo was behind the bar, and Sienna was half perched on one of the stools, a beaded and mirrored Indian bag slung over her shoulder. Emilio turned around with a stack of menus in his hand. He waved Gigi over.

"Cara." He kissed her on both checks then stepped back to look at her face. *"Mama mia*, what is it? Another accident?" He whirled around toward the oven, where Carlo was sliding a pizza out on a long, wooden paddle. He snapped his fingers. "A whiskey, Carlo, for our Gigi."

Carlo put the pizza on the counter and reached for the bottle. "What's wrong?" he called over his shoulder.

"Nothing. I'm fine," Gigi protested as she waved the whiskey away. "I can't. I'm driving. Although not very well," she added as she perched on the edge of the stool.

"An aperitif, then." Carlo selected another bottle and a tiny glass. "It's just a drop of vermouth." He pushed the glass across the bar toward Gigi. "It can't hurt you."

Gigi took a cautious sip and turned toward Sienna. Her face was blotchy, and her eyes were red and puffy, as if she'd been crying.

"What's wrong?" Gigi asked in alarm, putting a hand on her friend's shoulder.

Sienna shrugged then gave a halfhearted smile. "Nothing, really. Just the same old, same old. This time I really thought . . . you know. But the test was negative." She swiped at a tear that had escaped and was rolling down her cheek.

"I'm so sorry." Gigi knew how anxious Sienna was to have a baby. The thought gave her a pang. She'd been hoping that she and Ted would consider a family as well. Now she didn't know if motherhood would ever be in the cards for her.

Sienna looked away. "It's not that." She looked back at Gigi briefly, then down into her lap. "I think Oliver is losing interest in . . . in . . . having a baby."

"Why? What makes you think that?"

"Nothing, really." Sienna kneaded her hands in her lap.

"It's just that I think he's seeing someone in the city," she blurted out.

Gigi wasn't sure what to say. She took a sip of the vermouth Carlo had poured her.

"Is there something in particular . . ." Gigi paused, trying to think of a way to put it delicately. She didn't want to ask outright if Sienna had found lipstick on her husband's collar or another woman's phone number in his pocket.

"No . . ." Sienna hesitated. "It's just a feeling. He's coming home late more and more often, and when he does, he goes straight to the computer and doesn't even want to talk. I know he's been under a lot of stress lately." Sienna threw her head back and shook out her hair. "Well, I'm probably just imagining it! I always get sort of . . . weepy . . . around this time. It's probably just my imagination."

Carlo disappeared through the swinging door into the kitchen and returned with a Styrofoam container in his hand. It made Gigi think of the Gourmet De-Lite box she'd given to Martha, and she felt her spirits sink again.

"Here we are," Carlo said, handing it to Sienna, "one Caprese sandwich to go. Made with toasted flatbread, a walnut-and-basil pesto, tomatoes and of course the freshest mozzarella." He kissed the tips of his fingers.

The front door opened with a discordant jangle of bells and Alice strode up to the counter. "What the heck was that all about?" Her brows were furrowed in concern as she stared at Gigi. "You blew out of my office so fast I never got to show you that garter I bought Stacy or the cute miniature candy dishes we've settled on for the table gifts."

Gigi sniffled.

"Did something happen with Mertz?"

Gigi nodded. "The lab discovered the food I prepared for Martha was covered in peanut oil. I know I didn't use any peanut oil in making Martha's lunch. Or anybody else's for that matter."

"The police aren't blaming you." Alice ran a hand through her gray curls. "They think it was an accident."

"But that would mean I'd been criminally careless in preparing Martha's food," Gigi cried. She began to shred the edges of her cocktail napkin.

"That's obviously not the case, so someone must have gotten to the food and tampered with it." Sienna pulled her long hair over one shoulder and began to plait it.

Gigi shivered. "But that would mean someone did it on purpose. To try to . . . harm . . . Martha." She couldn't quite bring herself to use the word *kill*.

"Who would do something like that?" Carlo pulled a large jar of sliced olives from under the counter, emptied the contents into a stainless steel bowl and put it next to similar bowls filled with grated cheese, sliced mushrooms and chopped onions.

"Who knew Martha was allergic?" Alice looked from one to the other of them.

"Obviously, I did," Gigi began.

"It's news to me." Sienna tossed the finished braid over her shoulder.

"Me, too," Carlo said, and turned around to busy himself with some bottles on the bar.

"Why would anyone want to hurt Martha?"

Alice snorted. "Maybe it was a restaurant owner upset by one of those savage reviews of hers."

"Which restaurants has she reviewed lately?" Sienna opened her Styrofoam container and picked at the crust of her sandwich.

There was a crash, and everyone looked toward Carlo, who was quickly righting a toppled wine bottle and swabbing at the spilled liquid with a bar cloth. "Don't be silly," he laughed. "No one would kill because of a bad review." He glanced toward Emilio, who was busy serving a table of six businessmen in dark suits. "Would they?"

"They'd have to get in line," Alice laughed. "Martha hardly ever liked anything she reviewed."

"I heard her arguing with someone on the phone at the theater that day," Gigi said.

"Who was it?" Sienna broke off another piece of her sandwich.

Gigi shook her head. "I don't know."

"Doesn't matter." Alice eyed Sienna's sandwich longingly. "Martha argued with just about everyone at one time or another."

"Does someone benefit with Martha dead?" Sienna said.

"Everyone?" Alice said, and began to laugh.

"Seriously," Gigi pleaded. "There must be someone who benefits."

"Find out who benefits and who hated her, and you'll probably have your man."

"Or woman." Sienna leaned forward with her hands clasped on the bar.

"That's what I have to do, then," Gigi declared, slipping off her stool in her excitement. "I have to find out who might have wanted Martha dead, tell the police and let them investigate. Then everyone will know it wasn't my food that killed the poor woman."

If only it were that easy, Gigi thought later as she prepared plank-grilled salmon with garlic, ginger, lime and teriyaki glaze. What was she thinking? She didn't know the first thing about investigating. She could certainly ask a few questions and keep her ears open, but what good was that going to do? She pulled the strings off snow peas and blanched them briefly in boiling water before plunging them into cold. The couscous was ready—she just had to add the fresh vegetables and pineapple.

Gigi fluffed the couscous with a fork. It wouldn't hurt to find out if anyone had been seen loitering around her or Martha's cars that afternoon. Maybe someone had seen something and just didn't realize its importance. Because someone had to have gotten into her car to doctor Martha's meal, and the theater was the only place they could have done it.

Tonight, though, she wasn't going to think about Martha, peanuts, Detective Mertz, Gourmet De-Lite, Branston Foods or much of anything at all. Tonight she was going to enjoy herself. As soon as she'd delivered her meals, she was heading to the Silver Lining. The owner, Yvette Mathieu, was having an opening for a young silversmith she'd recently discovered in Soho, and Gigi was invited. Sienna and Oliver were going to be there, too, and she'd heard that Adora had been invited, as well as Barbie and Winston Bernhardt. If she kept her ears open, she might learn something of interest. And if not, at least it would be an evening out.

When Gigi arrived downtown, all the parking spaces along High Street were taken, and she had to circle the block twice before she found a spot for the MINI. The front door to the Silver Lining was propped open with a rock, and the sounds of a string quartet, combined with the low murmur of voices, drifted out to her as she made her way toward the brick-fronted building. She'd dressed up in an ice blue silk sheath and strappy, high-heeled silver sandals that made negotiating the uneven sidewalk a challenge.

In front of the shop, tethered to a parking meter, was a rakish-looking West Highland white terrier. He tilted his head to one side and watched as Gigi approached. He looked so earnest, she had to stop to say hello. She stooped down, as carefully as she could in her tight skirt and unaccustomed footgear, and gave his head a scratch. He licked her face, and Gigi giggled. She would love to have a dog. It got lonely at times in her little cottage, and it would be wonderful to have a companion. She gave the Westie a final scratch. She wondered whose dog he was—perhaps his owner was inside the Silver Lining.

The store was packed with people standing shoulder-to-shoulder in the small space. Gigi hesitated on the doorstep, craning her neck to see if she spotted anyone she knew.

"Excuse me." A man brushed past her and leaned out the open door.

It was Winston Bernhardt, rather formally dressed in a dark suit, white shirt and striped silk tie. "I just need to see what that beastly cur is up to." He gestured toward the dog Gigi had been petting.

"That's your dog?" Gigi looked out the window to where the little Westie was lying, his head resting dejectedly on his front paws. She didn't think he looked beastly.

Winston grunted. "He's my penance, you might say," he sighed, "for being far too easygoing. The beast belonged to Martha, my ex. There was no one else to take him on, so I offered. Otherwise he would have been put down. Still might do it in the end," he muttered half under his breath.

"Oh no!" Gigi exclaimed. "He's such a sweet little guy. What's his name?"

"Reg. Stupid name for a dog, if you ask me."

"You wouldn't really put him down, would you?" Gigi glanced out the window again to where the Westie, seemingly aware of the sudden attention, cocked his head to one side, looking bright and alert.

"Just might," Winston grunted.

"I'll take him," Gigi blurted out, surprising herself.

"Really?" Winston had stepped just outside the door and was lighting a cigarette, his hand cupped around the match. He looked from Gigi to the dog and back again.

"I won't take him back, you know"—he drew on the cigarette hungrily—"if you change your mind."

Gigi shook her head. "I won't change my mind."

"He's all yours, then." Winston took a few more puffs on the cigarette, dropped it to the sidewalk and ground it out with his heel before elbowing his way back into the crowd massed inside the Silver Lining.

Well, it looked as if she had a dog, Gigi thought. She went back to the curb, gave little Reg a pat and told him not to worry, she wouldn't be all that long.

Inside, the Silver Lining was hot and crowded with bodies pressing against the glass display cases, drinks in hand. Gigi inched her way toward the bar and accepted a glass of tepid chardonnay from the white-jacketed bartender. Waiters circulated with silver trays of hors d'oeuvres. She spotted a platter of bacon-wrapped water chestnuts, did some mental math and realized she was looking at over one hundred calories per mouthful. She hoped none of her clients would go near that particular appetizer.

Yvette Mathieu, the owner of the Silver Lining, stood in the middle of the room, arm-in-arm with a young man in a nineteenth century–looking frock coat, his black hair pulled into a tail at his nape and tied with a velvet ribbon. Yvette, appropriately enough, had prematurely silver hair cut in an asymmetrical bob. She wore a simple black dress accessorized with an elaborate silver necklace and had a burnt velvet shawl over her bare shoulders. Guests swirled around them, shaking the young man's hand and air-kissing Yvette.

Gigi looked around. The room swarmed with the sort of people who lived in the enormous houses that were springing up around the town—Wall Street types who spent their days in the city and only came home to Woodstone to sleep. They bought up older homes, tore them down and replaced them with "McMansions." On weekends they roared up and down High Street in their fancy cars, spending money in the shops long-time residents couldn't begin to afford.

Gigi clutched her drink, feeling slightly ill at ease in the midst of such an upscale crowd. Her dress, which had seemed perfectly appropriate in the sanctuary of her bedroom, suddenly felt common and uninteresting. She sighed with relief when she spotted Sienna in front of one of the display cases, her elbows on the glass. She was wearing a floaty pair of *I Dream of Jeannie* pants and a gold silk Indian blouse with a tiny, raspberry red handbag with silk tassels hanging from her shoulder.

"Where's Oliver?"

Sienna whirled around. "I wish I knew." Her shoulders sagged dejectedly. "He was supposed to meet me here"—she consulted her watch—"over an hour ago. There's no answer at his office, and his cell phone is turned off."

"Maybe his train is late?"

Sienna gave a small smile and patted Gigi's arm. "I've run through every excuse I could think of already." She shook her head. "Something is going on. I'm afraid I put too much stress on him with this whole baby thing."

Personally, Gigi thought Sienna was being too kind. If Oliver was really all that stressed out, he needed to talk to his wife, not pull disappearing acts.

"I don't think he's as invested in our life here in Woodstone as I am." Sienna swirled the swizzle stick around and around in her drink.

Gigi raised her eyebrows questioningly.

"He's staying in the city later and later. I suspect he misses our life there—the openings, parties, first nights. It *was* fun." Sienna smiled sadly at Gigi. "I guess I'm ready to move on to the next step, but he isn't. I shouldn't have talked him into moving to Woodstone so we could have a baby."

Gigi opened her mouth, but then closed it. She didn't know what to say to comfort her friend.

"Can you see the price tag on that bracelet?" Sienna said, changing the subject. She pointed to the display case.

Gigi stood next to her and peered through the glass. She squinted at the tiny square that hung from the silver bracelet by a white silk thread. She shook her head. "It looks like the tag has been turned over. It's probably expensive. Everything in here is." She gave a last look at the hammered silver cuff. "It's beautiful, though."

Gigi felt an arm slip around her waist.

"*Cara*, you look lovely tonight." Emilio kissed both her cheeks heartily. His whiskers felt scratchy against her skin, and he smelled of garlic and herbs. Gigi found it oddly comforting.

He motioned impatiently at Carlo, who stood nearby, his hands hanging at his sides. "Come say hello to our beautiful Gigi."

Carlo kissed her shyly on the cheek. Gigi felt equally shy. The spot where he kissed her tingled, and she had to stop herself from putting her hand to her cheek.

Carlo looked at her nearly empty glass. "You need a refill," he declared, and bolted for the bar.

Emilio rolled his eyes. "*Dio mio*, that nephew of mine!" He slapped his thigh as he glared at Carlo's retreating back.

Gigi wanted to laugh. Half the town was intent on fixing up her and Carlo. She felt a warm rush at the prospect. She liked Carlo, and she certainly found him attractive. Very attractive, she thought, as she watched him maneuver his way through the crowd toward the bar. But he was a little young for her, and besides, she didn't want to get involved. She'd created a good life for herself; why ruin it? The thought that it might already be ruined made her breath catch in her throat.

"What is it, *cara*?" Emilio put a hand on her shoulder gently.

Gigi shook her head. "Nothing. It's just a little warm in here," she lied, not meeting Emilio's eye.

"These are delicious!" A brash voice cut across her thoughts.

Georgia Branston elbowed her way through the crowd and came to stand next to Gigi. "I'm not losing anything on that diet plan of yours," she brayed in her horsey voice. Several people turned and glanced in their direction. She was roughly the size and shape of the Liberty Bell. *And just as cracked*, Gigi thought. She was wearing a plaid taffeta dress that was as far from slimming as it could get.

"Mrs. Branston, those appetizers are hundreds of calories each. You won't lose weight unless you stick to the diet."

"Nonsense!" Georgia grabbed a ham croquette from a passing waiter's tray and brandished it under Gigi's nose.

"Nothing to these. Can't be more than a few calories each. Look at the size of them, my girl."

Gigi felt her face burn. If only Georgia would stuff the darned croquette in her mouth and be quiet! She glanced around. Victor Branston was headed their way. If Georgia kept bad-mouthing Gourmet De-Lite, would Branston Foods still want to do business with her?

"Here's the gal who makes the dinners you think are so good." Georgia snagged her husband's elbow and pulled him over to where they were standing. He had the autocratic air of a typical CEO, but there was a kindly look in his gray eyes. "It's a shame I haven't lost a pound on the stupid diet." Georgia popped the rest of the appetizer in her mouth and chewed enthusiastically.

Gigi felt her stomach plummet. Great, just what she needed. An enthusiastic endorsement in front of the owner of Branston Foods—from his wife. They'd never go through with the deal now.

"You haven't lost any weight because you cheat," Branston admonished with a wink in Gigi's direction. "No diet will work if you don't stick to it. You should know that."

"Let's just hope the food doesn't kill me," Georgia brayed. "Like that other poor woman."

"What's this?" Branston's bushy gray brows rose in alarm.

Gigi felt a cold shiver trace its way down her spine. If only the fool woman would put something else in her mouth and be quiet! Gigi was ready to grab her another hors d'oeuvre herself, calories be damned.

"I'd rather not talk about it here." Gigi tried to smile reassuringly, but her face felt stiff and her mouth would hardly move.

Branston gave a curt nod. "So right. This is hardly the time or place. I'll give you a call. Come on, Georgia, I've had enough. Time to go." He put a hand on his wife's arm and led her away.

Gigi's knees shook. How on earth had Georgia gotten wind of the fact that the police had questioned her about Martha's death? She had to find out what really happened that day. Or else she and her business were going down faster than a cold soufflé.

She glanced around the still-crowded room. Barbie Bernhardt was talking to Yvette, their heads nearly touching, over one of the display cases. There was a velvet pad placed on top of the glass on which an elaborate and expensive-looking silver necklace had been arrayed. Gigi sidled closer. Maybe she would be able to grab a moment to talk to Barbie. Barbie had been sitting outside in Winston's Mercedes the day Martha died—perhaps she had seen someone go near Gigi's car.

Barbie and Yvette were busy examining the necklace and didn't notice Gigi inch closer. Barbie wore a pink, Chanel-type suit and kitten-heel slingbacks and had a black velvet headband holding back her blond hair. She always dressed very conservatively, although expensively, and Gigi wondered again where she had come from. She had the impression that Barbie was trying just a little too hard to look the part.

Both of them were intent on their examination of the necklace, and Gigi took the opportunity to squeeze in a little closer. She peered over Barbie's shoulder. The necklace was exquisite—and obviously very expensive—with detailed silverwork studded with diamonds and pearls.

"I have to have it," Barbie said breathlessly. She ran a

well-manicured finger lovingly over the ornate design and looked up at Yvette with a sly smile.

"And with that bitch, Martha, out of the way, Winston is no longer stuck paying alimony. He won't have any excuse not to buy it."

Chapter 5

"You stay here." Gigi knelt down and tied Reg's leash to a parking meter along High Street. "I doubt they allow dogs inside." She gave him a pat, and he sat obediently, his attention focused on a woman and a brown miniature poodle headed their way.

Gigi gave one last, backward glance, then pushed open the door to Abigail's. She'd peered through the windows but had never ventured inside before. She knew, without even turning over a single tag, that the prices were out of her league.

Although she doubted that Barbie would have killed Martha just to get some fancy-schmancy necklace, it was quite possible that Barbie was after more than that. Like a wholesale shopping spree and lifestyle upgrade. She figured Abigail's was as good a place as any to start investigating.

"May I help you?" A saleswoman glided forward, her forehead creased into a slight frown, as if she wondered at

Gigi's nerve on entering the sanctity of her shop. Her hip-
bones protruded through the simple but expensive white
linen sheath she wore, and her black hair was twisted into
an elaborate knot at her neck. She had a black cashmere
cardigan draped loosely around her shoulders and an enormous cocktail ring on her right hand. Her gold name tag
read *Deirdre* in fancy script.

Gigi stammered a greeting. "I'm just looking, thanks."

"Anything in particular?" The clerk positioned herself
adroitly between Gigi and the nearest rack of dresses.

"Er . . . no . . . not really." Gigi spotted a flash of pink
sleeve on the rack behind her. "Pink. I was thinking of something pink."

"With your coloring?" Deirdre shrugged and began click-
ing through the hangers. Each garment had its own padded
hanger, and there was a plastic sleeve over the shoulders to
keep off the dust.

Gigi began to sweat even though the shop was well air-
conditioned. How was she going to get out of this? She got
a glimpse of the tag, and there were way too many zeros for
her extremely meager budget.

With a stiff back, the saleswoman started toward the back
of the store.

She spun around abruptly, and Gigi nearly crashed into
her. "How did you come to find us?"

Well, you're right in the middle of Woodstone's main
street, was Gigi's first thought, but she bit her tongue and
managed to resist that little bit of sarcasm, satisfying though
it would have been. "Mrs. Bernhardt recommended you.
Barbie Bernhardt."

The saleswoman nodded solemnly. "Mrs. Bernhardt is
an excellent customer," she intoned with the deepest respect.

Gigi wondered how much you had to spend to earn that

appellation. More than she was prepared to, that was for sure.

"Now, if you'll follow me." The clerk opened a door with a flourish and snapped on a light.

The dressing room was bigger than Gigi's bedroom, with walls papered in red toile and a gold brocade bench in the corner. The clerk hung a number of garments from an ornate hook in the wall. She gestured toward the clothes. "I've chosen a few things that I think will work for you." She looked Gigi up and down. "Size eight, I believe?" She arched her thin, black brows.

Gigi nodded.

"This color would suit you better than the pink." She brandished a watery blue-green silk dress at Gigi. "Of course if you insist on the pink, that's up to you."

Gigi supposed that was her own version of "the customer is always right."

The clerk pulled the door closed behind her, and Gigi was left standing in the dressing room with thousands of dollars' worth of dresses she couldn't possibly afford. A handkerchief, maybe, but certainly not a whole dress.

She pulled off her T-shirt and slid out of her denim skirt. Her underwear, the kind that came six to a pack, looked tatty in such regal surroundings, even though she'd bought them at the grocery store just last week. She sighed and freed the blue-green dress from its hanger and plastic cover. It really was pretty. She held it up to her and looked in the mirror. The color brought depth to her eyes and made her hair shine. She wondered what Carlo would think if he saw her . . .

She wouldn't think about that. She couldn't. Gigi slid the dress over her head. It probably wasn't going to fit, and if it did, it would look terrible. She pulled the garment into place, and the silk floated coolly around her bare legs. She risked a glance in the mirror.

It was perfect. Absolutely perfect. She had to give the arrogant Deirdre her due—she knew her clothes.

She wondered if just maybe, if she really cut down her expenses—nonessential things like food, electricity, toilet paper and the like—if there was any way she could possibly afford such a heavenly piece of clothing. She peeked at the price tag with one eye half closed, as if that would lessen the shock.

Gigi gasped and put her hand to her mouth. She shouldn't even be trying something like this on, let alone contemplating buying it. What if it ripped when she took it off? What if she accidentally drooled on it—not that she was in the habit of drooling, but you never knew. Very carefully, she pulled the dress over her head and placed it back on the hanger.

"Can I help with anything?" The clerk's snooty tones filtered through the door.

"No, everything's fine," Gigi called back.

"How was the blue silk? Did you like it?" The clerk swung open the door abruptly.

Gigi grabbed her T-shirt and held it in front of her. "It's very lovely. But I'm afraid it's just a bit—"

"Would you like me to hold it for you? You're not going to find anything more perfect in Woodstone, I assure you. Unless, of course, you're planning to shop in the city." She said *city* as if it were a bad word.

"No, no, it's perfect. It's lovely. It's perfectly lovely," Gigi stammered. She couldn't possibly buy the dress. It was more than her rent for the month. For six months.

"What name shall I put on it?" The clerk held a thin, gold pen poised above a tiny blue card with *Abigail's* engraved across the top.

"Gigi Fitzgerald. But I'm not—"

"Don't worry. This is the only one we have in stock in this style. You won't be seeing yourself coming and going."

Did she really look as if she worried about that sort of thing? Gigi wondered. "And Mrs. Bernhardt—" Gigi blurted trying to turn the conversation back to Barbie.

"Oh no, that dress wouldn't suit her at all."

"She told me she had her eye on several things . . ." Gigi proffered, hoping Deirdre would take the bait.

Deirdre sniffed haughtily. "Mrs. Bernhardt was in yesterday afternoon. She has excellent taste. We managed to completely flesh out her summer wardrobe. They are going to the south of France in August, and she needed the perfect things to take with her." Deirdre's mouth clamped shut suddenly as if she realized she shouldn't be gossiping about her customers.

"Oh, yes, that's right. She mentioned that." Gigi crossed her fingers behind her back.

Putting the dress on hold couldn't possibly commit her to its purchase, could it? Gigi wondered as she stumbled out of Abigail's with a sigh of relief. At least her trip hadn't been wasted.

Barbie was off to Europe. With a suitcase full of new clothes that certainly had cost a small fortune. It sounded as if Winston and Barbie were throwing plenty of money around all of a sudden.

Were they just lucky that Martha had died, or was it more sinister than that?

Reg followed Gigi out to get the paper the next morning. She yawned and stretched her arms over her head. She was exhausted after tossing and turning all night, until even Reg got fed up and jumped off the bed. Gigi had heard him snuffling around the dog bed she'd bought him, which he had, up to now, ignored with a disdainful sniff.

She couldn't get Martha's death out of her mind. If it wasn't an accident, that meant it was on purpose—which was basically how the dictionary defined the term *murder*. It was a word Gigi was used to hearing on television or radio but certainly not in her everyday life.

Gigi retrieved the *Woodstone Times* from the end of the driveway and walked back toward the house, Reg trotting happily at her heels. The cottage was full of the aroma of coffee—her favorite, Sumatra Mandheling—and she inhaled appreciatively. She poured a cup and spread the newspaper open on the kitchen table. She was turning away to get her toast from the toaster when the lead article caught her eye. Her knees buckled, and she sank gratefully into one of the chairs. The headline was bold and black and nearly jumped off the page. "Local Restaurant Reviewer Felled by Peanut-Laced Food."

Gigi propped her elbows on the table, her coffee forgotten, as she read the story. They'd interviewed Detective Mertz, and he had told the reporter how Martha's last known meal had come from Gigi's Gourmet De-Lite. "We believe it was an accident," he was quoted as saying. "Somehow peanut oil was mistakenly introduced into the production of Mrs. Bernhardt's meal."

Gigi groaned. After this article, her business was toast. Burnt toast. Who would trust her to prepare a meal for them now? She flipped to Martha's obituary on page thirty.

According to the article, Martha had been born in Bronxville, New York, an upper-class village less than half an hour from Grand Central Terminal and Midtown Manhattan. She'd attended Bryn Mawr and married Winston Bernhardt shortly after graduation. Her career had been varied—newspaper reporter; book, theater and restaurant reviewer; director of a nonprofit and animal-rights activist.

The picture with the article was of a slightly younger Martha with longer hair and a softer expression. Gigi sighed and closed the paper. Even though she knew she wasn't responsible for Martha's death, she still felt guilty. As if she had failed Martha somehow. Maybe if she found the person who really did it, she'd feel better.

Gigi cleaned up her breakfast dishes, put some fresh water in Reg's bowl, exchanged her pajamas for a pair of jeans and a bateau-necked top and tucked her grocery list into her purse. She had to make a trip to the Shop and Save just outside of town but her first stop would be Bon Appétit. She needed a few things she wouldn't find anywhere else like black truffle oil and a new tart pan. And, even more importantly, the owner, Evelyn Fishko, was near neighbors with Martha Bernhardt. Who knew what gossip she might be persuaded to share?

Evelyn was behind the counter when Gigi pushed open the door to Bon Appétit. A small bell announced her arrival with a melodic tinkle. Evelyn looked up from the jar of lemon curd she was wrapping in tissue paper and glanced at Gigi over the top of her glasses. She had an apron with *Bon Appétit!* in scrawling black script fastened around her middle and a black cardigan tied loosely over her shoulders.

She nodded at Gigi as she lowered the jar into a glossy white bag with *Bon Appétit* in the same black script. She pushed it to one side and leaned on the counter. "Morning. What can I get you?"

She knew Gigi always came in with a list and was an

efficient shopper, unlike so many of the housewives who trolled the aisles for an hour and left empty-handed.

Gigi pulled the piece of paper from her purse. "Some truffle oil to start."

Evelyn pushed off from the counter and went to a well-stocked display to the right of the checkout. She ran her finger along the shelves until she found what she was looking for. "This do?" She adjusted the glasses on her nose and peered at the label. "It's the Sabatino Tartufi from Italy. I've only got the smaller size." She glanced at Gigi over her shoulder.

"That's fine," Gigi reassured her. "I only need the slightest bit." The last thing she planned to do was drown her clients' food in hundreds of calories of expensive oil. She wouldn't use more than the barest drop—just enough to provide the maximum flavor with the minimum of calories.

Evelyn put the bottle of oil on the counter and stood poised with her hands on her hips.

"Do you have a nine-inch tart pan? Preferably nonstick?"

Evelyn snorted. "Of course I do. What kind of a cookery store would this be if I didn't stock the most basic necessities?" She spun on her heel and disappeared into the warren of shelves opposite the cash register.

Gigi wondered about a tart pan being a basic necessity. Most people these days did little more than take out, eat out or microwave.

She glanced at the counter and noticed that Evelyn had received the day's *Woodstone Times*. It was folded and still in its plastic wrapper. Obviously Evelyn hadn't had a chance to read it yet. Gigi felt heat crawl from her feet to the top of her head. Once Evelyn—and everyone else in Woodstone—read about Martha's Gourmet De-Lite meal and the peanut oil, she'd be ruined. She'd never be able to hold her head up again.

Evelyn returned, brandishing the pewter-colored pan. She plunked it down on the counter. "What else?"

"That's it for today." Gigi was itching to get out of there in case Evelyn had the only case of X-ray vision ever known and could see through the newspaper wrapper to the damning article inside on the front page. But that wouldn't solve anything. If she was going to clear her name, she'd have to learn more about Martha, and Evelyn was a good place to start. She reached into her purse for her wallet.

But how to introduce Martha into their nonexistent conversation? Perhaps she'd start with the usual pleasantries and find a way to weave it in. Surely Martha's murder—she stumbled over the word, even in her own head—was on the tip of everyone's tongue.

"Nice day today." Gigi slid her credit card across the wooden counter.

Evelyn grunted. She fiddled with her glasses and squinted at the card before running it through the processing machine. "Shame about Martha Bernhardt."

"What?" Gigi was startled. Here she'd been searching for a way to bring up Martha's name, and Evelyn had done it for her.

"She a client of yours?" Evelyn paused with the bottle of truffle oil half in and half out of a Bon Appétit shopping bag.

Gigi hesitated. Had Evelyn heard about the peanut oil and Martha's allergy? Maybe she'd already read the paper and then carefully folded it back up and put it back in its wrapper? Gigi could feel her face getting red.

"Neighbor of mine," Evelyn offered in her usual terse style. She pulled a sheet of tissue paper from a roll and carefully wrapped both pieces of the tart pan.

The front bell tinkled, and Gigi groaned inwardly. Just when she might have gotten somewhere with Evelyn!

A bright-eyed, middle-aged blond woman approached the counter. She wore white capris, a lime green T-shirt and matching lime green canvas shoes.

"I'll be with you in a minute." Evelyn looked up from placing Gigi's pan in the shopping bag.

"Oh, that's okay." The woman waved a hand toward Evelyn. "I'm just looking." But instead of moving toward the shelves of merchandise, she continued to hover near the counter.

"Sure I can't help you with anything?" Evelyn handed Gigi her credit card receipt.

Gigi hesitated. Just when she'd gotten Evelyn talking! "It really is a shame about Martha," she agreed with an emphatic nod.

The blond woman approached the counter eagerly. "Is that the woman who died in the car accident?" She lowered her voice. "I heard her death wasn't completely natural . . . that some are calling it foul play." She looked back and forth between Gigi and Evelyn like a spectator at a tennis match.

Evelyn pursed her thin lips. She leaned over the counter, closer to Gigi and the blond. "I've heard the same thing." She looked over her shoulder briefly. "I heard that something caused her to have that accident." She crooked her left brow. "And I don't think it was a heart attack like they'd have us believe," she finished triumphantly.

"I heard she was only in her fifties." The blond looked from Evelyn to Gigi. "I don't know about you, but that's not old enough for a heart attack in my book." She laughed huskily and patted her chest in the region of her own heart.

Evelyn fiddled with a ball of twine that was sitting out on the counter. "Martha lived two doors down from me. And she was always working in that garden of hers—hauling bags of fertilizer, mulch and top soil as if they didn't weigh a thing. Then she'd be off on a long hike up the hills, swinging that walking stick she always took with her."

"There you go, then." The blonde shook her index finger at them. "She was in too good shape to have a heart attack."

"Unless it was all that arguing that did her in. Bad karma." Evelyn drew her lips back over her horsey teeth and brayed loudly.

Gigi's ears perked up. "Arguing?"

"Yup. Martha and her neighbor, that woman who's running the old Woodstone Summer Theater . . . what is her name? Give me a minute, it'll come to me."

"Adora Sands?" Gigi prompted.

Evelyn snapped her fingers. "That's it. She moved in alongside Martha about six months ago, and it's been nonstop crabbing at each other ever since."

"Oh?"

"Bicker, bicker, bicker, they're always at it." Evelyn said. "First it's Martha's dog doing its business in Adora's yard, then it's Adora's cat chewing on Martha's prize roses. If it wasn't one thing, it was another." She looked at Gigi. "Not that Martha was all that easy to get along with, mind you. We had our fights, too. The time my Howard accidentally blew some snow onto her driveway . . ." She raised her eyes and threw her hands into the air.

"Well, you want to know what I heard?" The blonde paused dramatically. "I heard it was something quite different that caused Martha's accident."

And she turned and looked straight at Gigi.

Gigi held her breath. Had she read the story in the day's paper? Soon everyone would know, and she'd have to leave Woodstone . . . go back to the city. She panicked and for a moment didn't realize what the blonde was saying.

"I heard"—the blond paused dramatically—"that her car had been tampered with."

Gigi expelled her breath in a loud *whoosh*. She raised a hand to her forehead and realized it was shaking. She quickly shoved it into her pocket, hoping the others hadn't noticed.

"Really?" Evelyn breathed.

The blond nodded. "Do you think maybe that neighbor of hers, what was her name—Adora? Do you think maybe she had something to do with it? Maybe she got tired of arguing with Martha and fiddled with her brakes or something?"

Evelyn brayed again. "I don't think Adora would know one end of a car from the other, let alone how to disengage the brakes. Besides"—she pulled her cardigan tighter around her shoulders—"you wouldn't kill someone just because their dog had piddled in your flower bed, would you?"

Chapter 6

The scent of onion, garlic, oregano and mint wafted from Gigi's oven as she pulled out a pan of turkey meatballs with Greek seasoning. The fragrant vapor curled around her, and she inhaled deeply, her stomach growling. She was hungry. She spent so much time feeding others that sometimes she forgot to feed herself. She plucked one of the tiny meatballs from the sheet and popped it into her mouth. She fanned her face furiously. It was hot! But very good, she decided as she chewed carefully. Her clients would like them. This recipe was a keeper.

Gigi set the pan on the counter and began to crumble feta cheese for the salad. She thought back to her conversation earlier with Evelyn and the blond lady at Bon Appétit. Was it possible that Martha had irritated Adora enough to kill? She shook her head—she couldn't see it. If Adora had clubbed Martha over the head with a garden gnome in a fit of pique . . . maybe. But this must have been premeditated.

Someone had to have doctored Martha's lunch with the peanut oil. It didn't make sense.

No, money was far more likely to be at the root of poor Martha's death. And who had the most to gain? Barbie and Winston. With Martha dead, Winston's responsibility was effectively over. He and Barbie could spend the alimony money any way they wanted.

Gigi passed her calendar and stopped to flip the page. The new sheet boasted a stunning shot of St. Andrew's Episcopal Church in downtown Woodstone. Lush, white peonies bloomed against the darker brick of the church, and the trees were thick with fresh, green leaves. Gigi realized it was the first of June already, and her rent was due.

She retrieved her checkbook from its accustomed spot in her desk drawer and opened it to a fresh check. She stopped with her pen poised above the blank "Pay to the order of" line. With Martha dead, who was she to send the check to? Worry niggled at the edges of her mind. What if Martha's heir wanted to move into the cottage? Where would she go? One of those featureless, boxy apartments near the train station? She shuddered. This place was home. But surely the new heirs, whoever they were, would want the income from the rent?

She pulled the telephone directory from her lower desk drawer and thumbed through it. Simpson and West were the only lawyers in town, and most people went to them for their everyday legal needs. Perhaps Martha had done the same.

William West wouldn't tell Gigi anything over the telephone, save confirming that Martha had been a client of the firm's, but he would see her in his office that afternoon.

Gigi hung up the phone, made a note in her diary and headed back to the kitchen to begin boxing up the day's lunches of salad with low-fat yogurt dressing, the grilled turkey meatballs, tzatziki sauce and a half a pita.

Humidity hovered over Woodstone like a malignant cloud. Gigi rolled the MINI's windows up and punched the button for the air-conditioning. She had all the food packed in a giant cooler—too bad she couldn't pack herself in one as well.

The Woodstone Players were deep into rehearsals for the upcoming start of the season. Gigi had been delivering more and more of their meals directly to the theater. She didn't mind—it made it easier for her.

She pulled the MINI into the theater parking lot under the spreading branches of an elm tree whose roots were starting to buckle the macadam. The hot, close air hit Gigi like a wet washcloth when she opened the front door and slid between the car and the tree. She went around to the passenger side and wrestled the cooler out. It bumped and gyrated with its wheels twisting and sticking as she pulled it across the rutted parking lot. She was a few yards shy of the theater door when the cooler jerked and landed on its side.

Gigi was tempted to kick it as she set it back on its feet and made sure that the contents were all still intact. She pushed a curling strand of hair out of her face as she wrangled the cooler up the steps and into the theater lobby.

She cracked open the door to the theater and peeked inside. Emilio and Barbie were on stage, and Alice was slumped in a seat at the back of the theater, her legs stretched out on the seat in front of her. Pierce was in the front row, arms crossed over his chest. All four looked hot, tired and disgruntled. Gigi glanced at her watch. She was a few minutes early—she'd let them finish this scene before bringing in the lunches.

The old theater was damp and close with a musty smell rising from the nearly threadbare carpeting. To save money, they only ran the air conditioner during performances. Gigi fanned herself. Suddenly, she had doubts about what she was doing. Would her business ever really take off? If the deal with Branston Foods came through, things would certainly change. But with everything that had happened, she had lost her optimism. Victor Branston would probably make some excuse and politely but firmly decline the opportunity to do business with Gigi's Gourmet De-Lite. She really couldn't blame him. How could he trust her product after everything that had happened? She knew that she hadn't used any peanuts in the preparation of Martha's meal—but it didn't look as if anyone else believed her.

Gigi lifted her hair off the back of her neck. She should have worn it up. She felt her face turning red. She'd worn it down because she thought Carlo liked it that way, and although she didn't like to admit it, she was hoping to see him. He sometimes joined Emilio and the cast for lunch if Al Forno wasn't too busy. A trickle of sweat made its way slowly down her right side. She had to get some air. There was a side door that led to a small patio where champagne cocktails were served during intermission. Gigi thought they probably made more money on the drinks than on the tickets themselves, especially when the house was packed. The rickety old air conditioner did little more than blow tepid air from its vents, and by the second act the theater was an oven.

She opened the side door, stepped onto the brick terrace and breathed in the ever-so-slightly fresher air. The atmosphere was heavy and still. She could hear the hum of traffic in the distance and the squabbling of some birds in a nearby tree. Suddenly she became aware of raised voices coming from around the back of the theater.

Some sort of instinct she didn't even know she had made Gigi tiptoe as she made her way the width of the terrace to peer around the corner of the theater. Winston and Adora were standing under a dogwood tree dripping with showy white blossoms. Winston was leaning against the trunk, his hands stuffed into his pockets. He was wearing a white broadcloth shirt with the sleeves rolled up, and, in spite of the heat of the day, a red paisley ascot was tucked into the open neck. Adora was in costume, and Gigi couldn't help noticing that her shorts had not become any looser. She worried her bottom lip with her teeth. Was she giving Adora too many calories, or was Adora cheating? Probably the latter, but Gigi would be the one blamed no matter what.

Even if she hadn't been able to hear their raised voices, it was obvious they were arguing. Adora's fists were clenched at her sides, and her back was rigid. Winston looked more annoyed than angry—the way you would be if a mosquito or fly were buzzing around you. Gigi half expected him to swat at Adora. What were they arguing about?

Suddenly, Adora drew back a hand and slapped Winston on the side of the face. He shouted, "What the—?" and put a hand to his cheek.

Gigi retreated into the shadows as Adora stomped toward where she was standing. If Adora put that much emotion into her acting, she must be dazzling on stage, Gigi thought. Maybe Adora *had* gotten mad enough to kill Martha.

Adora flew around the corner of the building, her fists still clenched, and nearly collided with Gigi. Her face was glowing red, although from the heat or from her confrontation with Winston, Gigi couldn't tell.

"That man is impossible," Adora cried. "He won't listen. He just won't listen."

She looked like she was playing to the back row, but Gigi sensed this wasn't any performance. Adora really was mad.

"What did he—?"

"He's going to ruin everything." Adora swept a hand toward the theater. "Everything I've worked for. I don't know what I'll do—" Tears sprang into her eyes. "Oooh." She stamped her foot suddenly.

"What's wrong?" Gigi tried again.

"I hate him, I really do." Adora stamped her other foot. "He's going to sell the theater. He's been threatening to do it for months."

"Maybe if someone else buys it, they'll put some money into it." Gigi looked around her at the overgrown gardens and the faded and splintered siding of the old barn-turned-theater.

"Don't be so naïve." Adora raised an eyebrow cynically. "No one's going to pay to repair this place. They'll tear it down and build more of those McMansions that are going up everywhere. Like the one Winston lives in with that gold-digging wife of his."

Adora threw herself into one of the wrought-iron chairs that were scattered around the terrace. She tugged at the waistband of her shorts. "These miserable things are still too tight."

Gigi started to say something but had barely opened her mouth when Adora interjected.

"He'll get a fortune for this land from some developer. They'll turn the place into another one of those insipid developments—'Harvest Harbor Homes' or something equally dreadful, with huge houses that all look the same."

"Can't the theater move?"

Adora shook her head. "There's no place to go. We don't have any money—or hardly any money." She tugged at her shorts again. "This is our first season, and now it looks as if it's going to be our last."

She burst into tears and bolted through the door.

Gigi found Alice backstage, organizing the props table. She noticed that Alice's long, cotton skirt was noticeably loose around the waist. There was something else different, too. She studied Alice through narrowed eyes. It was her hair. Alice had smoothed her normally frizzy locks into a wavy bob that was very becoming. And Gigi thought she detected a hint of pink lipstick and a bit of eye shadow as well. Gigi smiled to herself. She'd seen it many times before—a woman needed only to lose a bit of weight before she began to fix herself up.

"You brought my grub?" Alice placed a very realistic-looking gun in one of the taped-off squares on the prop table. "This goes off in the third act." She gestured toward the pistol.

Gigi shuddered. "Is it real?"

"Real enough, I guess. But the noise of the report will come from off-stage, just to be on the safe side. Some of these props are practically as old as the theater itself."

She glanced up at the dusty rafters soaring above them. "This place has been here since eighteen ninety-two. Of course, it was a working barn then."

She put out a hand, and Gigi handed her the Gourmet De-Lite container with her name on it.

"When was it turned into a theater?"

"Some Broadway actor came out here in the early seventies and decided to turn the place into a theater." Alice opened her container and inhaled deeply. "How do you manage to make everything so delicious, and yet I'm still losing weight. See?" She pulled at her loose waistband. "The fellow—I don't remember his name—caused a bit of a scandal because he was living with another man. They claimed to be friends, but the townspeople eventually caught on." She gave Gigi a wicked grin.

"I thought Adora was the one who—"

Alice shook her head. "The theater did quite well. In fact, it had a good, long run. But then there was Black Monday in 1987, and he lost a lot of his backing. He had to close the doors."

"So Adora has only been here—"

Alice nodded. "She descended on us quite recently and decided she wanted to try to get the place going again. Winston kicked in some money, and here we all are. Our own little version of hell."

"What do you mean—?"

"Just kidding, don't look so shocked. It's the same whenever you get a group of people together and put them under stress. This one doesn't like that one, the other one won't play fair. Someone else wants all the attention. Same song every time."

Gigi thought about *Wedding Spectacular* magazine and the feuds, the pettiness, the sulking. Alice was right—it was the same everywhere you went. She really was glad to be rid of it.

"But Adora just told me that Winston is planning on selling this place."

"What?" Alice stopped with one of the turkey meatballs halfway to her mouth. "Are you sure? We've only just got this place up and running again."

"That's what Adora just told me. She and Winston were outside arguing about it. At least, I think that's what they were fighting about."

Alice popped the meatball into her mouth. "Mmmm, these are delicious. How do you make everything taste so good and yet be so low in calories?"

Gigi shrugged. "Flavoring, mostly. Herbs, spices, things like that. And good ingredients." She shuddered. "I don't believe in things like fat-free dressings. They taste awful. It's better to have a little of the good stuff than a lot of the artificial stuff."

Alice licked the tips of her fingers. "I can second that." She looked thoughtful for a moment. "Why is Winston selling now, I wonder? Why let Adora go through all this trouble if this is going to be the beginning and the end of the Woodstone Theater?"

"I can answer that." Adora stomped in. "He had to wait until that bitch, Martha, was out of the way."

"What do you mean?" Gigi and Alice both spun in Adora's direction.

Adora peered into Alice's lunch container. "Those look good. Except I'm too angry to eat." She began pacing, her fists clenched at her side. "I could kill Winston!" She stopped pacing abruptly and turned toward Alice and Gigi with her hands outspread. "I didn't mean . . ."

"What makes you think that Martha's dying has anything do with Winston's sudden decision to sell this place?" Alice tore off a piece of her pita half and wiped the sauce from the inside of her container before popping it into her mouth.

Adora's shoulders sagged. "Because Martha owned half of the theater"—she waved a hand toward the moth-eaten, red velvet curtain—"and the land it's on. And while this pile of rubble isn't worth a dime, the acreage could be worth a fortune to some developer."

"I still don't see what that—" Alice began.

"Martha refused to sell," Adora snapped. "And Winston couldn't do anything without her approval. Now that she's dead . . ." She shrugged her shoulders.

"But didn't they divide everything up when they divorced?" Gigi thought about the hours she and Ted had spent apportioning the few belongings that had fit into their miniature New York apartment.

"According to Winston, the property wasn't worth nearly as much when they first divorced. But they suspected the value was only going to go up. They agreed to hang on to it together to wait for a better time. Which, according to Winston, is now." She stamped her foot.

"Won't Martha's half go to one of her heirs?" Gigi thought about her cottage again and the prospect that someone might show up at her door demanding she leave.

"They agreed that if one of them died, the other would get that person's half share," Adora moaned. "So it looks as if this is going to be the last of the Woodstone Theater. Winston thinks we should be able to finish this season's run, but then . . ." Adora burst into tears and rushed off.

Gigi jerked her head in Adora's direction. "She's taking this really hard."

"Oh, the dramatics come with the territory, don't you think?" Alice closed her empty Gourmet De-Lite container with a sigh. "But this place does mean a lot to her. She's put a good deal of work into it, and now . . ." She kissed the tips of her fingers.

Gigi was thoughtful as she walked back toward her car. Sunshine was breaking through the clouds and puffs of steam were rising from the damp macadam. She held her hair off the back of her neck with one hand and pulled open the driver's door to the MINI with the other. She rummaged briefly in the glove compartment and found a slightly bent aluminum hair clip. She stabbed it through the untidy bun she had created and breathed a sigh of relief.

As she was pulling out of the parking lot, she thought about what Alice had said—how, whenever you got a group of people together, there were bound to be petty disagreements, dislikes, arguing. She could testify to that from her own experience. There was just one thing.

Someone didn't usually wind up murdered.

Chapter 7

Simpson and West, Attorneys at Law had offices on the second and third floors above the Knit Knack Shop on High Street. They had cornered the market on wood paneling, which graced the entire reception area as well as each of the offices. Gigi half wondered if she would find the same dark mahogany boards in the restrooms and employee break room.

A middle-aged woman with a short, lacquered blond hairdo led Gigi to a closed door with a brass nameplate announcing *William West* in elaborate script. She rapped gently against the wood panels with the back of her hand. A deep baritone bade them enter.

West crouched behind a massive partner's desk, hands folded across a substantial paunch only partially camouflaged by his expensively tailored pinstripe suit.

Gigi traversed what seemed like an acre of antique Oriental carpet before sliding into the stiff armless chair strategically placed in front of West.

He steepled his fingers, glared at Gigi over their tips and raised caterpillar-like eyebrows. "I understand you are here in the matter of the death of Mrs. Martha Bernhardt."

Gigi nodded and sat up straighter in her chair. She wasn't going to allow this overstuffed, pompous ass to intimidate her. "All I need to know is to whom do I make out my next rent check?" Gigi could not actually recall ever having used the phrase *to whom* in conversation before. West, however, did not look particularly impressed.

"Ah, yes, the cottage." His face relaxed into the deep lines of a bulldog's mug as he gave this his consideration. Finally, he spoke. "The cottage now belongs to a client of mine."

At the word *belongs*, Gigi felt her chest tighten, and all the air in her lungs bellowed out. "Do they . . . do they want it back?" Gigi gulped.

West shook his head slightly. "For the moment they are content to leave things as they are. You will make out your rent checks to Simpson and West, and we will see that they are put into the hands of our client."

Gigi fidgeted with the thin gold band she now wore on her right hand. "Do you think your client is going to want to sell . . . ?" She could hardly get the words out. The thought made her heart speed up and her mouth go dry.

West shrugged large, padded shoulders. "I would assume so, given time to think about it."

"Will you let me know . . . when . . . if . . . ?"

West's caterpillar-like eyebrows crept upwards as his mouth turned down. "If my client should decide to sell, I am sure you will receive ample time to seek shelter elsewhere."

He made it sound as simple as buying a new dress. Gigi kneaded her hands in her lap. "But what if I want to buy it myself?" she blurted out.

West gave a bark of laughter. He plucked a fountain pen from his desk and twirled it between his fingers. "Given the current price of property in Woodstone, I think it is highly unlikely that you will, er, be in the market for my client's cottage."

Gigi felt her face glow red. "I don't think you're in a position to know that, now, are you, Mr. West?" Gigi lifted her chin and stared straight into West's tiny black eyes.

He dropped the fountain pen he'd been fiddling with, and it rolled across the desk, over the edge and onto the plush Oriental carpet. He stared after it for a moment before looking up at Gigi.

He sighed. "In that case, if you would leave your name and contact information with my receptionist, Mrs. Walker, I will see to it that you receive notice when my client decides to put the cottage up for sale." He pulled a sheaf of papers across the desk toward him. "Now, if you'll excuse me . . ."

Gigi delivered everyone else's dinner first that evening so she could swing by Winston and Barbie's house and not worry about how long she was taking. People got so testy when they were hungry and on a diet. Although you could hardly call the delicious plank-grilled salmon she'd prepared yesterday "diet food." Or the couscous salad brimming with peas, corn, scallions, tomatoes, pineapple chunks and fresh parsley grown in her garden.

She'd been delivering Barbie's food to the theater for the last couple of weeks, packing her dinner in a cooler for her to take home and eat later. She'd gotten the distinct impression that Barbie hadn't wanted her coming around the house for some reason.

That reason became obvious when Gigi pulled up in front of Winston and Barbie's house later that evening. The house was set well back from the road with a circular drive curving around under a porte cochere. The house itself was large and impressive, trimmed in fieldstone, with three chimneys rising above the roofline. There was a three-stall garage designed to look like a stable block with hitching posts and a cobblestoned forecourt. But instead of the manicured lawns and gardens of its neighbors, the grass was overgrown and the flower beds choked with several weeks' worth of weeds.

Although that was about to change. As Gigi watched, two men on riding mowers swooped down the drive and got to work on the acre of front lawn. Three other men, their ball caps tilted against the lowering sun, waded into the weed-infested gardens, shovels at the ready.

Gigi retrieved Barbie's dinner from the backseat of the MINI and started up the front walk. The noise from the two mowers was deafening, and she jumped when one of them cut a bit too close to the brick path. By the time she was at the front door, a large swath of lawn had already been sheared, the cut grass forming a feathery blanket on top.

Gigi rang the bell and waited. She rang again and waited some more. Nothing. And a third time, but still no response. She looked at her watch. She'd told Barbie to expect her at six o'clock, and she was a few minutes early.

She was heading back down the path when a lady walking a black standard poodle came down the street, tottering on a pair of red canvas espadrilles that laced up her ankles.

"Looking for the Bernhardts, my dear?" she called to

Gigi. She pushed large, oval sunglasses to the top of her head.

Gigi nodded and hurried down the walk to where the woman was waiting, her dog sniffing in an ever-widening circle around her.

"I saw their car leave about an hour ago," the woman told Gigi. She glanced over her shoulder where the men were working furiously on the lawn. "I must say, it's a relief to see them taking care of things again. Fifi, no," she commanded abruptly as the dog attempted to relieve itself on the Bernhardts' property. "They've been letting it go for weeks. The neighbors were starting to complain. I offered to go ring their bell and see what was what, but we voted to wait another week." She wrapped the dog's leash around her fist and yanked it off the grass where it had wandered again. "I was rather relieved. I have to say, that Winston gives me the creeps. Always skulking about in those ascots of his. Honestly, what year does he think it is?"

"It's odd that they've suddenly got people working on things again." Gigi watched as one of the men yanked the power cord on a hedge trimmer, and it roared to life with a belch of sooty exhaust.

"Isn't it? But I think they were caught in the recent stock market plunge like a lot of people. The Martinsons on the hill"—she pointed up the street with a hot pink manicured finger—"never did recover. They actually had to sell." She shivered. "We had a few sleepless nights ourselves, but everything has turned out okay. Same for the Bernhardts, it looks like."

"Did they come into some money?" Gigi tried to sound offhand, but her heart was hammering.

The woman jerked the dog's leash again and pulled it closer. "It certainly looks like it, doesn't it?" She looked over her shoulder at the swarm of men cutting the grass and tending to the garden. "And just the other week I saw"—she lowered her voice and leaned closer to Gigi—"I saw Barbie vacuuming her own living room. The shades were up, and you could see right through those enormous windows of theirs . . . and there she was! Pushing the vacuum herself." She shivered. She sounded as shocked as if Barbie had been caught running naked down the street. "That just isn't done around here. They must have let Linda go," she said with relish.

The woman turned her dark, beady eyes on Gigi. "How do you know the Bernhardts?"

"Mrs. Bernhardt subscribes to my meal plan. Gigi's Gourmet De-Lite. For weight loss . . ." Gigi trailed off. The woman was staring at her most peculiarly, with her thin, penciled-in eyebrows practically disappearing into her hairline.

"Do people actually lose weight? Does the stuff taste good?"

"Yes. Hopefully on both counts. My clients do claim to enjoy the food, and since it's low in calories, you ought to lose weight unless you have some sort of medical problem . . . or you cheat."

"I hope you don't use a lot of that fake stuff they put in the frozen diet dinners."

Gigi shook her head. "No. Nothing you wouldn't find in regular food."

"Do you have a card?" The woman stuck out her hand. Her dog had finally exhausted itself and lay panting by her feet.

Gigi dug in her purse and pulled out one of the cards she'd had printed at Folio in town. The possibility of getting another client was certainly an unexpected bonus. She realized she hadn't heard back from Branston Foods yet. She really hoped that didn't mean they'd changed their minds.

The woman took Gigi's card and finally walked on, the poodle straining on the leash ahead of her, and Gigi got back into her car.

It certainly did look like Winston and Barbie had come into money from somewhere, Gigi thought as she waited for them to come home. Was it just good luck that Martha had died right when they needed money so desperately?

Or was it something else entirely?

Chapter 8

Winston and Barbie zoomed up the drive in their shiny, dark Mercedes half an hour later. Gigi had dozed off in the front seat of her car, her cheek pressed into the steering wheel, and she stretched awkwardly. The air inside the car was hot and stale despite the open windows. Barbie gave her a peculiar look as they whizzed past in a cloud of dust and cut grass.

Gigi got out of her car, retrieved Barbie's container of food, and followed them on foot down the long, circular drive. Winston had already parked and was waiting for her on the front step when she got there.

"What have we here?" He held out a hand to take the glossy Gourmet De-Lite box from Gigi.

"It's Barbie's dinner—"

"Ah, yes! Especially prepared in your kitchen so we don't have to dirty ours. How thoughtful of you." Winston bowed with a flourish.

"It's not that, it's low-calorie food," Gigi began before he interrupted her again.

"But of course. So my charming wife doesn't even have to make the effort to diet. You do it all for her."

The scent of wine washed over Gigi—some expensive vintage, no doubt. Winston had obviously been drinking. As if to confirm it, he swayed slightly and grabbed at one of the white pillars holding up the portico.

"Well, not exactly. She still has to—"

"Just another way to spend my money," Winston sighed.

"If you'd rather I didn't—" Gigi was seriously tempted to bolt back down the stairs, leap into her car and drive off.

"Do I owe you some money for this?" Winston began to pull a tan leather Gucci wallet from his back pocket.

"No." Gigi shook her head. "It's all been taken care of already."

"Will wonders never cease?" Winston swayed again and grabbed for Gigi's shoulder.

His grip was strong, and she tried not to flinch as he held on while regaining his rather precarious balance. She thought of what Alice had said about being careful, and a tremulous shiver ran up and down her spine. There was an underlying ruthlessness about Winston that was frightening.

Gigi cleared her throat. She wanted to ask him if he knew anything about Martha's cottage, but she was half-afraid. He swayed again, and Gigi moved backward on the step, out of arm's reach.

"I wonder if you might be able to tell me," she began, taking a deep breath, "who owns my cottage now that Martha is dead. I know that you and Martha owned the theater together . . ."

"Ah, yes, Martha's twee little cottage." Winston burped. He pointed to his chest. "I own it. It's all mine. At least until

I find a buyer. I don't know why Martha bought that place. It's too small to be of any use. But"—he hiccoughed this time—"the land it's on should fetch a pretty penny." He looked thoughtful. "A pretty penny, indeed."

"So you're planning on selling?" Gigi tried to keep the disappointment out of her voice, even as she felt her spirits plummet.

He nodded. "Martha was very savvy, you know. Very savvy. She was the one who suggested we invest in that miserable old barn they call the Woodstone Theater. Too bad she didn't live to see our investment come to fruition." He wagged a finger at Gigi. "We got it at an excellent price, too. Martha knew how to drive a bargain." He looked thoughtful again. "She knew how to"—he hesitated—"overlook things, as well." He glanced back toward the house, where mellow lights had suddenly appeared in the windows. He cackled gleefully. "And she knew when and how to exact her revenge."

"Revenge?"

He waved a hand at Gigi. "Ancient history now, my dear. Ancient history."

The front door creaked open. "Winston!" Barbie stood on the threshold, hands on hips. She was wearing white linen slacks and a pink cotton twin set. There was a matching pink headband holding back her blond hair.

"Coming, my dear, coming." He winked at Gigi. "I've got your nummy, yummy dinner here." He brandished the Gourmet De-Lite container at Barbie.

Her lips thinned. She nodded at Gigi. "Thank you for bringing it." She glanced out at the lawn as if trying to gauge how far along the men had been when Gigi arrived and how much she had seen.

Gigi turned around and looked, too. "They're doing a

good job," she commented, carefully watching Barbie's expression.

Barbie's face became even more pinched. "Yes. Well. We had some trouble with our previous landscapers, and it took me simply *decades*"—she drawled the word out slowly for emphasis—"to find someone new. You have absolutely no idea how much trouble it was. And here we were, *stuck* with this dreadful mess. It made me positively *sick* every time I looked out the window."

"Yes, indeed, positively sick," Winston parroted. Barbie shot him a dirty look.

"I've got my dinner now." Barbie turned her back on Gigi. "Thank you and good night." She nodded curtly at Gigi and grabbed Winston by the arm.

He followed her inside, stumbling slightly on the doorstep.

"Wait," Gigi cried out. "What about the cottage?"

"What about it?" Barbie swiveled around to face her.

"I . . . I'd like to try to buy it." Gigi thought of her last bank statement and felt her face getting hot. She really wasn't in any position to make Winston an offer. But perhaps they could work something out. She'd had the idea while driving over. If he would agree to put her rent money toward a down payment, perhaps she could get a loan for the rest of it.

Winston wiggled his arm away from Barbie's grasp. He leaned against the doorjamb and examined the fingernails of his left hand. "If you really want to take the place off my hands, who am I to stop you?" He named a price and then began a minute examination of the nails on his right hand.

Gigi gasped. "But I can't afford that much," she blurted out.

Winston pulled a sad face. "That's a pity. It would be

wonderful to have the whole issue so handily taken care of."
He took a white, monogrammed handkerchief from his
pocket and blew his nose loudly.

"I don't suppose you'd reconsider the price?"

"No way," Barbie snapped. She linked her arm in Winston's and began to pull him away from the door. "We've
waited long enough to get rid of the place as it is. It's time
we got our money's worth."

She slammed the door loudly in Gigi's face.

Gigi stood at the counter and tore red leaf lettuce into small
pieces before putting them in the large, hand-turned wooden
salad bowl she'd bought in Bon Appétit when she first moved
to Woodstone. She was creating her signature salad—a
delectable combination of lettuce, chunks of tomatoes, slices
of avocado, crumbled feta cheese, pine nuts, sliced red
onion, black olives and plumped raisins—tossed with a
dressing of balsamic vinegar whisked with extra virgin olive
oil. Reg hovered underfoot, hoping for a treat. Gigi slipped
him a piece of cheese, and he licked his lips appreciatively.

The sun was setting, creating a golden glow that lit the
small kitchen with mellow warmth. Gigi felt her stomach
clench at the thought of having to give it all up. The cottage
had helped her grow whole again after her flight from the
city and her divorce from a marriage she had been convinced
was going to last forever.

She dabbed at her eyes with the corner of her apron. She
wouldn't cry. She couldn't. Sienna was arriving at any
moment, and she had more than enough troubles of her own.
Oliver was staying in town for the night—again—and Gigi
was making her dinner to take her mind off her problems.

She was hoping that it would help take her mind off her

own troubles as well. There was no way she could afford the price Winston had mentioned for the cottage. The thought had gnawed at her all the way home. *Unless the deal from Branston Foods comes through*, a little voice whispered inside her head. Of course, she hadn't heard from Victor Branston since the opening at the Silver Lining. It seemed quite likely that he had changed his mind.

She would just have to resign herself to moving. There were plenty of apartment complexes in Crestfield, the next town over. It lacked the charm of Woodstone, but she couldn't afford to be picky. It was still near enough to make delivery of her meals relatively easy. A thought suddenly struck her. What if she couldn't take Reg? A lot of places only allowed cats, if that. She glanced down at where Reg lay at her feet, his glance faithful and trusting. She wasn't giving him up, no matter what. She'd live in her car if necessary.

If she didn't want to lose it all, she was going to have to figure out who killed Martha herself. Winston and Barbie had one of the oldest motives known to man—greed. Martha's death was a windfall to them. They'd had opportunity, too. They could have easily gotten into Gigi's car to doctor the food without being seen.

Gigi grabbed the bottle of extra virgin olive oil from the cupboard and measured half a cup into a bowl. Now that she thought about it, she realized that Martha's murder couldn't have been a spur of the moment decision. The murderer must have come prepared with the peanut oil. People didn't generally run around with a bottle of it in their car or purse.

So that person, whoever it was, must have known Martha would be at the theater that day.

All she had to do was figure out who that person was.

* * *

Gigi pulled into the parking lot of the Woodstone Theater, the wheels of her MINI kicking up a splash of dust and gravel. She'd just delivered her clients' breakfasts, and she had a few minutes to spare before she had to head home and start all over again. She maneuvered into a parking space and hauled herself out of the car. She was so tired! Her body ached, and her eyes felt as gritty as sandpaper.

The theater was empty when Gigi pushed open the door. Strange shapes loomed in the darkness that shrouded the stage. Gigi shivered, let the door close behind her, and made her way down the corridor toward Hunter Pierce's office.

Light was visible behind the frosted pane of glass. Gigi knocked and waited. A deep rumble came from behind the closed door, which she took as an invitation to enter.

Pierce was seated in front of a desktop computer that looked incongruous among the jumble of dusty outmoded furniture that filled the office. He stared at Gigi over a pair of wire-rimmed glasses that perched halfway down his long, imperious nose.

"Can I help you?" His tone indicated that he thought it unlikely.

Familiar butterflies jostled for position in Gigi's stomach. It didn't feel right going around asking people questions, but if she was going to get to the bottom of Martha's death, she had to do it. "I hope so. I was wondering what Martha Bernhardt was doing at the theater the day she had the accident. She didn't normally spend time here, did she?"

"Spend time here?" Pierce reluctantly took his hand from the computer mouse and swiveled around to face Gigi. "Not really, no. But I believe she had an appointment of some sort. Although, apparently things went awry, and the fellow never showed."

"What fellow?"

"A repairman of some sort. For the air conditioner, I believe. Martha was furious at having her time wasted like that."

"Do you know his name?"

"His name?"

"The repairman." Gigi squelched a sigh of impatience with difficulty.

"I'm afraid I don't. Martha handled those sorts of things for the theater. It was her property, after all." He gave a sniff as if to say that *artistes* like him were above such petty details.

"Is there an address book, a file or Rolodex or somewhere the name might be recorded?" This time, a brief hiss of annoyance escaped Gigi's lips.

"I believe there's a sticker on the unit itself with the repair company's name and other vitals." He fingered the computer mouse and began to turn back toward the monitor.

Gigi cleared her throat. "Can you show me where it is, then?"

It was Pierce's turn to give a sigh of exasperation. He gave one last glance at his computer screen and hoisted himself from the chair.

"All the heating and cooling systems and the like were placed in an addition that was made to the barn when it was turned into a theater." He drew out the word *theater*, giving it the English pronunciation.

Gigi followed him down the corridor toward an unmarked door at the end of the hall.

Pierce opened the door and reached inside the small, dark

room, his hand waving in the air as if he were trying to catch something. He swore softly under his breath.

"Where is the danged cord?" Finally he grasped something and pulled. A dusty lightbulb glowed dimly in the gloom.

"I believe this is what you're looking for." Pierce slapped a square piece of machinery and it gave a hollow *thump*. "Phone number should be on the side somewhere." He held the door open for Gigi and edged out of the small space.

Gigi peered at the piece of equipment, searching for a label. Of course it was on the back, where she could barely see it. She leaned over the air conditioner and peered upside down at the square, white patch affixed to the back side. The phone number was just visible. She repeated the numbers over and over in her head as she scrabbled in her purse for a pen and a piece of scratch paper.

"Got it?"

Gigi nodded, and Pierce let the door slam shut behind them.

The air conditioner repairman wasn't in when Gigi called, but his assistant said he was expected back any minute. Rather than wait to telephone again, Gigi decided she would stop by, since it was on her way home.

Tom's Heating and Cooling was on the second floor of a small building just off of High Street. Gigi pulled into the parking lot and parked next to a shiny red truck that she hoped meant the repairman was back in his office.

He was. Gigi found him sitting at one of the two desks crammed into the tiny office space. He had a piece of waxed paper spread open on top of a helter-skelter stack of papers and was about to take a bite out of a very large bagel that oozed cream cheese and smelled like onions.

Gigi caught him mid-chew. He nodded and reached for his napkin, swiping it across the three-day-old growth of beard on his chin.

"Help you?" he asked as he gulped down his bite of bagel.

Once again Gigi felt the familiar butterflies churning in her stomach. Investigating was nerve-wracking. She hated going around asking such nosy questions! She closed her eyes and curled her toes under.

"Did you have an appointment to meet with Martha Bernhardt at the Woodstone Theater last week?" She opened her eyes to see Tom—at least she assumed that was his name—shaking his head furiously.

"No!" he thundered making Gigi jump. She took a step backward, but there was no place to go in the small space.

"Sorry." Tom smiled and wiped a hand across his face. "It's just that that woman, Ms. Bernhardt, gave me a terrible time about missing our appointment. Problem is, we didn't have no appointment. It wasn't in my book"—he flicked a thumb at a dog-eared appointment book open on the desk—"and Shirley"—this time he jerked a thumb at the empty desk in back of him—"didn't have no record of it, either." He shook his head. "The woman wouldn't believe me. Kept saying someone had called her to tell her that we had an appointment that morning, and that I was late." His voice rose in indignation.

"Did Martha, er, Ms. Bernhardt, say who told her about the appointment?"

"Afraid not. I just know it wasn't Shirley here, else she would have written it down in the book." He thumped the coffee-stained planner with the flat of his hand.

"Do you know if it was a man or a woman—?"

But he was already shaking his head. "I don't know much of anything about it. Just that Ms. Bernhardt was mistaken. We didn't have no appointment that day, or any other, for that matter, either." He picked up his bagel. "I offered to come out another day and see to the air conditioner, but she just slammed the phone down in my ear."

Well, that seemed to be that, Gigi thought as she opened her car door and got in. Even the repairman didn't know Martha was going to be at the theater that day. It was all a mix-up. She paused suddenly with her hand on the ignition key. Maybe it wasn't such a mix-up after all. Maybe someone had told Martha about the appointment to lure her to the theater. Knowing full well, of course, that Tom's Heating and Cooling had no idea Martha was expecting them.

But that one person, the *murderer*—Gigi still couldn't wrap her mind around that word—knew Martha was going to be there. And they had come prepared.

Chapter 9

Gigi's palms were sweating when she hung up the phone. She leaned against the wall, hands on her knees, and blew out such a huge breath that her bangs flopped up and down. She grabbed her mug of coffee off the kitchen island, and the dark brew sloshed back and forth in the cup. Her hands were still shaking.

She leaned her elbows on the island where she had a dozen open Gourmet De-Lite containers waiting for their contents—this morning it was a low-fat yet very tasty breakfast frittata. Everything swam in a hazy sort of light. She wiped her eyes with the corner of her apron and tried to will her heart rate to slow down.

She'd just gotten off the phone with Victor Branston. And he was still very much interested in a deal with Gigi's Gourmet De-Lite. He would be presenting the idea to his board that very day at a lunch meeting. And he wanted one dozen Gourmet De-Lite lunches to serve to the board members.

It was a tall order, but Gigi couldn't afford to say no. Somehow, she'd have to get the meals prepared and delivered on time.

Mentally, she ran through her repertoire of lunch dishes. She wanted something that seemed substantial yet was obviously low calorie. Something extremely tasty and maybe a little unexpected. She pulled her black binder from the drawer and began to flip through the pages. Nothing grabbed her interest.

She fished a yellow pad from the same drawer, plucked a pencil from the empty jam jar next to the telephone and grabbed her mug. It was almost empty. She refilled it and carried everything over to the kitchen table.

She thumbed through the pages again, but nothing caught her eye. She sat for a minute, chin resting on her palm. The majority of the board members were probably men. And men liked something that felt good and solid for their meals. She might have to cheat a bit calorie-wise. When she had to do that with her clients—because she wanted to give them an extra-special something for lunch—she always made up for it with a lighter dinner. But the board of Branston Foods wasn't specifically on a diet. She had a sudden mental image of all these fat cats in jackets straining at the buttons, sitting around a beautifully polished wooden table. Gigi shook her head and rubbed a hand across her eyes. No use in stereotyping her audience.

She'd slice up some lean flank steak very, very thinly, then soak it in an Asian marinade with plenty of garlic, sesame and ginger, then she'd grill it and serve it over a salad of baby field greens dressed with a rice wine vinaigrette. She might mix some water chestnuts into the salad as well and a handful of chopped walnuts. Lots of nice crunch there.

She grabbed her pad and began working out a list. She

glanced at the clock, and her heart sped up in panic. She had to finish packing up the Gourmet De-Lite breakfasts and get them delivered, then she had to prepare a dozen of these special lunches, plus the regular ones, and get all of those delivered before noon.

She was really going to have to hustle.

Gigi pulled into the parking lot of the Shop and Save just outside of town and looked around in dismay. Cars vied for every available spot, and it looked as crowded as if it were three o'clock on the Wednesday before Thanksgiving. Had everyone in Woodstone decided to go shopping this morning?

She found a narrow spot next to the Dumpster around back and once again blessed the compactness of her MINI. She could barely open the driver's door but managed to slip through the sliver of an opening between her car and an oversize SUV that had been parked crookedly.

Inside, the store hummed with chatter, with shoppers tangling carts, blocking aisles and toppling displays. Gigi's hands clenched on the handle of her cart as a woman in a pink velour Juicy Couture sweatsuit cut her off without so much as a *sorry* tossed over her shoulder. She took a deep breath and maneuvered down the aisle and in front of the meat counter, where expensive steaks and roasts gleamed pinkly on artfully arranged beds of curly parsley.

Gigi punched the button on the number machine, and it spit out a ticket with *33* in large, black numerals. She glanced at the board over the counter and was dismayed to see *22* prominently displayed. She looked at her watch. This was going to take forever.

The flank steaks were toward the back of the crowded

meat counter, fanned out on a black tray. They looked excellent. Flank steak is a potentially tough cut of meat because it's so lean, but Gigi had had a lot of success using marinades and cutting the slices as thin as possible. Technically, flank steak isn't even steak—it's the belly muscle of the cow—but she had no plans to tell her customers that. All they needed to know was that it contained almost no fat and, when properly prepared, had a wonderful flavor.

The line went quickly until the woman just ahead of Gigi got to the counter. The butcher spent an eternity trying to explain the properties of hanger steak versus those of skirt steak. The woman had recently eaten one of each at some trendy New York bistro and wanted to create a similar dish for her upcoming dinner party.

Gigi sweated as the rather plump blonde and the butcher—Gus, according to his name tag—discussed the relative merits of each. Finally, it was her turn, and she placed her order quickly. Gus wasted no time in wrapping the meat in butcher paper secured with old-fashioned string. Gigi dropped the package into her cart and began to wheel away, but ran smack into someone's back.

Gigi was already apologizing when the fellow whirled around, and she realized it was Carlo.

"Carlo! I'm so sorry. I wasn't watching where I was going."

Carlo shook his head. "No, no, that is okay. I am fine." He smiled shyly and pointed at Gigi's cart. "What are you cooking today?"

Gigi looked up into Carlo's dark eyes. She felt her heartbeat jerk slightly, and she was a little breathless as she explained about the order from Branston Foods.

"You will need some help, then," Carlo declared decisively.

"But the restaurant—" Gigi countered as he took control of her cart and began to wheel it away from the counter.

"Closed for lunch today. The water heater sprang a leak." He made a gesture with his hands. "So we had to get the plumber to come and fix it."

"Oh!" Gigi cried. "That's too bad."

"Not at all! It's a stroke of luck. Now I am free to help you." Carlo smiled broadly, and Gigi felt herself flush.

To cover her awkwardness, she bent her head over her list.

"Where do we go next?"

"Produce." Gigi pointed toward the first aisle, and Carlo wheeled the cart around.

They went up and down the aisles collecting ingredients, and, in what seemed like no time at all to Gigi, Carlo was pushing the cart toward the registers, arguing amiably with her about which was the shortest line.

"This is so charming, *cara*." Carlo looked around Gigi's small kitchen. Sunlight slanted through the bay window and made a warm puddle of light on the wood floor where Reg was curled in its center. Carlo hoisted three bags of groceries onto the counter. He wouldn't let Gigi carry anything heavier than her purse, and she felt foolish walking up the drive empty-handed. "What do we do first?" He emptied the last of the contents of the bags and lined them up on the island.

"I'll put together the marinade if you don't mind slicing the beef? It needs to be super-thin."

"I'd be delighted." Carlo took off his tweed blazer and slung it over the back of a chair. It was gently worn, with patches at the elbows. He pushed up his sleeves and contemplated Gigi's knife block before selecting a knife with a long, thin blade. He pulled out the old-fashioned sharpening steel and began to run the knife back and forth with dazzling speed—like a virtuoso violinist wielding the bow.

Gigi watched as light glinted off the sharp blade, and she shivered slightly. Somewhere in Woodstone a murderer was loose. What if it were Carlo? She was alone with him in the house, and he had one of her sharpest knives in his hand. She shook her head firmly. She was being ridiculous. Carlo wouldn't hurt anyone!

She got busy assembling her marinade ingredients and whisking them together in a white ceramic bowl. Carefully, drop by drop, she drizzled in some sesame oil.

"Your steak will soften up nicely if you soak it in some olive oil." Carlo stood with the bottle of extra virgin olive oil poised above the thin slices of steak he'd arranged on a plate.

"No," Gigi shouted, lunging for the bottle.

"I'm sorry." Carlo's face fell. "I did something wrong?"

"No, it's just that oil has a lot of calories—one hundred per tablespoon, to be exact." Gigi took the bottle and carefully put it back in its place in the cupboard. "My customers can't afford to eat that many calories. They're all trying to lose weight."

Carlo looked baffled. "And yet I see them eating all kinds of bad foods." He made a frustrated gesture with his hands. "What you call junk food, I think. Your Adora, for instance"—he pointed at Gigi—"when I went to see Emilio at the theater one day, I found her hiding something in the prop box. When I asked her what it was"—he made a helpless gesture with his hands—"she said it was a bag of chips." He shook his head. "That is not good, no?"

"No," Gigi agreed.

Carlo laughed and came to stand right behind her as she covered the beef he'd sliced with the garlic and ginger marinade. "People are funny, no?"

Gigi could feel his breath whisper against the side of her neck. She turned around, and they were face-to-face, inches apart. Heat flashed across her cheeks as if someone had suddenly opened the oven door. She tried to take a step backward, but she was already pressed against the edge of the counter. Carlo was close enough that she could see the flecks of gold in his brown eyes. Gigi held her breath as they stared at each other, momentarily as frozen as an ice sculpture.

The tick of the clock behind her made Gigi jump. She swiveled her head around and gasped. "We'll never make it. I have to get the food there by noon . . ."

"Then we must hurry." Carlo spun on his heel and grabbed the bag of lettuce from the counter. He held it up toward Gigi. "To be washed, yes?"

She nodded thankfully. Her hands shook a little as she retrieved the olive oil from the pantry and carefully measured some into a small bowl.

Carlo raised an eyebrow at the miserly amount but didn't say anything, merely gave a shrug of feigned indifference. He filled the sink with cold water and plunged the lettuce under with both hands.

Gigi watched as he gathered the tender leaves from their icy bath and dropped them into her salad spinner. "Are you sure this won't make the lettuce too . . . too . . . tired?" Carlo gestured toward the spinner.

Gigi laughed. "No more tired than I am."

"You are tired. I can see it in your eyes." Carlo's face drooped in concern. "But this is important, no?"

"Yes." Gigi nodded.

"Then we will make it happen."

The salad spinner whirred feverishly as Carlo spun the lettuce dry. He emptied it into a large bowl Gigi had set on the counter. "You have some dressing, or do they have to eat it plain?" He pulled a silly face, and Gigi laughed.

"There's some dressing, don't worry. I'll mix it up as soon as I finish with this." Gigi carefully turned the slices of meat grilling on her cast-iron stovetop grill.

"It smells delicious." Carlo sniffed appreciatively. "I think your lunch will be a big success."

"I hope so." Gigi's shoulders drooped. "I hope Victor Branston likes the meal. I really need this deal to go through."

Carlo looked at her inquisitively.

Gigi made a gesture that encompassed the kitchen and the rest of the cottage. "I want to be able to afford to buy my cottage whenever the owner is ready to sell."

"But your business does quite well, no?"

"No." Gigi shook her head. "Yes. Yes, I'm doing quite well, but I don't know how long it's going to last with people thinking that I . . . I . . . poisoned Martha with peanut oil." Gigi's voice cracked, and Carlo's eyebrows drew together in concern.

"But no one would think that, would they?"

Gigi nodded. "They might."

Carlo's frown deepened, and a dark cloud descended on his bright eyes. "It makes me very sad to hear that." He looked down at his hands, and Gigi could see the muscle in his jaw clenching and unclenching. He turned toward her and opened his mouth, then shut it again with a decisive click. He bent his head over the lettuce, quickly tearing it into bite-sized pieces.

Gigi wondered what he had been about to say. She

thought of Martha with her face perpetually creased into sour lines of discontent. She tried to feel sad that Martha was gone, but she just felt empty.

"No one could ever think you would hurt anyone. Certainly not poison them." Carlo looked up abruptly. "The police, that detective, they don't really think you had anything to do with it?"

"I don't know. The problem is, there don't seem to be any other suspects." Gigi carried the platter of grilled meat over to the island where she had a dozen Gourmet De-Lite boxes open and ready. She gestured toward them. "Here, let's put some salad in each of these."

"I think that Martha was really not very nice," Carlo said as he helped Gigi fill each container with freshly washed greens. "Many people didn't like her. Adora, Barbie, Winston," he ticked the names off one by one on his fingers.

"I don't suppose her restaurant reviews made her a lot of friends, either," Gigi said thinking back to one she had read upon her arrival in Woodstone. Martha's review had been scathing, and the place had closed shortly afterward. She handed Carlo the bowl of dressing, and he began spooning some over the lettuce in each of the containers. "Did Martha ever review Al Forno?" Gigi glanced up at Carlo.

His arm jerked, and the sauce flew into the air, landing in a puddle on the counter. "I'm so sorry." He grabbed some paper towels and blotted up the spot. "No. No, Martha did not yet review Al Forno. We had hoped she would come, but . . ." He spread his hands wide.

"So she never even ate there?"

Carlo shook his head quickly. "No. Never. I had planned to make her our famous vegetable lasagna, but now . . ." He shrugged.

He looked at Gigi, his glance sliding to a spot above her right ear.

He was lying. She was sure of it. But why? Surely Carlo didn't have anything to do with Martha's death.

Did he?

Gigi drove slowly down High Street, head swiveling, searching for a parking place. There was a small space tucked between a shiny new Escalade and a battered vintage nineties Volvo station wagon. Gigi bit her lip. Parallel parking wasn't one of her strong suits, but she thought the MINI ought to be small enough to fit.

She pulled alongside the space and began turning the wheel. The angle was wrong. She looked in her rearview mirror, but no one was hovering impatiently behind her. She straightened the car and tried again. It still wasn't quite right. She was ready to give up and head for the lot at the end of town when she noticed someone watching her.

It was Detective Mertz. And there was a funny look on his face. If she didn't know better, she would almost think it was a smile. She straightened the car again. Now she had to get it into the space. She couldn't let Mertz get away with laughing at her like that.

Gigi's hands were slippery on the wheel. She worried her lower lip with her teeth as she concentrated on the parking maneuver that had always seemed to come so easily to Ted. And men in general. Just the thought made her mad.

There was a knock on the window, and Gigi stopped, her foot jammed on the brake. She zapped her window down.

Mertz's face was grave, but she thought she saw a brief, dancing glint in his steel gray eyes. He bent down until their heads were almost level. "I need to ask you some questions about the death of Miss Martha Bernhardt."

"Now?" Gigi scowled, glancing at the clock on her dashboard. She was starving, and had planned to stop in at Al Forno to pick up something quick for lunch. By the time she was finished making all the Gourmet De-Lite meals, the last thing she wanted to do was cook for herself. She hadn't eaten much since the day before—an attack of nerves had sidelined her appetite. She had no idea how soon she'd be hearing from Branston Foods, but with Carlo's help, they'd delivered all the meals promptly on the stroke of twelve noon.

Mertz nodded. "I apologize for the inconvenience, but it would be most helpful if you could spare me a few minutes."

"Fine. Just let me park my car."

"I'd be happy to do it for you."

Gigi glared at him as she zapped her window closed.

Mercifully, the car slid into the spot this time without a hitch. Gigi wiped a trickle of sweat off the back of her neck with a tissue. Her hand inched toward her purse and her lipstick and compact, but she stopped herself. What did she care how she looked in front of Detective Mertz?

She had the feeling that he was watching her as she slid out of the car, but when she glanced at him out of the corner of her eye, his face was as unreadable as a statue's, and he was standing straight and tall with his hands clasped behind his back.

"Okay." She squinted up at him when he didn't move.

He nodded. "Would you mind if we got a bite to eat while we talk? I haven't had lunch yet."

Gigi felt her own stomach grumble. "Sure." She looked down the street toward the Woodstone Diner. The place was clean, even if the most imaginative thing on the menu was a black-and-white milkshake.

"I think you'll like Al Forno." Mertz inclined his head toward the red and green striped awning.

"Oh." Gigi was caught by surprise and hesitated.

"If you would rather some place else?"

"No. Al Forno. That's fine." Gigi took a determined step in that direction. She pushed aside the extremely irrational thought that she didn't want Carlo to see her with Mertz and get the wrong idea. That was ridiculous. It was none of Carlo's business who she had lunch with, and she wasn't really having lunch with Mertz—they were just killing two birds with one stone by having something to eat while he asked her his questions.

It was slightly past the lunch hour, and the crowd at Al Forno had already thinned. A group of men in business-casual khakis and golf shirts were nursing cups of coffee and picking at the remains of dessert, while at another table, a group of women toasted a very pregnant coworker as she unwrapped gifts covered in pastel-colored paper. A lone man sat at the bar, the remains of his lunch pushed to one side, his briefcase open on the empty stool next to him.

Emilio rushed forward when he saw Gigi. "*Cara*, come in, come in. We have a wonderful *pasta e fagioli* today that you are going to love." He smacked his lips. "Come sit at the bar and talk to me while I polish the glasses."

Mertz stepped out of the shadows and stood next to Gigi.

"Oh." Emilio's hand flew to his mouth, and his face froze. "A table for two?" he asked in a stilted voice.

Gigi nodded.

"This way, please." He spun on his heel and turned his back on them.

He led them to a large table, set for four, that stood smack in the center of the room. Gigi almost laughed. She wasn't here to canoodle with Mertz, and if she were, Emilio's choice of table almost guaranteed they'd have no privacy.

Emilio busied himself removing the extra two place settings as Mertz pulled out a chair for Gigi. Emilio's normally open and friendly face was settled into a deep frown. Gigi tried to smile at him, but he kept his eyes down and averted.

Emilio snapped his fingers, and a waitress came running to their table. She had blond hair piled on top of her head in a loose bun and was wearing a low-cut white shirt and candy pink glossy lipstick. She had a water pitcher in one hand and two menus in the other. Emilio grabbed the menus and plunked one down at each of their places as the waitress filled their water goblets.

"Lara will be back to take your order," Emilio said stiffly before walking away.

"Do you need a few minutes?" Lara smiled at Mertz, and Gigi could see a piece of bright orange gum parked in the back of her mouth.

Mertz nodded curtly, his eyes on his menu. Lara shrugged and flounced off toward the kitchen.

Gigi flipped open her own menu and scanned the luncheon entrees. Her appetite had suddenly deserted her. Carlo was nowhere to be seen, but she expected him to appear at any moment. What would she say? Not that she owed him an explanation. She sat up straighter. She had every right to be sitting in Al Forno with Detective Mertz. Especially since it was official business.

And even if it weren't, Carlo had never asked her out . . .

She stopped with her water glass halfway to her mouth. Where had that thought come from? She'd never before even admitted to herself that she wanted to go on a date with Carlo. And she didn't. She really and truly didn't.

Mertz slapped his menu closed. "I've decided. And you?"

Gigi nodded. She'd hardly glanced at the menu, but she'd been to Al Forno enough times to know what was on it. "I'll have the *pasta e fagioli* Emilio mentioned."

Mertz nodded and turned around to look for the waitress. He waved, and Lara rushed over to their table.

Lara leaned over the table as Mertz gave their order, but if she expected to catch Mertz's eye, she was doomed to disappointment. Gigi almost laughed. Mertz kept his glance averted and his face rigid.

Finally, Lara flounced off toward the kitchen again, and they were alone. Mertz cleared his throat. "I appreciate your meeting with me over lunch." His mouth quirked to one side in a semblance of a smile. "Otherwise I wouldn't have a chance to eat until dinnertime."

Gigi glanced at Mertz's impressive shoulders. He probably needed plenty of nourishment to feed all those muscles.

Mertz looked around the room. "I've never been here before, but I've heard the food is good."

"It is." Gigi fiddled with her water glass. Emilio stood behind the bar, furiously polishing glasses and throwing glances their way. So far there was no sign of Carlo.

Mertz ran a finger around his collar as if it were choking him. "The only Italian food I've ever had is pizza."

"You'll like it," Gigi reassured him. "I think it's some of the best food there is."

Mertz nodded. "Ma had to feed six boys, so we were a real meat-and-potatoes kind of family."

Six boys? No wonder Mertz was so uncomfortable

around her, Gigi realized. Growing up with all those boys, he probably knew very little about women.

He cleared his throat. "Did you see anyone around your car the day Ms. Bernhardt was killed?" he asked, getting down to business. Obviously he had depleted his entire stock of small talk.

Gigi sat up straighter. She thought back to the day of Martha's car accident. "I don't remember seeing anyone. But I wasn't paying very much attention." Gigi pleated the napkin in her lap.

"What exactly did you do that day?" Mertz's expression was intense. "Try to remember it step-by-step. If you did see someone, it might come back to you."

Gigi closed her eyes and mentally retraced her steps on that fateful day. She ran through it like a movie playing in her head—ending with Martha driving away and eventually hitting the tree. She felt her hands clench at the memory and opened her eyes to see Mertz watching her intently. She shrugged. "I'm sorry. I just don't remember if there was anyone near my car. There may have been, but I just can't remember."

Mertz nodded. "That's okay. But if something does come to you, be sure to give me a call." He reached into his jacket pocket, pulled out a card and pushed it across the table toward Gigi.

Gigi was about to pick it up when someone slid a plate in front of her. She looked up. It was Carlo.

His eyes were dark and miserable, and his mouth was set in a thin, tight line. Gigi started to say something but then closed her mouth. What could she say? She really didn't owe Carlo any explanation. None at all. Still, she felt terrible seeing the look on his face.

Carlo slid a grilled chicken pesto panini in front of Mertz. Mertz looked at it doubtfully.

"Could I get a cup of coffee, please?" Mertz nodded stiffly at Carlo.

Carlo nodded back, and Gigi could tell by his expression and the rigid set of his shoulders that he disapproved. According to Carlo and Emilio, the only thing to drink with lunch or dinner was a glass of an appropriate wine or, if for some reason you chose not to drink, a glass of bottled Italian water. Coffee was for after dinner only.

Carlo brought over the coffeepot nonetheless and deftly slid a cup and saucer onto the table at Mertz's place. He began to pour the dark, vibrant brew they served at Al Forno when his arm jerked and hot liquid was suddenly pouring onto the table and into Mertz's lap.

Mertz jumped up, nearly upsetting the table. Gigi's glass of water toppled over and mingled with the spilt coffee.

"*Merde*," Carlo muttered as he put the coffeepot down on the table. "Please excuse me. My mistake." He grabbed the napkin Gigi handed him and began to mop up the spilled coffee.

"Lara." Carlo snapped his fingers, and the waitress bustled over with a roll of paper towels.

"I am so sorry about that." She twinkled at Mertz as she dabbed at his trousers with a wad of paper towels. "At least it wasn't my fault this time." She ripped off some fresh towels and dropped them on top of the puddle on the table. "Carlo went ballistic last week when I spilled a drop of water on a customer."

Gigi was surprised. That didn't sound like Carlo.

"She was someone real important," Lara continued, as if she had read Gigi's thoughts. "I don't remember her name, but Carlo seemed to think she might say bad things about Al Forno on account of it." Lara shrugged. "It wasn't my fault that's the day the chef decided to overcook the chicken."

"What did the woman look like?" Gigi righted her now empty water glass. The liquid had flooded Mertz's plate, leaving his panini a soggy mess.

"Ordinary," Lara replied snapping her gum. "Dark hair. About so tall." She held a hand out roughly level with her own head. "Nothing special, you know?"

Gigi's stomach plummeted. She had a pretty good idea who the woman might have been.

And if she were right, then Carlo was in big trouble.

Chapter 10

"Carlo a murderer?" Sienna squealed.

Gigi put a finger to her lips and looked around. "Shhh, not so loud."

Sienna grabbed Gigi by the elbow and pulled her through a beaded curtain and into the storeroom of the Book Nook. She leaned against a towering stack of dusty volumes, chin in hand. "Okay, now tell me everything."

Gigi explained about the waitress and Carlo getting all upset about her spilling water on the woman. "It must have been Martha," Gigi declared.

"Not necessarily." The books Sienna was leaning on began to wobble, and she grabbed them quickly. "It could have been any good customer that Carlo didn't want to upset."

"I wish that were true. But I know Carlo. He wouldn't act like that for no reason. It had to have been someone very important. And that someone had to have been Martha. She was probably planning to review Al Forno."

Sienna frowned. "We don't know that—"

"Believe me. I don't want it to be Carlo, either," Gigi said, wondering why she was trying so hard to convince Sienna of just that.

"You *are* falling for him!" Sienna thumped the stack of books, and they wobbled dangerously.

"I'm not," Gigi said, but the denial felt halfhearted, even to her.

"You are." Sienna clapped her hands. "We knew it. Everyone has been—"

"What?" Gigi demanded. "Has everyone been talking about me?"

"No, no, it's just that anyone can see Carlo is crazy about you." She glanced at her watch. "Come on. It's teatime. Let's sit down with a cup and figure out what we're going to do."

"What *are* we going to do?" Gigi followed her glumly to the coffee corner and collapsed on the sagging sofa while Sienna fiddled with the tea things.

"First, we have to find out if Martha planned to review Al Forno. Because if not, then it doesn't matter what happened to this mystery woman Lara claims ate at Al Forno."

"I can stop by the newspaper on my way home and talk to the editor," Gigi interjected. "You're right. If Martha had no intention of reviewing Al Forno, then Carlo had no reason to murder her." Her tongue stuck a little on the word *murder*.

Sienna nodded as she poured hot water from the coffeemaker into two mugs.

"Carlo has been acting rather weird, though. Like yesterday, when he was helping me with the lunches for Branston Foods—"

"What? You didn't tell me that." Sienna stamped her foot in mock offense and water sloshed over the side of one of the mugs.

"Don't look at me like that. Nothing happened!" Gigi thought about that moment when she and Carlo had come face-to-face, pressed together in her tiny kitchen and how, just for a second, she had thought he might kiss her. She could feel heat coloring her cheeks, and it wasn't from the hot tea.

Sienna smiled smugly and took a sip from her cup. "All the more reason to prove Carlo had nothing to do with this whole business." She plopped down in the chair opposite Gigi, moved a stack of books out of the way and leaned back. "So what do you mean by *weird*?"

"Kind of jumpy. I mentioned something about Martha reviewing Al Forno, and he spilled dressing all over the counter."

"Hmmm." Sienna fiddled with one of the sequins scattered across her long, gauzy skirt. "But this woman the waitress told you about—it could have been anyone, right?"

"Lara said she had plain, short hair, not very tall, rather severe."

Sienna snorted. "That describes half the population of Woodstone. It doesn't prove it was Martha."

"It had to have been. Why else would Carlo get so upset?"

Sienna turned her tea around and around in her hands. "True. You're probably right. That's not like Carlo." She stared into her mug for several long seconds. "So, if that was Martha, and things didn't go well with the dinner, chances are she would have been giving them a pretty bad review. Assuming she'd been planning to review Al Forno in the first place."

"It could have ruined them. Like that other place—"

"The Woodstone River Grill?"

Gigi nodded. "They closed shortly after Martha's review appeared in the *Woodstone Times*."

Sienna frowned. "Then that gives Carlo a pretty good motive for murder, doesn't it?" She looked up at Gigi, her face pinched and her mouth drawn downward.

Gigi's face mirrored Sienna's. "I'm afraid so."

Traffic crawled through downtown Woodstone. Gigi sat behind a double-parked Sweet Kleen laundry van and watched as the numbers on her dashboard clock ticked toward the hour. The offices of the *Woodstone Times* would be locking their doors any minute now, and she had no idea whether Devon Singleton would leave with the staff or not. There was no point in even blowing her horn, since the van's driver was still inside the Woodstone Medical Group with his delivery.

And she had to get home, fill her Gourmet De-Lite containers, and get them delivered. Fortunately, dinner was cooking itself today—the slow cooker was a wonderful tool for producing low-fat dishes. Tonight it was a savory beef barbecue that she would serve over whole-grain buns with a low-fat coleslaw.

The thought of food made her feel slightly queasy. She couldn't believe Carlo would murder anyone—not even the acerbic Martha. But if Martha had been planning to pan Al Forno, it really was quite possible. She wasn't in love with Carlo, no matter what Sienna thought, but the idea of his not being there behind the counter of Al Forno as usual made the area in the region of her heart ache in a strange way.

A sharp-faced woman in a long denim skirt and Birkenstock sandals was locking the front door to the *Woodstone Times* when Gigi got there, hot and breathless.

"Has Mr. Singleton gone?" she panted. The only parking place she'd been able to find was in the lot at the other end of High Street.

The woman paused in the process of putting her key in the lock and looked at Gigi. "We're closed." She turned the key decisively.

"Yes, I can see that, but I need to talk to Mr. Singleton. If he's here."

The woman gave a sigh that heaved her sloping shoulders up and down. "Suppose it's okay." She slid the key back into the lock, turned it and pushed the door open with one broad hip. "Devon," she called through cupped hands. "Someone here wants to see you."

"All right," came the grumbled reply from somewhere down the hall.

"I'll be going then." The woman headed toward the glass-fronted door.

Gigi perched on a chair in front of the reception desk and flipped through a dog-eared copy of the previous day's paper. Finally she heard footsteps shuffling down the hall. She realized she'd never met Devon Singleton before. She also realized she had no idea what she was going to say.

She'd been expecting an older man, Gigi realized, as Devon Singleton ambled into the reception area, running a hand through black hair that was already standing on end. He looked to be about twenty-five years old and was wearing low-slung jeans with a rip at one knee and a faded white T-shirt upon which the red letters *BU* were faintly visible.

"Hey," he said, and stood looking at Gigi, one foot on top of the other, one hand scratching his belly.

"Devon Singleton?"

He nodded and gave a grin that made him look even younger. "What's up?" He tilted his head to the side and stifled a yawn with the back of his hand. "Sorry. I haven't been getting much sleep. New baby." And he grinned again.

"Congratulations." When had newspaper editors become so young? Gigi wondered.

He gestured behind him. "Want to go sit in my office? I left my coffee on the desk."

"Sure." Gigi followed him down the hallway, where framed copies of the front pages of the *Woodstone Times* were hung every few feet.

Devon's office was surprisingly neat, with an aerody-namic computer chair and an ergonomic keyboard. A Nerf ball hoop stood in one corner and a scrolling computerized picture frame was in a prominent position on his desk.

He picked up a cardboard container of coffee from the Woodstone Beanery and motioned toward a low-slung chair in front of his desk.

Gigi sat down, and her knees immediately jackknifed to a position under her chin. She hoped she didn't look as stu-pid as she felt.

Devon threw himself into his chair and took a big gulp of his coffee. "So, what's up?" He glanced at the picture frame, where a drooling baby was staring up at the camera.

Gigi fiddled with the strap of her purse. She couldn't just come right out and ask him if Martha was planning to review Al Forno, could she? She cleared her throat. Devon was still staring at the rotating pictures of his new baby.

What if she pretended to have some connection to Al Forno? Devon wouldn't be likely to know one way or the other.

"It's about Al Forno, actually."

Devon reluctantly peeled his eyes away from his newborn to glance at Gigi. "The place down the street?"

"You know it?"

"Sure." He poked a finger through the hole in the knee of his jeans and scratched idly. "Can't afford it now, though. Even if we could get a sitter."

Gigi nodded and wet her lips. *Here goes nothing*, she thought. "I'm doing some freelance marketing for Al Forno." She put both hands behind her back and crossed her fingers. She still couldn't tell even a tiny white lie without thinking of the nuns back in grade school.

Devon nodded, and his head swiveled back to the baby pictures.

"And I'm wondering . . ." Gigi cleared her throat again. "Are there any plans for the *Woodstone Times* to review Al Forno?"

Devon tore his gaze from the baby pictures long enough to look slightly startled. "I guess you didn't hear about Martha. Martha Bernhardt. She'd been reviewing for the *Woodstone Times* for, like, forever—"

"Yes. I heard about what happened. Terrible, just terrible." Gigi tried to look suitably sad. She really was sad, but if she started to think about it now, she wouldn't be able to concentrate. "Are there any plans for anyone to take her place? Not that anyone could, of course . . ."

Devon grunted.

"And maybe they would consider reviewing my client's restaurant."

"It's funny . . ." Devon began, when his attention was caught by a particularly adorable baby picture that had rotated to the screen. It changed again, back to the beginning this time, and he returned his attention to Gigi.

"What's funny?" she prompted encouragingly.

"Well, Martha told me she was planning for her next review to be Al Forno. As a matter of fact, she said she was really looking forward to it."

"So Martha was planning on reviewing Al Forno."

"Apparently." Gigi sighed. "And now she's dead. Murdered." She choked the word out.

Sienna rolled a wide swath of white paint across a piece of scenery intended to suggest part of the elegant drawing room that was the setting for the first act of *Truth or Dare*. She had a smudge of paint on the end of her nose and a streak of it through her golden hair.

Gigi sat with her back against a large armoire that would be wheeled into place during the third act while Sienna worked on her piece of scenery. She'd volunteered to help in order to keep busy during Oliver's increasing absences.

"Do you really think she was murdered because of that? I mean, a bad review isn't life or death."

"It isn't, of course, but it depends on how you look at it. If Al Forno closed because of it, where would Carlo and Emilio be? I'm pretty sure Emilio only got a visa because he's helping Carlo with the restaurant."

"But still"—Sienna dipped her roller in paint—"I can't picture either Emilio or Carlo murdering Martha."

"Maybe they just wanted to scare her, or delay the review, and things backfired. It's not like they held a gun to her head or stabbed her in cold blood. All they had to do was add some peanuts to the food I'd prepared and then let nature take its course."

Gigi sprang to her feet and began pacing. "Remember the day Martha was killed? Someone had stolen her purse. Why? She said she didn't have much money in it—barely more than a five dollar bill."

"Maybe the thief was after something else?" Sienna dipped her roller in the paint tray again and ran it back and forth to remove the excess paint.

Gigi stared out into the darkened theater where the ghost light flickered feebly—a light left burning to prevent hapless actors from breaking their necks when entering an unlit theater, or to keep ghosts at bay, depending on your beliefs. "If not money, then what?"

Gigi thought back to the times she'd seen Martha at the theater or around town. She always carried the same purse— a large, black leather satchel with handles that she looped over her arm or tucked over her shoulder. She closed her eyes and tried to picture it more clearly. She snapped her fingers and whirled around toward Sienna.

"Her notebook," she announced triumphantly. "It was spiral bound with a brown cover. About so big." She held her hands about six inches apart. "I saw her at the Wood-stone Diner once, making notes in it. Then, when she came to ask me about Gigi's Gourmet De-Lite, she wrote everything down in the same notebook."

Sienna stopped mid-roll. A blob of white paint dripped onto her foot, but she didn't notice it. "And maybe her notes about her dining experience at Al Forno were in the same notebook."

Gigi paced faster, her hands clenched in front of her. "And maybe that's why her purse had to disappear." She whirled around to face Sienna. "Carlo said something when he was helping me prepare the lunches for Branston Foods." Gigi realized she still hadn't heard from Victor Branston, but she pushed the thought out of her mind. "He said Adora is hiding chip bags in the prop box."

Sienna pointed the roller at Gigi, and another blob of white paint slid down her calf and landed on her big toe. "And how would he know that if he hadn't been going in there himself?" Sienna made a wide gesture with the roller and paint splattered in every direction, like an airborne Jackson Pollock. "He stole Martha's purse with her notebook and stuffed it in the prop box."

Gigi and Sienna whirled around as one and headed for the prop box. They lifted the lid and began to root through the contents. Finally, they pulled out the last item—a rather moth-eaten stuffed bear—and stared into the now-empty depths.

"Okay, there's nothing here now, but what if this was merely a temporary hiding place?"

Sienna looked at Gigi with one eyebrow raised.

"Okay, let's go back to the day Martha's purse was stolen." Gigi had a sudden flashback to Martha's car swerving unsteadily across the yellow line before heading straight at the roundabout and the sturdy oak tree in its center. She rubbed a hand across her forehead. "Someone—and we don't know who that is yet," she added defiantly, "steals Martha's purse. This place is crawling with people. I've just arrived with the lunches, Barbie flits out to have lunch in the car with Winston. Who knows who else was coming and going at the time."

"So this person has this purse, which, of course, they can't possibly be seen with," Sienna added.

"Yes." Gigi turned on her heel and began pacing in the other direction. "So what do they do?" She looked up at Sienna.

"Ditch it," Sienna said succinctly, "in the prop box."

She pointed to the wooden steamer trunk with its lid flung back.

Gigi nodded. "But they can't leave it where it is. Anyone might go into the prop box at any time."

"Especially Adora, who is hiding goodies in there."

"That's right. So, as soon as no one is looking, they retrieve the purse and take it with them to—"

"Dispose of it somewhere else."

Gigi whirled around. "The question is where."

"There." Sienna pointed out the open stage door at a hulking, rectangular-shaped object, shrouded in darkness, squatting next to the theater.

"The Dumpster?"

Sienna nodded. "Come on. Let's go check it out." Sienna grabbed Gigi by the arm and pulled her through the open door.

Gigi's stomach did flip-flops as unappetizing aromas drifted toward them on the warm, humid air.

"How are we going to get in there?" Sienna stood on tiptoe and peered over the edge of the Dumpster. "I can't see anything from here."

"Is there a stool around here somewhere?"

"There's one in the dressing room. I'll get it. Be right back," Sienna tossed over her shoulder as she headed toward the back door of the theater.

Gigi stood in the darkness, trying to quell the faint sense of nausea caused by the smells wafting from the Dumpster and the thought of having to get up close and personal with its odiferous contents.

An owl hooted in the distance, and she jumped. Goose bumps prickled along her arms and legs. She glanced toward the door, willing Sienna to hurry. Being out here alone in the dark was giving her the creeps.

The door opened, and a rectangular chink of light spread across the gravel drive. Sienna eased through the opening, holding the stool in front of her, much like a lion tamer.

"This is the tallest one I could find." She set it next to the Dumpster.

Gigi put a hand on Sienna's shoulder and stepped up onto the stool. It put her waist-high with the top of the Dumpster. She leaned over the edge and peered into the darkness. "You didn't, by any chance, happen to grab a flashlight while you were at it, did you?"

Sienna shook her head. "No, but we can turn that light on at least." She pointed toward a bare floodlight hanging over the back door to the theater.

Gigi gripped the edge of the Dumpster and swallowed hard. The smell was much worse up there. She closed her eyes and tried to remember why she was doing this and how important it was to find out just what had happened to poor Martha. Because if she didn't, she was pretty sure the public planned on pinning it on her. They might call it an accident, but it would ruin her business nonetheless.

The bulb flashed on, and the top of the Dumpster was illuminated with watery light. A quick glance told Gigi that Martha's purse wasn't part of the top layer. She leaned over the edge, held her breath, and began pushing the contents to one side. She just prayed she'd find Martha's handbag without actually having to get in the Dumpster. Her stomach was giving little warning heaves as it was.

Gigi jumped down from the stool, and they dragged it to the other end of the Dumpster.

"Want me to try this time?"

Gigi shook her head. "I'm already up to my elbows in ick." She held her hands away from her. "No need for both of us to get dirty."

Once again, Gigi gingerly sifted through the contents she could reach—discarded tissues clotted with face cream and makeup remover, rotting banana peels, half-eaten sand-wiches and crumpled-up wads of paper. Something black and leather-looking was sticking up out of the disgusting morass. Gigi stretched out a hand, but it was just beyond reach. She couldn't be sure, but it looked like it might pos-sibly be a strap from a handbag. Then again, perhaps that was just wishful thinking.

She stood on tiptoe and reached forward again.

"Careful. You're going to fall in." Sienna rushed forward and grabbed Gigi around the ankles.

Gigi shuddered. There wouldn't be enough water and soap in the world to make her feel clean after tumbling around in this disgusting stuff.

With Sienna's grasp strong on her legs, she reached even farther. This time her fingertips brushed the object briefly. It definitely felt like a leather strap. She took a deep breath, heaved herself up a little higher onto the edge of the Dump-ster and stretched.

Gigi's feet shot out from under her, and Sienna lost her grip on her ankles. For a moment, Gigi teeter-tottered on the edge, flailing for purchase with her feet and failing.

She tumbled headfirst into the putrid contents of the Dumpster.

"What's that smell?" Sienna sniffed and looked around her.

"It's me!" Gigi declared on an anguished note. "I can't wait to get home and shower. I can barely stand myself."

"Phew, you can say that again." Sienna pulled a cord, and the theater passage lit up. "Let's take it in here." She pushed open the door to the dressing room and felt along the wall for a switch. "There's a sink, so you can at least wash your hands and face."

As tempted as she was, Gigi couldn't wait to begin exploring the notebook she'd unearthed from the contents of the Dumpster. A quick glance had revealed that it was most definitely Martha's. They may not have found Martha's purse—the leather strap had turned out to be a black plastic garbage handle—but this was even better.

Gigi peeled back the cover and glanced at the first page. It was college-ruled in grayish blue. Martha's handwriting had been small, neat and precise. Her notes were easy to read.

Gigi flipped through the pages. With each one, her heart thudded harder and harder until she could hear it echoing in her ears like a drumbeat. She came to some notes about Sprouted Goodness, the new health food restaurant on Cherry Street. She remembered the review. She read through Martha's notes. Yes, she hadn't like Sprouted Goodness all that much—the wait staff had been pretentious and the bread moldy. A few pages beyond she found Martha's reactions to Surf and Turf—a place catering to the weekend and summer crowd and their opinion that the best meal included either lobster or steak.

That review had been quite recent. She checked the date on Martha's notes—a week before she'd died. Gigi turned the next page with clumsy fingers. Her heartbeat went into overdrive, and she felt light-headed and slightly breathless. She should be getting to the notes Martha had taken about her visit to Al Forno. She crossed her fingers. Maybe things hadn't gone as badly as all that.

The page wasn't there.

"What?" Gigi looked up at Sienna, her mouth open in surprise. Gigi showed her the notebook. "That's it. The last notes are on the Surf and Turf, and then that's it." She fluttered the pages at Sienna.

Sienna grabbed the notebook. "Maybe she flipped it over and started again from back to front, like you do with steno pads." She flipped through the pages but soon realized that hadn't been the case. She handed the notebook back to Gigi.

"What do we do now?"

"I don't know." Gigi sat with her chin in her hands, finally oblivious to the smell that surrounded her like a noxious cloud. "She must have started a new notebook and thrown this one away."

Sienna groaned. "We'll never find it, then."

Gigi thought for a moment. "Maybe she tore those pages out—the ones with her notes about Al Forno."

"Why would she do that?"

"Maybe she changed her mind about the review?"

"Why does that sound like wishful thinking?"

"Okay, maybe she was already working on the review of Al Forno and needed her notes close at hand." Gigi turned the hot spigot on the sink to full blast, added a bit of cold water and plunged her hands under the stream. "She might have torn the relevant pages out and left them by her computer."

Sienna nodded. "Makes sense."

Gigi lathered up to her elbows with soap. "Which means we need to get into her house and look around for those pages."

"But how are we going to do that? I'm sorry, but I draw the line at breaking and entering." Sienna handed Gigi a wad of paper towels.

"Maybe there's one of those hide-a-key thingies. You know, the ones that look like a rock, and people keep them by their front door in case they've misplaced their regular set."

"That does sound like Martha. I can imagine her having something like that."

"What are we waiting for then?" Gigi tossed the towels in the trash with a flourish.

"Are you sure you don't want to go home and shower first?" Sienna fanned the air in front of her nose.

"Do I still smell?"

"Well . . . yes, but I'm starting to get used to it."

"Let's go, then."

"Great idea to bring Reg. It will look like we're just out walking the dog."

Gigi glanced at the sky, where dark clouds swirled across the moon. "Yes, except I'm not about to walk the three miles to Martha's house. We can drive over, park and then saunter up her drive with Reg." She opened her car door, and Reg hopped into the backseat of the MINI obligingly.

A slight drizzle, barely heavier than mist, was falling when Gigi and Sienna turned onto Martha's street. Gigi cut her lights and coasted to the curb in front of Martha's house. She looked at the houses on either side—the one to the right was dark except for a lit globe over the front porch, and the one on the other side had a light burning in what was probably the kitchen.

"Which house is Adora's?" Sienna hissed under her breath.

"That one over there with the light over the front door, I think." Gigi shut her door and winced at the quiet *thunk* it made. She opened the back door, and Reg bounded out, stretched and immediately began to sniff the ground, his tail wagging furiously.

"Do you think he smells Martha?" Sienna came around the car and joined Gigi.

Gigi shrugged. "Probably. Their sense of smell is so much keener than ours."

"Too bad we can't tell him to sniff out the key to the front door," Sienna grumbled as they made their way up the drive. "I don't want to be standing out here where we can be seen any longer than necessary."

"That makes two of us," Gigi whispered.

A car came around the corner, its headlights sweeping the street in a flash of brilliance. Gigi and Sienna pressed into the bushes as far as they could and held their breath. Gigi realized she would have a hard time explaining what she was up to if someone called the police. She could just imagine Detective Mertz's poker face at the news. He already thought she was guilty as sin—this would clinch it.

The car disappeared down the street, the red taillights fading slowly to nothing. Gigi let out her breath in a loud *whoosh*. Reg strained at the end of his leash, his nose twitching furiously.

"Where should we start?"

Gigi reined Reg in as best she could. "Let's look by the front door. That's where most people hide their spare key."

They edged their way up the walk toward the front door. "I should have worn black," Sienna hissed as another car appeared around the corner.

"If anyone asks, we're just here to pick up some of Reg's things," Gigi said with more conviction than she felt.

Gigi knelt and felt around the bushes that flanked Martha's front steps. "Nothing here." She got to her feet and brushed at the dirt clinging to her knees. Now she not only smelled dirty, she looked dirty as well.

Sienna explored the two pots of petunias on either side of the front door but also came up empty-handed. She lifted the edge of the doormat, and a spider scurried out. Sienna squealed and dropped the mat back into place.

"Shhh," Gigi reminded her.

"I can't help it. I hate spiders."

"Here, hold Reg's leash." Gigi handed Sienna the strap and bent down and picked up the doormat. She felt around with her foot, but there was no clink of a metal key against the flagstone landing.

"Maybe there's one by the back door?"

"Let's hope."

Sienna followed Gigi across the small lawn and through some budding flower beds around to the back porch.

Gigi reached for the handle of the porch door. *Please let it be unlocked*, she prayed silently. The knob turned, and Gigi pushed open the door.

They stumbled inside, feeling their way around the porch furniture, still shrouded in sheets.

"Looks like poor Martha never even got a chance to get ready for the summer." Gigi felt the seat of the sofa and behind the cushions, but came up empty-handed. "Did you find anything?" She turned toward Sienna, who was just a vague shape in the dark, her halo of curly golden hair faintly visible.

"Quiet, Reg," Gigi whispered to the dog, who was scratching and whining at the back door. Gigi tried the handle, but, as she suspected, it was locked.

She dropped Reg's leash and used both hands to feel under the throw rug by the door. "Nothing here, either." She got back to her feet, her hands pressed against the small of her back.

"Where's Reg?" They both turned toward the open door,

nearly crashing into each other as they made their way through.

"Reg?" Gigi called softly into the enveloping darkness. She grabbed Sienna's arm. "I think I see him." She pointed. "Over there."

They felt their way across the lawn toward some bushes, where Reg was a white smudge against the greenery.

"What's he doing?" Sienna peered at the spot where Reg's tail peeked out from beneath some evergreens.

"It looks like he's digging or something." Gigi tried to see under the bushes, but it was too dark.

Suddenly, Reg began to back out of the shrubbery, dragging something along by his teeth.

Sienna shuddered. "I hope it's not a dead animal." She took a step backward.

"I don't think so. I don't know what it is." Gigi bent over to get a better look.

She straightened suddenly. "You won't believe it."

"What?"

"I think Reg has found Martha's purse!"

Gigi struggled to wrest the handbag from Reg's mouth. He seemed to think she was after a brisk game of tug-of-war. Finally, she was able to remove his jaws from around the straps. She held the bag up and turned toward the nearest streetlight.

"It looks like Martha's. At least, I'm pretty sure it is."

"Let's go put it in the car. We can empty it out at your house. Maybe the missing pages will be in there."

"Should we still try to get inside to look around?"

Gigi shook her head. Suddenly she couldn't wait to get out of there. The hair on the back of her neck was standing on end, and she felt all goose-bumpy—as if they were being watched.

"Come on, let's go. We can come back another time if we don't find the pages." Gigi grabbed Reg's leash and wrapped it around her hand.

They tiptoed back across the lawn, sticking to the shadows under the swooping trees. A branch smacked Gigi in the face, and she stifled a scream. She couldn't wait to get in the car and drive away from there as fast as she could. She had one hand on the car door when they heard someone calling. She stiffened.

"What's that?" Sienna whispered.

"Sounds like it's coming from next door. Maybe someone calling their cat. Come on, let's get out of here."

"Stop," the voice yelled, more clearly this time.

"Is she talking to us?"

"Who cares?" Gigi began to open the car door. "Let's just go."

"I've called the police," the woman shouted over the bushes that divided the two houses. "They'll be here any minute now."

"Isn't that Adora?"

Gigi craned her neck over the roof of the car. "It does sound like it's coming from her house." She listened, but the only sound was the rumble of thunder in the distance. "Let's go before she sees us."

Gigi had one foot in the car when they heard it. Sirens. Headed their way. They stood frozen as two patrol cars screeched onto the street, their headlights sweeping the darkened houses, and their siren lights turning the landscape into a kaleidoscope of red and blue.

Chapter 11

Gigi watched as the two patrol cars slowed to a stop in front of Martha's house. She ordered herself to run, but her feet refused to move. Of course, the clouds parted just then, and moonlight flooded the street. Now she wasn't just visible, she was practically casting a shadow.

"Adora," Gigi yelled through cupped hands over the din of the rotating sirens.

Sienna was equally rooted to the spot, looking like an exotic plant with her gauzy skirt blowing in the faint breeze. Gigi grabbed her by the arm. She swore as they pushed their way through the bushes that ran between the two driveways.

"Ouch."

"What's the matter?"

"Nothing. Just a scratch."

They could see the outline of someone standing on the front porch of Adora's house. Gigi waved. "Adora. It's us."

Adora peered into the darkness. "Gigi? What on earth are you doing—?"

"What on earth are *you* doing?" Gigi countered. "Why did you call the police? We're just out walking the dog." She gestured toward Reg, who sat at her feet, casting a baleful eye at Adora.

They mounted the three steps to the front landing of Adora's house. Sienna had several leaves and a small branch caught in her hair. Gigi's knee was bleeding where she'd scratched it on the bushes, and she was breathing heavily.

"What's that funny smell?" Adora sniffed and looked around.

"I don't smell anything." Gigi was glad it was dark, and Adora couldn't see how red her face was.

"I don't smell anything, either."

"I thought someone was breaking into Martha's house." Adora put a hand to her chest in a dramatic gesture. She was wearing a lacy, white slip dress that accentuated her ample curves, and she had a glass of white wine in one hand.

"She's channeling her inner Maggie the Cat," Sienna whispered to Gigi.

"What on earth are you doing walking the dog all the way over here? You live, what, two, three miles from here. It's hardly the sort of night for a long walk." Adora looked up at the sky.

Sienna started to open her mouth, but Gigi gave her a look, and she shut it again. She raised her eyebrows inquiringly.

"It's like this," Gigi began. Her mind was whirling furiously. What possible explanation could there be for her and Sienna to be skulking around Martha's house like a pair of cat burglars?

"Well?" Adora waited, her head titled to one side.

"Yes?" Sienna echoed with her head titled in a similar fashion. Gigi wanted to pinch her.

"As you know, Reg was Martha's dog, and I recently adopted him, and we just came over to get some of his things so he would feel more at home in his new home . . . that is to say, my place."

Sienna nodded dutifully and hastened to wipe the surprised expression off her face.

Gigi risked a look over her shoulder. Four policemen were standing in the street, hands on their holsters, looking toward Martha's house.

Adora opened her screen door. "Come on. You'd better get inside. I'll deal with the police."

But before Gigi and Sienna could disappear from view, Detective Mertz called out.

They all stopped where they were. Mertz's tone of voice made Gigi feel like she ought to put up her hands. She had the feeling it wasn't going to be that easy to talk her way out of this one.

She became conscious of Martha's large, black handbag looped over her arm. Suddenly it felt enormous. She hoped she could pass it off as her own. Surely Mertz wouldn't know the difference? Adora, though, *had* looked at it strangely. Gigi crossed her fingers that Adora wouldn't say anything until the police had gone. By then, hopefully, she would have come up with a plausible story.

Mertz paused at the foot of the steps and looked up at them. He sniffed deeply. "What's that awful smell?"

"I don't smell anything," Gigi, Sienna and Adora chorused in unison.

Adora batted her eyelashes. "I'm so sorry, Detective. It seems I've made an enormous boo-boo." She laughed, a hand resting on her ample hip. The white satin of her dress reflected the moonlight. "Why don't we all go inside and have a glass of wine. Or"—her voice went all husky—"perhaps a man like you would prefer something a bit stronger?"

Gigi felt her blood boil. Adora was actually flirting with Detective Mertz! Not that she cared. She didn't care a bit. Not a bit. It was just absurd, that was all.

"I'm sorry, ma'am, but I'm afraid I'm going to have to ask you to explain what this is all about." Mertz shifted from one foot to the other. "Did you or did you not place a call to nine-one-one?"

Adora rolled her eyes and fanned her face. "It's just so hot out here, Officer. And I've got the air conditioner running inside and a frosty cold bottle of white wine." She brandished her glass. "It's an excellent pinot grigio. I'm sure you'd like it."

Gigi couldn't help notice how Mertz's gaze swept Adora's body from head to toe. He didn't linger, but he certainly looked. His expression, however, didn't change. It remained stern and downright frightening.

"My friends here"—Adora rested a hand on Mertz's arm, and he looked at it as if an insect had landed on his sleeve—"were walking their dog, when it got away from them. It chased a rabbit across Martha's property, and they followed trying to catch him. I"—she put a splayed hand flat against the billowing mounds of her chest—"made the mistake of thinking someone was attempting to break into Martha's house and called the cavalry." She pointed a pink tipped finger at Mertz. "That would be you."

Mertz scowled. "That true?" He looked from Gigi to Sienna and back again.

They both nodded.

Mertz waved an arm toward the other three officers who were quickly approaching Adora's front door. "False alarm. Come on. Let's get out of here."

He looked backward briefly, toward Gigi, then headed to the patrol car parked at the curb.

They watched as the police slammed their doors shut and pulled away from the curb.

"Now, you"—Adora turned toward Gigi and pointed at her this time—"must tell me what on earth you're doing with that hideous old purse of Martha's."

"Do you think she believed you?" Sienna took a sip of the chilled chardonnay Gigi had pulled from her fridge along with some cheese and other goodies. She dropped a crumb of Cheshire to Reg, who waited expectantly at her feet.

"I don't know and, frankly, I don't care." Gigi spread some St. André on a cracker. Their adventure had left her starving. She held a nibble out to Reg, and he took it eagerly. Gigi laughed as she thought of the look on Adora's face when Gigi told her that the purse was hers. She'd admired Martha's so much, she'd bought one exactly like it for herself. Fortunately, she had left her own cute straw bag in the car.

"Shall we look inside now?" Sienna gestured toward the clunky, black bag squatting on the porch floor between them like a large toad. She pushed it toward Gigi with her foot. Reg gave it a perfunctory sniff, but then immediately went back to keeping vigil over the cheese.

Gigi wasn't anxious to see what they'd find. Would Martha's new notebook be in it? Would there be evidence that incriminated Carlo? There must be something—or why would her bag have been stolen? It seemed too coincidental.

She was fairly certain that the person who'd stolen Martha's bag was the same one who'd put the peanut oil on the food.

Gigi sighed and pulled the purse onto her lap. It was heavy, and the leather was rough beneath her fingers. A zipper with a round, burnished brass toggle ran the length of the bag. Gigi slid it open and peered inside. Martha's wallet was still there, along with a compact and a tube of lipstick, some hand sanitizer, Band-Aids and a packet of tissues. She stuck her hand into the purse, feeling along the sides and bottom. She came up with a wad of crumpled papers.

"What's that?"

"I don't know." Gigi smoothed the pages out on the coffee table. "They look like they come from Martha's notebook."

"What do they say?"

Gigi held her breath. Maybe Martha's experience at Al Forno hadn't been as bad as Carlo thought. He was something of a perfectionist, after all.

Gigi began reading Martha's tidy, precise handwriting, and her hopes fizzled like wet firecrackers. Martha hadn't enjoyed Al Forno at all, that was for sure.

"Bad?" Sienna asked.

Gigi nodded, wadding the papers back up into a ball. "Yes. It doesn't look as if Carlo and Emilio would have gotten a good review."

"But that doesn't mean they had anything to do with Martha's death, does it?"

Gigi shrugged. "I don't know. Carlo did tell me that he'd sunk virtually all of his money into the restaurant. He couldn't afford for it to fail. That certainly gives him a solid motive for wanting her out of the way."

* * *

Evelyn was nursing a mug of tea behind the counter of Bon Appétit when Gigi pushed open the door the next morning. She needed a half pound of Kalamata olives, a tube of anchovy paste, oyster sauce, mini-gherkins and a new lemon zester.

Evelyn looked up from the paper she was reading as the bell over the front door tinkled melodically. She pushed the paper to one side and leaned her elbows on the counter as Gigi approached.

"Morning." Evelyn's greeting was as economical as she was.

Gigi smiled and returned the greeting. She dug around in her purse with one hand and triumphantly pulled out her shopping list. She spread it out on the counter, and Evelyn peered at it upside down.

"Anchovy paste," she read as she reached for the shelf behind her and selected a tube with a red and green wrapper. She placed it on the counter and ran her finger down the list to the next item.

The bell over the front door tinkled again, and Evelyn looked up, a curtain of bobbed gray hair falling over her cheek. Gigi swiveled toward the door as well.

"I thought that was you through the window," Alice trilled. She was wearing new-looking khaki pants and a crisp, fitted white shirt. Gigi could tell right away that she'd lost more weight.

"I had to tell you," Alice exclaimed as she approached Gigi and Evelyn, "I've just been to the doctor, and I've lost another ten pounds! And all those numbers he always goes on about have improved, too! The bad ones are down, the

good ones are up, and I'm thrilled," she finished triumphantly.

"You on Gigi's plan?" Evelyn cocked her head in Gigi's
direction.

"Yes." Alice nodded. She twirled around as she
approached the counter. "Like my new outfit?"

"You look fantastic," Gigi said. It made her feel so good
to see Alice's success. For a minute she almost forgot about
Carlo, Martha's purse, Al Forno and Branston Foods—who
still hadn't called her, but she wasn't going to think about
that right now.

"Anything I can get you?" Evelyn pointed at Gigi's shopping list. "Just need one or two more things for Gigi here."

Alice shook her head. "Not while I'm on Gigi's plan, I'm
afraid."

"Say." Evelyn spun around suddenly. "You hear about
the to-do over at Martha's place last night?"

"To-do?" Alice asked eagerly, her eyes alight with
excitement.

Gigi went very still—as if that would keep her face from
turning tomato red, which she could tell it was already
doing. She felt hot flames licking at her cheeks and faked a
coughing spell, hoping that would account for her crimson
complexion.

"Water?"

Gigi shook her head and fanned her face with one hand.
"No, I'm fine. Thanks."

"So tell us about this to-do," Alice demanded.

"Yes," Gigi chorused weakly.

"Well," Evelyn began with relish, resting her arms on the
counter and inviting them to lean in close. "It's like this."
She looked around, but the tiny shop remained as empty of
other customers as it had been moments ago. "I was watch-

ing television. A rerun of that cop show Jim likes. Then all of a sudden, sirens, lights flashing, the works." She blinked at them triumphantly. "Just like on the program."

"No kidding!" Alice licked her lips and leaned in even closer.

Evelyn nodded. "And get this. Two cop cars pulled to a stop right in front of Martha's house."

"No!" Alice's eyes were as round as two cherries. "Everything always happens on my days off! What happened then?"

Evelyn held out a hand. "I'm getting to it. Don't rush me." She put up a hand and readjusted her tortoiseshell hair band. "The cops spilled out and rushed up Martha's drive."

"And then?"

Evelyn scowled. "Well, I can't see much more than that from my house, can I?" She scowled harder, her brows nearly meeting in the middle of her broad forehead. "I was in my robe and slippers, and by the time I went upstairs and changed, they were gone." She snapped her fingers.

Gigi let out a breath she hadn't even realized she'd been holding. Obviously Evelyn hadn't seen much of anything. Certainly not her and Sienna skulking around in the bushes, or it would be all over town by now.

"Later Adora told me she'd called them," Evelyn continued, and Gigi's breath caught in her throat again. Her heart went to double-time as if she were running a marathon. "Apparently"—Evelyn's voice dropped even lower—"Adora thought she'd heard someone prowling around the yard."

"No!" Alice exclaimed again. "Did they catch the person?"

"Well, no." Evelyn's face settled into lines of disappointment. "It seems it was all a mix-up of some sort. Just someone out walking their dog, Adora said."

"Oh." Alice's face fell as well.

"Of course"—Evelyn pulled the edges of her cardigan together over her ample chest—"I could tell you about some other goings-on in our neighborhood that you wouldn't believe," she finished triumphantly.

"What do you mean?" Gigi tried not to sound interested, although she could feel the pulse in her neck speeding up.

Evelyn wagged a stubby forefinger at them. "I've seen a man coming and going from Adora's house at all hours," she sniffed, her stubby nose in the air. "Stocky fellow with dark hair. Couldn't tell who it was, of course. Too dark, and he was too clever to stand under the streetlight long enough to be recognized." She turned a beady stare on Alice and Gigi. "That Adora isn't as lily white as she makes out."

"Have you seen him recently?"

Evelyn nodded. "Last night, as a matter of fact. I was letting Oscar out for his last evening walk when I saw the fellow disappear around the back of Adora's house. Still didn't get a good look at him," she added ruefully.

"Who could it be?" Alice's eyes were calculating.

"Someone who doesn't want to be seen, that's for sure."

"But why?" Gigi looked from Alice to Evelyn.

"He's married," Alice offered. "What else could it be?"

Evelyn leaned back and brayed, her mouth pulled tight over her teeth. "Adora thinks she's so clever. But everyone knows," she crowed triumphantly.

Chapter 12

"Maybe Adora's mystery man isn't a lover," Gigi said as she swiped a soapy sponge across the hood of the MINI.

"What else could he be?" Sienna's voice was muffled as she bent over to scrub a stubborn spot just above the right wheel well.

"I don't know." Gigi dropped her sponge into the bucket of soapy water. "A cat burglar?" She waited until Sienna had finished her side of the car, then uncoiled the garden hose.

"Don't you think he would have struck by now?"

"Maybe Martha saw him sneaking into Adora's house, and he killed her?" Gigi turned on the spigot and motioned for Sienna to stand back. She aimed the stream of water at the car and hosed off the suds.

"Seems pretty extreme to me." Sienna grabbed a couple of towels from the stack they'd brought out with them and handed Gigi one.

"The whole idea of murder seems extreme to me," Gigi said, panting slightly as she rubbed down the hood of the car. Gigi finished drying the last section of the MINI and stood back for a moment to admire the shine.

Sienna unreeled the cord on the vacuum cleaner and looked around for the plug.

"Over there." Gigi pointed to a spot next to the garage door, half-hidden behind a slightly overgrown rhododendron. She opened the rear door of the MINI, and Sienna pushed the power button on the vacuum cleaner. Gigi took the hose from her and began on the backseat. "But how does the mystery man tie in with the notebook and Martha's purse?" She half disappeared into the backseat as she worked the vacuum cleaner wand over the upholstery. Reg didn't shed much, but there were still some white hairs clinging to the fabric, along with a fair number of crumbs.

"Maybe they aren't related." Sienna grabbed the bucket of used, dirty water and tossed it away from the car. It ran down the driveway in a sudsy stream.

"But don't you think that would be too coincidental? Martha's purse just happens to get stolen, and it happens to get stolen the same day someone kills her? I can't believe there isn't a connection between the two. And I'm afraid the connection points to Carlo."

Something glinted on the floor of the MINI. It was half under the passenger seat, and Gigi stretched out an arm to grab it. It looked like a pen. She'd probably dropped it at some point without realizing it.

Her hands closed around the object, and she pulled it out, steadying herself with one arm braced against the backseat. She was about to toss it into the glove compartment when she realized it wasn't a pen.

"What on earth . . . ?"

"What is it?" Sienna peered over Gigi's shoulder at the object.

"I thought it was a pen," Gigi began. She turned the item this way and that.

"It is a pen." Sienna held out a hand, and Gigi passed her the item. Sienna held it up to the light. "It's not a normal pen, though. It's an EpiPen." She slapped a palm to her forehead. "I should have thought of that!"

"Thought of what?" Gigi took the pen from Sienna and gave it a closer look. "What's an EpiPen?"

"It's really a hypodermic, see?" Sienna pointed to the needle just visible through the clear plastic of the barrel. "And it contains epinephrine."

"Epi-what?"

"Epinephrine," Sienna repeated. "People with severe allergies to peanuts or bee stings or things like that carry it. It keeps their heart beating and their airway open until they can get to the hospital."

"But what's it doing in my car?" Gigi stared from the pen to the backseat. "Unless . . ." She nibbled her lower lip with her teeth. "Unless it fell out of Martha's purse when I tossed it into the backseat."

"Was the zipper open?"

"Possibly." Gigi's brows drew together over her eyes. "I remember pulling it out of the car and fiddling with the zipper as we walked toward the house. So, yes, I think it was unzipped."

"This is what the killer was really after." Sienna held the pen aloft triumphantly.

Gigi nodded slowly. "I think you're right."

"Without her EpiPen, Martha would have no way of treating her reaction to the peanut oil the killer put on her food."

Gigi's heart contracted. The sun went behind a cloud, momentarily casting an ominous shadow across the driveway and the front lawn. Someone had taken Martha's purse to prevent her from getting at her EpiPen. She shuddered. How frightened Martha must have been when she felt her throat closing up as she reacted to the peanut oil the killer had added to her food.

There really was a ruthless killer out there somewhere, Gigi thought. And all evidence pointed toward its being Carlo.

Gigi circled through the tiny parking lot behind the police station. Two cruisers were parked perpendicular to the building, and the rest of the spaces were filled with an assortment of vehicles ranging from a bright yellow Hummer to an old model Volkswagen Beetle with peeling tape over a cracked rear window. There was no room for Gigi's MINI. And this was no place to double-park, even though she didn't plan on being more than a minute.

She pulled back out onto High Street. A spot had opened up right in front of the station, but it was small and cramped, and she wasn't taking any chances on parallel parking. It would be just her luck to have Detective Mertz come out and catch her struggling again.

Gigi pulled into the lot at the end of High Street in a space fairly close to the sidewalk. She retrieved a Gigi's Gourmet De-Lite container with Alice's name on it from the backseat.

The sidewalk was empty except for a dog panting in the heat outside of Brown's Hardware. Gigi had been tempted to bring Reg with her but didn't want to leave him in the car in such sultry weather.

Gigi pushed open the front door, and a uniformed receptionist buzzed her through an interior door.

"That for Alice?" She gestured toward the container in Gigi's hand as she reached for the phone. "That gal is sure losing some weight," she commented as she tugged at her belt, which created a slight indentation where her waist should have been. "I oughta give it a try myself." She laughed, then began to cough and wheeze.

Alice appeared around the corner, looking even slimmer than the last time Gigi had seen her. Her hair was attractively styled, and Gigi was surprised to see that its customary gray had become a flattering ash blond.

Gigi held out the container with Alice's name on it.

"Why don't you come on back?" Alice waved a hand in the direction of her cubicle. "I've got a fresh pitcher of iced tea. You look like you could use a cool drink. No sugar," she added with a twinkle in her eye.

Did she look that bad, Gigi thought? She put a hand to the back of her neck and lifted up her hair. She could feel the moisture there and could sense the hair curling messily around her face. She could even imagine the glowing shine on her nose and forehead. She mentally crossed her fingers that they wouldn't run into Detective Mertz. Although, she decided she wasn't going to think about why that should matter until later. Much later.

Of course, they ran smack into him in the hallway. He was exiting what looked like a conference room and had a sheaf of papers in his hand. They went flying like leaves in a windstorm.

"I'm so sorry." Gigi bent to retrieve them at the same time that Mertz did, and they bumped heads. Gigi felt the heat rising from her toes to the top of her head like molten lava spilling over the sides of a volcano.

Mertz gave her a crooked smile that disappeared so quickly she wasn't sure it had even been there. He fumbled awkwardly with the documents, seemingly engrossed in lining the edges up perfectly.

"Come on. Let me get you that cold drink." Alice linked her arm through Gigi's.

"I have some news for you," Mertz began, the words coming out in a bark that startled Gigi.

She stopped in her tracks. "Yes?"

"We've closed the case," he murmured looking everywhere but at Gigi. "The death of your client, Martha Bernhardt, that is." He gestured at Gigi with the stack of papers. "Accidental death. Somehow peanut oil was used in her food in spite of all precautions . . ."

Gigi noticed how he avoided the use of pronouns. As in the second person singular. As in the accusatory sounding *you* and *you put peanut oil in Martha's food*. The heat that had risen to her cheeks earlier intensified to blast-furnace level. She tried to say something, but her tongue had become stuck to the roof of her mouth.

"Anyway," Mertz shrugged. "I thought you'd want to know." He stared at Gigi for a moment, and she couldn't tell if he was blushing slightly or it was the red haze of fury in front of her eyes. "Well, I guess that's it." He spun on his heel suddenly and headed in the other direction, his shoulders stiff and set.

"Very interesting." Alice glanced at his retreating back. She turned an appraising eye on Gigi.

"What is?"

"I think he likes you."

The *Woodstone Times* made the most of the story. Gigi noticed the heavy black headline even before she slid the paper from her newspaperbox. She read the article as she made her way back up the driveway, Reg dancing around and around her feet.

She threw herself into one of the Windsor chairs arranged around the breakfast table and opened the paper to the second page and the continuation of the story.

It was just as Mertz had said. The police had concluded their investigation and determined that Martha's death was an accident caused by an allergic reaction to peanut oil. The reporter had obviously tracked down Barbie Bernhardt, because there were several quotes from her confirming that Martha's last meal had come from Gigi's Gourmet De-Lite.

Gigi's stomach did a belly flop and landed somewhere in the region of her knees. This was the final straw, the last nail in the coffin of her fledgling business. After reading this, no one would ever want to do business with her again.

As if to confirm that fact, the phone rang abruptly. Gigi answered slowly, half suspecting who it was going to be.

She wasn't wrong.

"Yes, of course I understand," she said politely, although of course she didn't understand at all. "Yes, I can see how there just isn't any other option."

She hung the phone up slowly. The deal with Branston Foods was off. Even though she had expected it, the news still hit with the force of a twister. Her stomach dropped even lower.

She was doomed.

"I don't know what to do," Gigi wailed, snapping the long, thin piece of crostini in half and then in half again. She put it down on the table without taking even a nibble.

She and Sienna were seated at the table Carlo and Emilio

kept for favored guests—tucked in a quiet corner, away from
the kitchen, with a view across the lawn and down to the
river, where heat shimmered off the sluggishly moving
water.

Sienna twirled her stemmed water glass in her fingers.
"Why did Barbie have to talk to that reporter? What a bitch!
She must have known that this would land you in the soup.
No pun intended," she added as she took a sip of her water.

Gigi tried to smile, but her face refused to cooperate. She
felt stiff with anxiety. What was she going to do if she
started losing all her customers? Waiting tables at Al Forno
or becoming a cashier at the Shop and Save wasn't going to
pay her rent, let alone all her other expenses.

"We're going to have to come clean about finding Martha's purse." Sienna drizzled olive oil on her bread plate and
tore a chunk of bread off the loaf on the table. "I'm sure
Detective Mertz will agree that the thief must have been
after the EpiPen."

Gigi poked at one of the pieces of crostini and watched
as it rolled away from her. "What good is that going to do?"

"For one, it establishes the fact that Martha's death wasn't
an accident. If someone went to the trouble of stealing her
medication, they obviously wanted her to die from the allergic reaction."

Gigi shivered. "But if we tell him, he, too, might make
the connection between Carlo and Martha's review and the
notes in her purse . . ."

"It's a chance we'll have to take. Otherwise people will
continue to think that it was your fault."

The Bernhardts' neo-Georgian mansion had been fully
restored to its former glory, Gigi noted as she pulled into

the circular drive. The flower beds were immaculate, the lawn verdant and carefully cut, the bushes pruned into pleasing shapes. The front windows were gleaming, and the entryway well swept. All of the former Bernhardt employees must have been reinstated, because she doubted Winston and Barbie had done it themselves.

Their knock was answered by a young woman whose scuffed athletic shoes were at odds with her pristine pink uniform. She scowled at Gigi and Sienna briefly before indicating with a languid sweep of her arm that they should enter.

They stepped through the door and stood uncertainly in the center of the plush Oriental area rug.

Winston wandered into the foyer just then, a quizzical expression on his face and a bottle of frosty champagne in his hands. He was wearing velvet monogrammed slippers, white linen trousers and a short-sleeve navy shirt. He stopped short when he saw Gigi and Sienna.

"Ah, delivering the goods are you?" He motioned finally with his head toward the Gourmet De-Lite container in Gigi's hands. "Just about to open a bit of bubbly to celebrate." He held up the bottle of Veuve Clicquot and grinned.

"Celebrating?" Sienna grabbed Gigi's arm and pulled her farther into the large, square foyer.

"We are indeed, and you must join us." He snapped his fingers at the girl in the pink uniform. "Sabrina—"

"Selena," she corrected, glowering at him, fierce, dark brows lowered over her black eyes.

"Yes, yes, Selena, of course. Please fetch us some glasses, would you?" He held up his left hand and counted. "Four to be exact."

"What are we celebrating?" Gigi asked as Selena stomped off without a word.

"Come in, and I'll tell you." Winston pointed toward an open door just off the foyer.

Sienna and Gigi looked at each other, shrugged and followed Winston into the other room.

The room had bookcases lining each of the walls with yards and yards of leather-bound volumes filling the shelves. Gigi wondered if Winston or Barbie had read any of them or if they had been purchased wholesale to fill up the space. Two voluptuous armchairs were pulled in front of a monstrous, yawning fireplace with a plump sofa opposite. Winston waved them toward the sofa, and Gigi and Sienna perched carefully on its quilted, black leather edge.

Winston put the champagne down on top of a walnut desk and began to wrestle the cork from the bottle. It was ejected with a satisfying *pop* as sparkling wine fizzed over the sides.

"Bravo!" he exclaimed, clapping.

Selena reappeared with four champagne flutes and plunked them on the desk, banging them so hard that Gigi was afraid the delicate crystal would shatter.

Winton poured them each a glass and was passing them around when Barbie strolled into the room. She was wearing white Bermuda shorts, a pink silk shirt and woven leather sandals. Her toes were painted the exact color of her top.

"Oh," was all she said when she saw Gigi and Sienna.

"I've invited your friends to join us, my dear." Winston swept a champagne flute in their direction.

Barbie's nostrils flared slightly, as if she had encountered a bad smell in the room, and Gigi had the distinct feeling Barbie was about to inform him that they were most certainly not her friends, when she clamped her mouth shut and graced them with a chilly smile.

If she hadn't wanted information so badly, Gigi would

have bolted. That and the fact that Sienna was clutching the edge of her skirt, holding her in place.

Winston handed Barbie the fourth champagne glass, and she held it to her mouth, although Gigi could have sworn she did little more than wet her lips with the expensive French wine. Obviously, Barbie was taking her diet more seriously than most of Gigi's other clients, Alice excepted.

Sienna raised her glass in a mock toast. "So what are we celebrating?" She looked from Winston to Barbie and then back again.

Barbie shrugged. "You started this. You tell them." She eased down into one of the armchairs, glass held aloft lest it spill. She glanced at Winston and crossed one slender leg over the other, her delicate designer sandal dangling from her bare toes.

"Yes, indeed." Winston rubbed his hands together briskly. He plucked his glass from the desk and thrust it toward them. "To Stuckey and Sons." He tossed back a gulp of champagne.

Gigi took a sip, her eyebrows raised questioningly.

"The deal is done. Signed, sealed and delivered." Winston smacked the desk, and a stack of documents bounced and trembled. "Or it will be as soon as all the legal ends are tied up. It will make me a very rich man. A very rich man, indeed." He threw back another gulp of wine before grabbing a long sheaf of papers rolled and fastened with a rubber band.

Gigi glanced around the room, wondering how Winston would describe his current situation.

He spread the papers out on the desk and stabbed the center of them with a long forefinger. "Say hello to the new Woodstone Mall."

Gigi and Sienna went to peer over his shoulder.

Gigi tilted her head, trying to read some of the writing, which was upside down. She pointed toward the blueprints. "Isn't that where the Woodstone Theater is?" She frowned.

"So it is." Winston drew his finger around the blueprint in a circle. "These will be the shops, here. High-end places like Gucci and Chanel and Louis Vuitton."

Gigi glanced at Barbie, and she could have sworn she saw her mouth water. Barbie walked over to the desk and peered at the plans splayed out on top.

"What's that?" She jabbed a spot with a pink-tipped finger.

"That?" Winston cleared his throat, and an uneasy expression smudged his features.

"Yes, that." Barbie tapped her foot. "Well? I'm waiting."

"That will be the new Woodstone Theater. New and improved." He smiled at Barbie and raised his glass in cheer.

"But you told me—"

Winston cleared his throat. "I wanted to surprise you, my dear."

"You bastard!" Barbie hissed, and flung the contents of her glass at Winston.

He sputtered, and wine dripped off the end of his nose onto the blueprints on the desk. "But Barbie! I thought you'd be pleased."

But Barbie had already stomped from the room, giving the door a resounding slam behind her.

"Well!" Winston pulled a handkerchief from his back pocket and wiped his face. "I guess my little sweetie is one of those people who don't like surprises." He laughed. "The joys of newly married life! There's always something fresh

to discover about each other." He beamed at Gigi and
Sienna, but Gigi could see the uneasiness clouding his eyes.
She glanced at Sienna, who shrugged her shoulders as if to
say, "What gives?"

Winston jabbed the center of the drawing with his finger
again. "I'm sure Barbie will be as excited about the theater
as I am as soon as she's had the chance to think it over." He
beamed at them. "We'll have the Woodstone Players in the
summer"—he winked at them slyly—"fortified with some
ringers from Broadway." He reached for his glass, and the
papers rolled together again with a *snap.* "And we'll have
traveling shows, and some single acts, but not"—he shuddered broadly—"any rock and roll."

"So the Woodstone Players will continue . . ." Gigi
looked from Winston to Sienna.

"Yes." Winston clapped his hands gruffly. "Isn't that just
splendid? And here"—Winston unrolled the papers again
and anchored them with a monogrammed crystal paper-
weight on one end, and a high-tech looking stapler on the
other—"we're planning an atrium with real, live trees—a
bit of a green oasis for weary shoppers."

Gigi felt Sienna's elbow in her rib and turned toward her.
Sienna raised her eyebrows questioningly, and Gigi silently
mouthed, "What?" Sienna rolled her eyes toward Winston
in a desperate pantomime.

Of course! Gigi had been so astounded by Winston's
revelation that she'd forgotten all about the questions
she'd planned to ask. But how to turn the conversation
toward Martha and her murder? Especially now that Winston was in full bore with his plans for the new Woodstone
Mall.

Gigi spied a copy of the *Woodstone Times* discarded on

the floor near Winston's desk. She gestured toward it. "Did you see the article in the paper about Martha's death? It seems the police have decided that it was an accident after all."

"Of course it was," Winston declared, polishing off the last sip of champagne in his glass.

Gigi felt herself bristle, and Sienna shot her a warning look.

"Unfortunately, people seem to think I was the cause of the accident." Gigi tried to keep the bitterness from her voice.

"You?" Winston went to the corner of the room, where he retrieved a golf club that had been leaning against the wall. He took a practice swing, sighing with satisfaction as he followed through.

"Yes. By process of elimination. My Gourmet De-Lite food was the last thing that Martha touched."

"Of course, she might have eaten something earlier while she was at the theater . . ." Sienna interjected helpfully.

"That's true." Gigi tried to act like the idea had just occurred to her. "Did you, by any chance, see her eating anything while she was there that afternoon?" Gigi looked hopefully at Winston.

Winston shook his head and moved his hands farther down on the golf club, taking a crack at a practice putt this time, gently tapping a phantom ball. "I'm afraid I can't help you."

"You didn't happen to see anyone lurking around my car that afternoon?

Winston had raised the club over his shoulder again, preparatory to swinging, but this time he let it drop unceremoniously with no follow-through. "See someone around your car?"

Gigi nodded. "Yes. You were sitting in your car, I remember, and Barbie came out to have her lunch with you."

"Well, if you say so," Winston said amiably enough, but his features had hardened, and there was a shadow behind his eyes that hadn't been there before.

"Did you see anyone?" Gigi prompted.

But Winston was shaking his head before she even finished the sentence.

Winston ran off to show the gardeners, who had just arrived amid a roar of engines, where he wanted his truckload of new Japanese maple trees planted, and Barbie reappeared to walk Gigi and Sienna to the door. Her eyes were red, and it was obvious she'd been crying.

"The property where the new mall is going to stand," Gigi began as they crossed the foyer, "is that the land that Winston owned jointly with Martha?"

Barbie nodded, her eyes wary.

"Adora seemed to think that Winston was planning on doing away with the Woodstone Theater altogether."

"Yes," Sienna chimed in. "And now it looks as if he's actually going to put a ton of money into it."

Barbie's pink mouth tightened into a sour line, and her slender shoulders stiffened, but she didn't say anything.

"I guess Winston changed his mind." Gigi glanced over her shoulder at Barbie.

Barbie's mouth tightened even more, as if she had to clench her lips to keep the words from spilling out.

Gigi hesitated on the doorstep, and Sienna dawdled as well, pretending to admire the large terra cotta pot of red and white geraniums on the brick entryway. They both looked at Barbie expectantly.

Her cheeks were puffed out as if they would explode, and a deep flush had spread from the open neck of her blouse to the roots of her blond hair. She had her hand on the door, and as soon as Gigi and Sienna were clear of the doorway, she slammed it hard behind them.

Chapter 13

"What was that all about?" Gigi said as she pulled out of the Bernhardts' circular drive.

Sienna pulled down the car's visor, flipped open the mirror and began drawing her hair into a wobbly knot on top of her head. "I don't think it's a *what*, I think it's more like a *who*."

"Who?"

"Yes, who."

"You're beginning to sound like that old Abbott and Costello skit."

Sienna laughed.

"Someone made Winston change his mind about the theater."

"And obviously it wasn't Barbie." Sienna stuck a final pin in the makeshift bun on top of her head.

"No. Who is the one person who cares more about the Woodstone Theater than anyone else?"

"Adora."

"I can't think of any other reason why he'd suddenly change his mind about the theater. She must have changed it for him."

"Now, that's a picture I don't want to contemplate." Sienna shuddered. "But why Adora? Winston already has his little trophy wife in Barbie. Why go after Adora? She's a good fifteen years older than Barbie and forty pounds heavier!"

"Maybe Winston's discovered that hanging out with someone half his age isn't as much fun as he thought it would be. Look at Prince Charles and Camilla."

Sienna grunted.

"Were you watching Winston when I asked him whether he'd seen anyone around my car the day Martha died?"

Sienna nodded, and the hair piled on top of her head bobbed unsteadily. "Yes, I was."

"What did you think? Does he know something?" Gigi glanced swiftly at Sienna, then back at the road again.

"Hmmm." Sienna pursed her lips. "He did seem a bit fishy to me."

"As if he were lying?"

"Maybe not lying exactly. More like there was something he wasn't telling us."

"That's what I thought. We do know one thing: Someone did go into Martha's car that day and steal her purse. And they went into my car and added peanut oil to the food. Surely someone saw something!"

Sienna shrugged. "You'd think so, wouldn't you?"

"I have an idea." Gigi was so excited, she slammed on the brake as they neared a stop sign at the corner of Monroe and High, and they both shot forward and backward in their

seats. "Sorry about that." She looked both ways before pulling across High Street. "What if I can convince Devon
Singleton to run something in the paper asking anyone who
might have seen anything that day to come forward?"

"Brilliant!"

"Someone might have been passing in their car or walking their dog . . . or something."

Devon Singleton was wearing the same Boston University
T-shirt he'd been in the last time Gigi had visited his office,
but she could tell the jeans were new—the holes were in
different places this time.

Gigi followed him back to his office, nearly stepping on
his heels in her excitement. Sienna was close behind, and
they both tried to go through the door at the same time.
Sienna took a step back and motioned for Gigi to go ahead.

Gigi graciously urged Sienna toward the low-slung chair
in front of Devon's desk. She had to suppress a smile when
the unsuspecting Sienna slid into the seat, her knees nearly
hitting her chin in the process. Gigi pulled an armless chair
away from the small round table pushed into the corner of
the office and wheeled it closer to Devon's desk.

Devon's computerized picture frame was scrolling
through a new group of pictures, Gigi noticed. Devon gave
it half of his attention, and Gigi and Sienna the other half.

"So," he began, tossing a glance in their direction.
"What's up?"

Gigi fiddled with the strap on her purse. She stole a
glance at Sienna, who looked equally dumbstruck. It had
seemed like such a good idea on the way over. Now, faced
with Devon Singleton's open and honest gaze, she wasn't

sure where to begin. Was she making a mountain out of a molehill simply to clear her own name?

No. Mertz had said that the food in the Martha's Gourmet De-Lite container was covered in peanut oil. Which meant it could only have been put there deliberately by someone who knew Martha was allergic and who wanted to do her harm. And that person was not her. And if the police couldn't figure it out, then she was just going to have to do it herself.

She raised her chin and looked Devon squarely in the eye. "You recently ran a story in the *Woodstone Times* that the police have closed the investigation into the death of Martha Bernhardt. They've decided it was an accident."

Devon nodded, his eyes sliding back toward the rotating picture frame.

"I just can't accept that, you see." Gigi could feel herself "getting her Irish up," as her mother used to say.

Devon made a gesture that might have been a shrug.

"The police believe I was the one who used peanut oil in preparing Martha's food. Which would make me criminally negligent because I knew perfectly well that Martha was deathly allergic to peanuts. I have all my clients fill out a form with their likes, dislikes, and most importantly"—Gigi could feel her face flushing and her voice becoming louder—"whether or not they have any allergies." She sank back in her seat and fixed Devon with a gaze so intent that this time he didn't dare look away.

She could sense Sienna silently cheering at her side, and she felt a glow of satisfaction. If she could just go shout that from the rooftops, maybe she'd feel better. And maybe then someone would listen!

Devon spread his hands open on the desk. "What is it you want me to do?"

Gigi inched forward in her chair and leaned her elbows on the edge of the desk. "I'd like you to run a story asking if anyone saw anyone around my car or Martha's the day she was killed."

"You're kidding, right?" Devon's mouth quirked into a smile, making him look even younger.

Gigi's "Irish" rose to unprecedented heights. "Why not?"

Devon leaned back in his hair, crossing one leg over the other. His finger snaked beneath one of the holes in his jeans and rooted around aimlessly. "Because it's not a story. The *Woodstone Times* prints stories," he explained as patiently, as if they were children. He leaned forward, and his chair snapped back into place.

"It doesn't have to be a big piece. It doesn't even have to be on the front page." Gigi was chagrined to notice that a wheedling tone had crept into her voice.

"Just a little bit on the back page," Sienna piped up. "You know as a . . . what do you call it . . . a filler."

"That's it." Gigi stabbed the air with her finger. "Instead of those little bits you always put in like 'Geriatric Finishes Marathon'—"

"Or, 'Child Wins Blue Ribbon at County Fair'," Sienna chimed in.

Devon was shaking his head. "But those things are news, even if they don't interest you. This. Just. Isn't. News." He stared at Gigi briefly before his gaze returned to his picture frame.

Gigi groaned inwardly. She couldn't give up. She couldn't. She looked at Sienna helplessly, but Sienna just shrugged and looked equally helpless.

What was it that Sienna was always urging her to do? *Ask the universe*; that was it. Well, she had nothing to lose by putting the question out there. *Okay, universe*, she intoned to herself, *tell me what to do.* She sat back in her seat, closed her eyes and waited.

"You could take out a classified ad."

Gigi's eyes flew open. Who said that? The universe had spoken, and it sounded an awful lot like Devon Singleton.

Devon watched her expectantly, his eyebrows raised and disappearing under his shaggy brown hair.

"Yes . . ." It was a possibility.

"One of those colored classifieds—" Sienna interjected.

"With a box around it," Devon added with satisfaction.

"Yes!" Gigi punched the air with her fist then subsided back into her chair. "How much?"

Devon named a figure.

Gigi groaned. Her budget was tight enough already, but she'd have to make it work somehow.

It was just too important not to.

"Anything?" Sienna asked the minute Gigi pushed open the door to the Book Nook. She was perched on ladder, a stack of books tucked into the crook of her arm.

Gigi shook her head. "No, not yet. And yes, I checked my phone and it's working just fine." She slumped into one of the overstuffed armchairs near the shelf where Sienna was shelving books and leaned her chin in her hands.

Sienna made her way down the ladder, kicking at her long, gauzy skirt to get it out of the way. "We've got to do something. I can't stand waiting," she pouted. "You know what I'd like to know?"

"What?" Gigi asked dejectedly.

"I'd like to know who has been sneaking around Adora's house and why."

"It has to be Winston, don't you think? It looks like he and Adora are having some sort of affair."

"Which means it probably doesn't have anything to do with anything. At least not anything to do with Martha's murder."

"We need to find out for sure."

"Meaning?"

"Meaning we . . . I mean *I* . . . need to stake out Adora's house one night and see if it really is Winston who Evelyn saw sneaking around."

"No way I'm letting you do that by yourself." Sienna grinned and jumped to her feet.

They decided to take Sienna's car because it was black. They parked around the corner from Adora's house, well away from the streetlight. Gigi felt a little foolish dressed in dark jeans and a black top. Though that was nothing compared to Sienna, who was wearing camouflage cargo pants and a black leather vest over a black T-shirt.

A sliver of a moon hung over the quiet street, making it just possible to negotiate the crooked sidewalk without tripping. Slowly, they picked their way along, sidestepping tree roots and yawning cracks. The houses were modest and neat with a light over most of the front doors. A perfectly ordinary scene, yet Gigi couldn't help but shiver.

They kept to the shadows as they made their way down the block and around the corner.

"Where should we wait?" Sienna whispered in Gigi's ear.

Gigi looked around. They weren't going to be inconspicuous no matter what they did. People just didn't hang out on street corners in Woodstone.

"Maybe we can crouch behind those bushes over there?" Gigi pointed toward some gnarly looking shrubs across the street from Adora's house.

They got into position and turned their gaze on their target. The light was on over Adora's front door as well as in some of the downstairs rooms. Gigi thought she saw a shadow cross the large bay window where the shades had already been drawn for the night.

An owl hooted in the tree behind them, and Gigi jumped half a foot.

"What is it?" Sienna whispered.

"Nothing. Just an owl. It just scared me, that's all."

Sienna grunted.

Within a few minutes they felt hot, cramped and bored. And not a little foolish.

"What if he doesn't come tonight?" Sienna hissed under cover of the noise from a passing car.

Gigi shrugged. "Then we'll have to come back until he does."

"I don't know why I thought this was going to be exciting," Sienna murmured. "It always looks exciting on television."

"I know. I don't think I could stand to be a detective if this is what it's like."

An hour later, Gigi rubbed her calf where a cramp had started and was growing. It felt like something was gnawing at her leg. She changed position to see if that would help. Suddenly there was a faint noise from across the street, along with a sense of motion.

Gigi and Sienna peered into the darkness.

"Is that him, do you think?"

"I don't know." Gigi squinted, straining her eyes to see in the darkness. The moon had ducked behind a cloud. The fixture over Adora's front door cast a pool of light that ended abruptly in inky blackness.

Gigi half rose, peering over the scrubby bush behind which they were hiding.

Another noise. "Get down." Sienna grabbed the edge of Gigi's T-shirt and pulled.

They waited a couple of seconds, then very slowly straightened their legs enough to see over the top of the withering boxwood hedge.

In a streak of tawny fur, a cat shot out of the shadows and disappeared down the sidewalk.

"Oh, my gosh." Sienna put a hand to her chest.

"Can I help you, ladies?"

A man came up behind them, and this time they both screamed.

"Sorry, didn't mean to startle you." He had a small, rat-faced dog tucked under his arm.

"We're just . . . just . . ." Sienna looked at Gigi helplessly.

"We're just fine," Gigi declared firmly.

But the fellow had already lost interest. His dog was straining to get down, and as soon as its paws touched the sidewalk, the two were off down the street. "If you're sure," he tossed over his shoulder, but he didn't wait for their answer.

"This is ridiculous." Sienna pulled down her vest. "No one's coming tonight. We might as well go home."

"Just a couple more minutes." Gigi listened as intently as she could over the rapid booming of her heart. She thought she heard a car—it sounded like it was a block or two away. Suddenly, the engine was cut, and the chirp of crickets filled the air again.

"Do you think—?"

"Shhh." Gigi tugged Sienna back behind the bush. "This might be our man."

"Winston?"

"Yes." Gigi watched the darkness intently, willing Winston to appear. She cocked her head. Was that the sound of someone approaching?

"We need those night goggles like they have on television."

"Shhh." Gigi shushed Sienna again. "I think I hear someone coming."

"I don't hear anything," Sienna grumbled, but she crouched down beside Gigi and clamped her lips shut.

"There," Gigi hissed excitedly, pointing across the street.

At first it looked as if the shadows were moving slightly, and Gigi stared hard, half-afraid to blink. Finally, a dark form took shape and separated slightly from the swaying shadows of the tree branches.

"Someone's there." Gigi grabbed Sienna's elbow, nearly knocking her off balance.

Sienna put down a hand to steady herself. "Where?"

"Right there." Gigi straightened, hoping to get a better view. There was definitely a dark mass stealthily approaching Adora's house. Any moment now it would be plunged into the pool of light over her front door. Gigi held her breath. Had she been right about Winston?

The outline of the creeping figure became clearer and better defined. Gigi could make out dark pants and a dark, short-sleeved shirt. Any second now the creeping figure would reach the light from the lamp, and she would have her answer.

Then the light went out.

Chapter 14

"Are you sure?" Sienna asked for the third time as they made their way back along the darkened sidewalk to her car.

"I'm positive."

"You're sure it couldn't have been Winston?" Sienna rephrased the question, perhaps hoping it would yield a different answer.

Gigi shook her head stiffly. "No, it most definitely wasn't Winston. I mean, I still think she's having an affair with Winston as well, but it was definitely Emilio I saw this time."

"I can't believe it."

"Neither can I." Gigi turned to face her friend. "I can't believe that Emilio is sneaking around under cover, having an affair with Adora!"

"I wish I had gotten a better look at him," Sienna lamented.

"I just saw him for that one moment. When Adora opened

the door, and the light from her living room shone onto the steps."

"But why sneak around like that?" Sienna stubbed her toe on a raised section of sidewalk and almost lost her balance. "They don't have anything to hide."

"She probably doesn't want Winston to find out. Especially if she's using Winston's attraction to her to get the things she wants, like a new theater for the Woodstone Players."

"That's true," Sienna murmured. "And if Winston killed Martha, Adora had better be careful."

"That's right," Gigi agreed. "There's nothing to stop him from killing Adora when he finds out she's been two-timing him."

"Or Emilio, too, for that matter."

Gigi felt as if someone had slid an icicle down her back. She shivered. Hopefully Sienna wasn't right—but you could never be too sure.

Gigi realized she had a problem the minute she walked into her kitchen. Martha's purse crouched on her counter like a large, poisonous spider. Sienna had been after her to turn it over to the police. But how was she going to do that without admitting to having kept it for as long as she had? Her only real option was to put it back where Reg had found it—in Martha's bushes. Gigi shivered. She did not relish the thought of creeping through the streets of Woodstone in the dark again. Even if she could talk Sienna into coming along. Their luck was not going to hold forever, and this time someone might see them.

The thought that it might be Detective Mertz catching them made Gigi shiver again. Although this time the shiver wasn't altogether unpleasant. She shook her head to chase away the thought. The last thing she needed was to develop fanciful notions about Detective Mertz. She was done with men. Done. D-o-n-e.

She was tipping some dry food into Reg's bowl and thinking about Adora and Emilio. Sienna thought she was being overdramatic in thinking that Emilio might be in danger, too. But news headlines she'd seen over the years flashed through her mind in bold, black-and-white, 72-point type. "Man Kills Cheating Wife and Lover." "Lover Killed by Jealous Boyfriend." All of a sudden, it seemed perfectly possible that Winston would go after Emilio. She'd have to warn him.

But then she'd have to admit to having spied on him. Maybe it would be better to approach Carlo and see what he knew. Perhaps she could put a bug in his ear to keep an eye out for Emilio—without actually telling him why.

Emilio was behind the bar polishing glasses when Gigi pushed open the door to Al Forno.

He immediately threw down his rag and bustled over to where she was standing, waiting for her eyes to adjust to the dimness of the restaurant's interior. The lunch rush was over, and the tables were empty but for a group of women in red hats laughing and talking in the back.

"Cara." He took her by the elbow and steered her toward the bar. "So good to see you. It has been too long, no?" He slipped behind the counter again and reached for a bottle. "A little port perhaps? I have a lovely white one from Portugal you must try." Before Gigi could answer, he took a small glass from the shelf, filled it, and pushed it toward her.

He snapped his fingers at Lara, the waitress, who was

refilling salt and pepper shakers at one of the stations. Her head jerked up, her blond ponytail flicking back and forth.

"Lara, please be a dear and bring our friend here an appetizer platter." He turned toward Gigi. "You are hungry, no?"

Gigi nodded, realizing that she was indeed hungry. She'd forgotten to eat lunch again. Although Emilio always assumed *everyone* was hungry.

"Me, too." Emilio patted his rather protuberant stomach. "We can share. A few roasted peppers, some giardiniera, a little grilled melanzana . . ." He smacked his lips in anticipation.

Lara put down the pepper mill she'd been holding, nodded in their direction and disappeared through the swinging door into the kitchen.

Gigi perched on the edge of her stool. Where was Carlo? She hoped she would be able to get him alone. She tried to see into the kitchen as the door swung to and fro, but it was impossible.

Several minutes later, the swinging doors flew open again, and Lara backed through them, a large platter in one hand and several small plates in the other. She eased them carefully onto the counter.

Gigi's stomach rumbled as she surveyed the contents of the platter. Emilio grabbed the serving fork, filled a plate and placed it in front of Gigi with the command to eat.

Lara retreated through the swinging door again, and, try as she might, Gigi couldn't see past the door into the room beyond.

She was nearly finished with the wonderful grilled and marinated vegetables Emilio had served her, and there was still no sign of Carlo. Finally, she couldn't wait any longer. "Is Carlo around?" she asked, as casually as possible.

"Carlo?" Emilio clapped his hands together, his eyes shining. He laughed. A deep guffaw that shook his belly and turned his face red. "Of course," he declared. "Carlo." He winked at Gigi, and she drew back in alarm. "Why would you want to talk to a silly old fool like me?" He thumped himself on the chest, leaned close and winked again. "Especially when there's a handsome young man like Carlo around, eh?" He turned toward the kitchen and bellowed, "Carlo?"

Gigi felt her face ignite. Now Emilio was going to think she had a crush on Carlo. How embarrassing!

Emilio waited expectantly, but there was no response. "*Dio, mio,* where is that silly boy?" He tossed his rag onto the counter and wagged a finger at Gigi. "You stay here. He must be in the stockroom."

He disappeared into the kitchen, and Gigi could faintly hear him calling Carlo's name.

She sat, waiting, hoping that Carlo had gone out and Emilio wouldn't find him. She slowly shredded the white paper cocktail napkin under her drink, becoming more hopeful as the minutes ticked by.

Finally, the kitchen door burst open and Carlo was propelled through it, Emilio's hand at his back. He smiled when he saw Gigi, and the intensity of the heat coloring her face increased.

Carlo's look of confusion turned to one of pleasure when he saw her. He glanced at her and then at the bar.

"I see my uncle has already given you something to eat."

Emilio made a big show of looking at his watch. "*Porca miseria.* I almost forget," he exclaimed. "I am supposed to call the suppliers about the delivery of the olive oil."

"But—" Carlo began before Emilio shushed him with a dismissive wave of his hand.

"I will take care of it, Carlo, don't worry." He motioned toward Gigi. "You two have a nice visit with each other, eh?"

They both stared at the swinging kitchen door as Emilio disappeared behind it.

"So . . ." Carlo began.

"So . . ." Gigi began at the same time. They laughed, and she felt herself relax. Although how on earth was she going to broach the subject of Emilio and Adora with Carlo?

Carlo pushed the empty appetizer platter to one side and leaned his elbows on the bar. "You wanted to tell me something?" he asked hopefully.

Gigi cleared her throat. "Yes." Better just get to the point, she thought. "I'm worried about Emilio."

"Emilio?" Carlo glanced over his shoulder at the closed kitchen door. "Why?"

Gigi fiddled with the pieces of her shredded napkin. She cleared her throat again. It felt dry and raspy. "I think he's been . . ." She paused, trying to think of a delicate way to put it. ". . . seeing Adora," she finished. "Not that there's anything wrong with that," she hastened to add, seeing the look on Carlo's face. "It's just that . . ." She paused again, wondering whether Carlo was going to believe her or think she was crazy.

"Yes?" Carlo nodded his head in encouragement.

"Well, we . . . I mean I . . . think that Adora is also secretly seeing Winston. I don't want to see Emilio get hurt." She broke off and took a sip of her port in an attempt to wet her parched throat. "Also, I'm terribly, terribly afraid that Winston might . . . might . . . get upset." Now, there was an understatement, she thought. "And possibly even do something to harm Emilio." It sounded lame, and she knew it.

She looked up to see that Carlo was shaking his head.

"What?" She asked.

"You don't have anything to worry about!" Carlo declared.

"No?"

He shook his head. "No. Emilio isn't seeing Adora."

"He's not?"

Carlo shook his head even more vigorously. "No."

Carlo plucked a swizzle stick from a container on the bar and began to fiddle with it, twirling it around and around between his fingers, rolling it back and forth across the bar and finally tapping it against Gigi's glass.

Gigi waited patiently. She couldn't imagine who on earth Emilio was involved with. She'd never seen him with anyone—not that she'd seen him with Adora, either, except that one night on her doorstep. She couldn't imagine why Carlo didn't just *tell* her, for goodness' sake!

"If I tell you this, do you promise not to tell anyone?"

Carlo's eyes were dark and serious pools that Gigi was afraid she might drown in. She nodded her head even as she reasoned with her conscience that telling Sienna wouldn't count.

"Okay." Carlo let out a big sigh. "I have been wanting to talk to someone for so long. I've been so worried."

"Worried about what?"

He leaned closer. "I followed Emilio once. I don't know why, but he wouldn't tell me where he was going, and I was curious." He gave an apologetic smile, as if inviting her to forgive him. "He'd put on his special aftershave—the one he saves for important occasions. So when he told me he was just going to get some air, I didn't believe him."

"So you followed him."

Carlo nodded.

"What did you find out?" Gigi prompted. Why was it taking Carlo so long to get to the point?

"You need a refill, no?" Carlo pointed at Gigi's half-empty glass.

"No. No, thank you. That's more than enough for me."

Carlo nodded abstractedly. He put his index finger on an empty cardboard coaster with *Al Forno* written on it and twirled it around and around. It wasn't till it slipped over the edge of the bar and onto the floor that he looked up at Gigi.

"Emilio went to Martha's house that night," he blurted out.

"Martha?" Gigi's voice rose to a high C, then squeaked off.

"I know. Can you believe it?"

Gigi shook her head. "My grandmother always said, every pot has its lid."

Carlo laughed, and although his dark eyes crinkled at the corners, the laugh sounded mirthless to Gigi. He began to shake his head even before the sound trailed off. "That's not it."

"What's not it?"

"You know—*amore*. Love. Emilio wasn't in love with Martha."

Gigi thought of Ted suddenly. Had he ever really loved her? This was no time to dwell on it. She'd think about it later. "Well, maybe it wasn't love exactly." She tried to picture Emilio and Martha together and failed. Martha had been so practical and almost severe, while Emilio had a love affair going with life itself. "Maybe it was more like companionship. Two lonely people getting together . . ." She trailed off when she saw Carlo's expression.

"It was more like—what do you call it?—a bribe."

"Emilio was bribing Martha?" Gigi's voice hit a high note again.

"Martha liked Emilio. I noticed it right away, and he did,

too. Her face got softer when he was around, and she would giggle like a little schoolgirl." Carlo took a glass off the shelf, picked up the rag that Emilio had dropped on the bar and began to polish it.

"I'm off," Lara called from the door. "I'll be back in time to get the tables ready for dinner."

"Yes. Thank you." Carlo flapped the rag in her direction. They both listened as the front door yawned open. A bright beam of sunlight pierced the interior of Al Forno and was quickly extinguished as the door squeaked shut.

"Where was I?" Carlo paused with the rag in one hand and the glass in the other.

"Martha liked Emilio, you were saying."

Carlo nodded. "Yes. And she decided she wanted to review Al Forno for the *Woodstone Times*. Emilio and I were very excited. Whenever Martha gave someone a good review, the place would be packed with people for weeks afterwards. And not just the people who lived around here"—he made a small, circular gesture with his hand—"but the weekend people from the city." He rubbed his fingers together. "They're the ones who bring the real money.

"But . . ." His attention strayed to a bottle of Famous Grouse that was out of alignment with the rest of the liquor on the tiered shelf behind the bar. He nudged it back into place carefully.

"But?"

He shrugged. "Someone must have put the evil eye on us that day. The chef was in a mood and burned the chicken. Lara spilled water on Martha."

So that *was* Martha who Lara had been talking about after all, Gigi realized.

"But don't you think that, since Martha had a kind of thing for Emilio, she would—"

Carlo shook his head so vigorously his hair flopped to and fro. "Not Martha. Emilio begged her to come back another day, to give us another chance, but no." He clenched his fists. "She could have ruined us with a bad review."

Gigi felt a sinking sensation in her stomach. Was Carlo trying to tell her that Emilio had actually done something to . . . kill . . . Martha's review?

If not Martha herself?

"Emilio had the idea that perhaps he could get Martha to change her mind by . . ." Carlo stopped, and Gigi thought he was blushing. "By making love to her. And pretending to be a little in love with her."

"Did it work?"

"When he asked about the review and perhaps not printing it, she just laughed at him."

"What did Emilio do?"

"I don't know. That is why I'm so worried." Carlo's dark eyes clouded over. "I'm afraid Emilio might have done something . . . drastic . . . to stop the review. Do you really think it is—how do you say it in English?—a coincidence that a couple of days later Martha was dead?"

Chapter 15

Gigi woke with butterflies in her stomach, and for a moment she couldn't remember why. Reg stretched lazily next to her, and she reached out to scratch his belly as she tried to remember why she had this strange feeling of excitement.

Of course. Today was the day she was meeting with Donna Small, the UPS delivery person who had answered her classified ad. Today, hopefully, she would be getting some answers. Donna had seen someone outside the theater the day Martha was killed, and she had even seen them hovering around Gigi's MINI. She had been passing by on her way to deliver a package to Simpson and West on High Street. And she'd promised to tell Gigi all about it over a glass of iced tea and a slice of pound cake at the Woodstone Diner.

Gigi rushed through her breakfast prep—she was doing scrambled eggs on English muffins with a sprinkle of low-fat cheese—and delivered her containers in what felt like a blur. She'd barely gotten home when it was time to think about what she needed to do for lunch. She always took care with each meal but even more so now. She was grateful to the clients who hadn't been put off by Martha's death and the insinuation that it had been negligence on the part of Gigi's Gourmet De-Lite.

Despite all the work she had to do, Gigi was convinced that the hands on the clock were crawling along at half their customary speed. Surely it had never taken this long to get to three P.M.

She arrived early at the Woodstone Diner and parked around back. There was only one other car in the lot, and it wasn't a UPS delivery van, but Gigi didn't expect Donna Small until three o'clock at the earliest.

The Woodstone Diner had actually been transported from some place in New Jersey and plunked down on Woodstone's High Street. It was as authentic as they came, right down to the obligatory open-faced turkey sandwiches, meat loaf specials and wisecracking but soft-hearted waitresses. The moneyed weekend crowd enjoyed it in a perverse, "anti-chic" kind of way.

Gigi nodded at the gray-haired, barrel-chested man sitting at the counter and slid into the last booth on the right. The waitress hurried over and slapped a menu down on the table.

"I'm waiting for someone. She should be here any minute." Gigi folded her hands on top of the menu.

"Gotcha." The waitress spun on her heel, returning several seconds later with a tumbler of ice water and two place settings.

Gigi took several sips of the water. Being nervous had made her throat dry. She watched out the window, scanning the street for the arrival of a UPS truck. The waitress had

finished wiping down all the booths and the counter before
the door opened and Donna Small walked in.

Gigi half rose in her seat, motioning with her arm, before
she realized it must be obvious that she was the only person
in the establishment named Gigi.

"Hi," Donna Small said with a smile as she slid into the
booth opposite Gigi. She wiped a hand across her forehead,
which glistened with perspiration. "Hot out there."

Gigi motioned for the waitress, who was already on her
way with a tall glass of iced tea and a straw. She put them
both on the table in front of Donna.

Donna laughed. "I always stop here on my break." She
peeled the wrapper off the straw and plunged it into her
glass. "They know what I like. Iced tea and a slice of their
delicious pound cake." She smiled ruefully and tugged on
the waistband of her shorts. "I don't need either of them, of
course."

That was good, Gigi thought. At least her reward of free
meals might mean something then. She'd omitted that little
detail from her ad in the paper, and most people would
probably assume a reward meant cash.

The waitress reappeared with a slice of pound cake and
slid it in front of Donna. She turned to Gigi and raised her
overly plucked eyebrows.

"I'll have a . . . a . . . diet soda." Gigi opened the menu
and tried to speed read. "And a dish of vanilla ice cream."

The waitress took her menu and retreated to the counter.

"That was a miracle I saw your ad." Donna brushed
crumbs off the front of her brown uniform blouse. "I don't
usually read the *Woodstone Times*, but someone had left it
in one of the booths so I picked it up to read on my break.
There wasn't much in it, and by the time I'd finished my
cake, I was up to the classifieds."

Gigi held her breath.

"I was surprised to see your ad," Donna continued as she tore the tops off two packets of sugar and dumped them into her glass of iced tea. "Not to mention curious. I mean, the classifieds are usually all about used cars, lost pets and personals." She grinned at Gigi.

"I didn't know what else to do," Gigi admitted. "I needed to know if anyone had been seen by my car that afternoon." She was quiet for a moment as the waitress slid her dish of ice cream in front of her. "I think someone might have tampered with the food I was bringing to my clients." She spread her hands out on the table. "I make diet meals for a small group of clients. Gigi's Gourmet De-Lite, it's called. I'm afraid this will ruin me."

Donna's head bobbed up and down as she nodded. "I noticed your car in the parking lot of that old barn where the theater is." She lowered her head shyly. "I'm saving for a MINI myself." She jerked a thumb in the direction of the diner parking lot. "I get sick of driving that enormous dusty heap around all day. A MINI seems like it would be fun."

"It is." Gigi fiddled with the wrapper from her straw. "But how can you be sure it was the same day?" she asked finally, holding her breath, hoping for the right answer.

"Well, I passed the theater first and slowed down to get a good look at your car. I'm thinking about a blue one myself, but the red sure is perky looking." Donna took a long draft of her iced tea and swiped a paper napkin across her mouth. "Then I delivered a package to Simpson and West, the law firm over there on High Street."

"Yes. I know them."

"It took forever. I had to get it signed for, and the girl at the desk was a temp and didn't want to risk giving me her

John Hancock in case it wasn't allowed, so I had to wait for the big guy's secretary to come out to reception and do it. She took her ever-lovin' sweet time, I can tell you." She ran a hand under the open-necked collar of her shirt and across the back of her neck. "Some people just like to show you how much better than you they are. It's annoying, but honestly, I feel kinda sorry for them."

Gigi tried to look interested, wondering if any of this had anything to do with anything.

"By the time I beat it out of there, there was all this commotion going on outside. Sirens wailing, police cars flying past. Turned out someone hit a tree in the middle of that roundabout where High Street veers to the left and goes up the hill," she pointed in vaguely that direction.

Gigi squirmed forward in her seat. "Yes, that was the day. The day I'm talking about."

Donna ran her fingers up and down her glass, leaving trails in the condensation. "Yeah, well, that's the day I noticed your car."

"Yes. And you did notice someone sort of hanging around my car?"

Donna wet her finger and pressed it against the crumbs left on her plate. She nibbled them off her index finger. "I did. And it worried me." She ducked her head. "In my mind, I was kind of pretending like your car was mine. Like I already had my own MINI, and there it was."

Gigi nodded eagerly. She had to stop herself from shrieking. It was taking Donna so long to get to the point, her ice cream had already melted.

"It was a young kid. A teenager, I think."

"A teenager?" Gigi asked. Disappointment settled in her gut like a stomach virus.

Donna nodded. "He . . . at least I think it was a he . . .

had short hair . . . and was wearing a T-shirt and a pair of shorts. Kind of khaki colored I think."

Gigi tried to swallow her disappointment, but it created a bitter lump in her throat that didn't want to move and nearly choked her.

"You're sure it was a young guy?"

"Yeah. Pretty sure." Donna tilted her glass back, extracted an ice cube and began to chew on it. "He looked to be in his late teens. And he had blond hair," she added triumphantly as if that was what Gigi was waiting to hear.

Gigi tried to smile, but her face felt paralyzed, and she was sure it looked like a Halloween mask frozen in mid-grimace.

Donna didn't seem to notice. "All I really saw was the kid hovering around your car. I can't say for sure if he actually touched it or opened the door or anything."

"No, of course not."

Donna looked at her with her eyebrows raised.

"That's really helpful," Gigi managed to get out, although her mouth had become so dry, it felt as if her tongue were permanently cemented to the roof of her mouth.

Donna swirled her straw around and around her empty glass. "You'd kind of mentioned a reward in the ad . . ."

"Yes!" Gigi declared brightly. "I'm offering a week of my gourmet diet meals for free!"

Gigi was gratified to see that Donna now looked as stunned as she felt.

The atmosphere inside the Woodstone Theater had shifted, Gigi noticed when she got there with her lunch delivery. The time till opening night was growing shorter, tempers were even shorter still and the air vibrated with unreleased tension.

Gigi eased open the inner door to the theater and stood for a moment to let her eyes adjust. Adora was center stage in mid-dialogue with Emilio's character. She turned suddenly and pointed toward the back of the theater. "Who opened the door?" she demanded.

"It's all right, *cara*, we can start over." Emilio tried to put a hand on Adora's arm, but she brushed it off. Alice and Barbie hovered stage left, shifting uncomfortably. Winston, who lounged in the second row with his feet propped on the seat in front of him, looked over his shoulder at the open door and then back at Adora again.

"We'll never get through this if we keep getting interrupted." Adora slammed the prop she'd been holding—a book—down on an antique-looking wooden side table that made up part of the living room set that surrounded them.

"I'm sorry," Gigi called out. "I didn't mean to interrupt. I've brought the food."

Adora put a hand to her eyes and looked out past the spotlight that illuminated the stage. "Then leave it in the lobby. We have to get through this scene, or we're not going to be ready for opening night. We'll just have to wait to eat."

"Sorry," Gigi said again as she backed out the door and let it close quietly behind her. She took a deep breath. She hadn't meant to interrupt. Usually when she arrived, everyone was standing around waiting for the food and practically pounced on her the second they saw her.

She sat down on a long, dusty, velvet-covered bench that had been placed under a row of framed posters announcing past Woodstone Theater performances. Her shoulders drooped. She still couldn't believe what Donna had told her. A teenage boy? Maybe it had been nothing more than a prank? A prank that had gone terribly, terribly wrong. It didn't seem possible now that she would ever be able to clear her name. The police had closed the case, and she had run out of ideas. She might as well give up.

The front door to the theater opened, and Sienna came in, her long cotton skirt swishing around her tanned legs. "I hoped I'd catch you here." She collapsed on the bench next to Gigi and used the hem of her gauzy tunic to blot her upper lip. "What happened with the UPS woman yesterday?" She turned to look at Gigi, her brows drawn together over her green eyes. "I'm assuming it's not good news, or you would have called me."

Gigi nodded, glumly. "She did see someone around my car the day Martha died. Unfortunately she was quite positive that it was a teenage boy wearing a T-shirt and shorts."

"Oh no." Sienna put a warm hand on Gigi's arm and gave it a squeeze. "That is bad news, isn't it? And she was absolutely positive?"

"Yes. She even noticed he had blond hair. She was quite certain about that."

The inner door to the theater burst open and Adora shot through it. Emilio followed close behind. Once again, he tried to put a hand on her arm, but she shook it off. "Where's my lunch?" she demanded as soon as she saw Gigi.

"There is no need to get so upset," Emilio began before Adora cut him off with a withering glance.

She snatched the wig off her head and glared at him, then turned her glance on Barbie and Alice, who had emerged from the theater, blinking in the sudden light.

"You don't understand. Any of you." She looked from

one cast member to the next. "Amateurs," she spat out, then turned on her heel and ran out of the theater.

Alice watched her go. "Temper, temper, temper," she chided. "Just because she once had a bit part in a Broadway play." She shook her head and held out a hand for her Gourmet De-Lite container. "You know"—she opened the lid and peered inside—"I used to think this was a ridiculously small amount of food. Couldn't imagine how someone my size was going to survive on so little. But now"—she ran a finger around the loose waistband of her trousers—"I can barely finish it." She looked up at Gigi. "Can you believe it?"

"Your appetite has shrunk back to normal."

At least someone had benefited from this whole enterprise, Gigi thought. Alice had lost weight and was really going to wow them at her daughter's wedding.

Barbie took her lunch and smiled warily at Gigi.

Winston materialized at Barbie's elbow. "Come on, old girl, let's go outside while you eat that. Hopefully we'll catch something of a breath of fresh air out there." He took her arm and led her toward the door.

Gigi was left holding Adora's container. She looked around, but Alice and Emilio had also disappeared. "I hope she isn't long. I've left Reg in the car. The windows are down, but still . . ."

Sienna gestured toward the bench. "Oh, just leave it there for her. Serve her right if it spoils."

"I don't know. I could put it back in the cooler and wait for her—"

"Don't be silly. Adora acted appallingly. There's no reason why you should hang around waiting for her to come back from wherever she's gone to have her temper tantrum."

"Well, if you're sure . . ."

"I am." Sienna held open the door. "Come on. I could do with some air myself."

The parking lot was empty as they bumped and dragged Gigi's cooler over the rutted macadam toward her car.

"I managed to snag a spot in the shade." Gigi pointed to where the MINI sat under the spreading branches of one of the trees.

"Aren't those seed things going to get all over it?" Sienna gestured toward the ground under the tree, which was littered with pods.

Gigi shrugged. "At least it will be cool." She craned her neck. "I guess Reg must have fallen asleep. Usually he's got his head hanging out the window watching every blade of grass twitch."

Sienna laughed. "He is a good watchdog, that's for sure."

"What's that on your windshield?" Sienna stopped and bent down to fix the strap on her sandal.

"I don't know." Gigi frowned at the square of white paper that fluttered under one of her wipers. She laughed. "It can't be a ticket, thank goodness."

"Probably some sort of advertisement. I'll heave this into the car"—Sienna kicked lightly at the cooler—"and you go check it out."

Gigi reached across the hood of the car, careful to keep her dress from brushing against the MINI, and grabbed the piece of paper. It was an ordinary sheet that looked like it had been torn from the kind of notepad you'd keep by the phone or on your desk. The top edge was jagged, and there was a corner missing. It had been unevenly folded in half.

"What is it?" Sienna asked, pausing as she tried to

maneuver the cooler into the backseat. "I think you're going to have to help me with this."

"Just a sec." Gigi unfolded the note.

She read the words, but at first they didn't make sense. They were easy enough to read, written in childish block capitals in black ink. For a second, the words swam before her eyes before coming back into focus.

"This note . . ." She held the piece of paper away from her. Her voice cracked, and she had to start again. "This note says that if I don't stop investigating Martha's murder, they're going to do something to hurt Reg." Her voice ascended to a crescendo, and she had to bite off a scream that rose in her throat like bile.

Suddenly she panicked. "Where is Reg? Is he in the backseat?"

Sienna's face went a ghostly white. She leaned into the car. "No." Her voice was muffled. "He's not here." She yanked open the front door, and both she and Gigi peered inside.

Nothing.

"He's gone." Gigi did scream this time.

And Sienna crumpled to the weedy ground in a dead faint.

Chapter 16

"Sienna!" Gigi screamed as she fell to her knees beside her friend. Sienna's eyelids fluttered.

Gigi took Sienna's wrist and felt for her pulse. Not that she had any idea what a person's pulse ought to be, but she'd seen it done in movies often enough. At least she could verify that Sienna did indeed have a pulse.

Sienna moaned softly and turned her head to and fro. Her eyelids fluttered again, then opened.

"What happened?" She ran a tongue over her lips.

"You fainted."

Sienna groaned again. "That's right." She struggled to sit up. "They've got Reg haven't they?" She put a hand to her forehead. "That's all I remember . . ."

"We've got to do something," Gigi sobbed as she tried to help her friend sit up. She was torn between helping Sienna and rushing off to find her lost dog.

She was squatting next to Sienna when she felt something push against her. It knocked her off balance, and she had to put a hand down to keep from toppling over.

"What the . . . ?"

Something warm and wet nuzzled at Gigi's side. She twisted around.

"Reg!"

The little dog put his paws on her shoulders and licked her face enthusiastically.

"Okay, that's enough, boy." Gigi gently pushed him aside and swiped a hand across her damp face.

Reg sidled up to the still-prostrate Sienna and began to lick her face. She giggled and hugged him fiercely.

"He must have gotten out of the car somehow." Gigi buried her face in Reg's fur.

"Or whoever left the note let him out. You said you'd left the windows down."

The note. Gigi had almost forgotten about it in her panic.

"We've got to show it to Detective Mertz. It's time to stop playing amateur detective. Someone is going to get hurt."

"And it's time to get you to the hospital," Gigi declared firmly. "You really scared me."

Sienna struggled onto her elbows. "Must be that flu bug I had last week."

"Well you're going to get it checked out before another minute goes by."

They dropped Reg off at Gigi's cottage, making extra sure that the doors and windows were all bolted and shut tight. Gigi was still nervous about leaving him, but they certainly weren't going to allow him into the Woodstone Hospital emergency room, and she wasn't letting Sienna out of her sight until she'd had a thorough examination. She didn't want any more scares like the one she'd just had.

An ambulance screamed past as they were pulling into the hospital parking lot. The noise and flashing lights made Gigi jump, although maybe she was just jumpy already. She pulled up to the automated ticket dispenser, but not close enough, and she had to open her door and slide half out of the car in order to reach the stub the machine spit out. She vowed that as soon as she got home she was making a cup of iced chai tea and sitting on the patio with her feet up even if it was only for five minutes. She had to do something to restore her equilibrium.

Gigi was relieved to see that the emergency room wasn't crowded. There was a young man sitting with his hand wrapped in a towel filled with ice, and a young mother cradling a baby whose red cheeks suggested it was suffering from a fever.

They found a seat as far as possible from the television, which was blaring an afternoon game show, and picked up dog-eared magazines.

They didn't have long to wait. A nurse with a clipboard called Sienna's name, and then the two of them disappeared through an open door.

Gigi tried not to think about Reg, home alone. What if the person who'd left that note tried to break into her house? She felt perspiration breaking out along her sides. She looked at her watch. They hadn't been gone more than half an hour. Surely Reg would be okay for a few more minutes. If this took any longer, she'd run home and check on him and then come back for Sienna.

Sienna returned relatively swiftly, and Gigi looked up,

surprised, from the magazine article on finding romance
after thirty that she'd been reading with more interest than
she was willing to admit to.

Sienna had a strange look on her face. Awe, joy, disbe-
lief . . . the emotions floated like clouds across her features.

"What is it?" Gigi tossed the magazine on the table and
stood up.

"You won't believe it," Sienna said in a voice that sounded
like she didn't believe it herself.

"What is it?" Gigi prompted again.

"I'm pregnant." Sienna plopped down in the seat Gigi
has just vacated, and burst into tears.

"I thought you wanted to get pregnant," Gigi said as she
tried to feed a dollar bill into the automated ticket station
that guarded the exit to the hospital parking lot. The bill
went half into the machine before being spit out again like
a naughty kid sticking out its tongue.

"I do," Sienna sniffled, and rummaged in her purse for
a tissue. "I don't know. I'm just surprised, I guess. And
emotional from the hormones. I've been a wreck lately. No
wonder."

Gigi finally got the machine to accept her rumpled dollar
and felt a very small surge of triumph as the barrier lifted
and she pulled out of the lot.

"I'll drop you at home, and you can call Oliver, and then
lie down and get some rest." She patted Sienna's hand.

To her surprise, Sienna burst into a fresh torrent of tears.

"What's the matter?" Gigi stole a glance at her friend out
of the corner of her eye.

"I don't know where Oliver is," Sienna wailed.

Gigi nearly stomped on the brake in her surprise. "What do you mean you don't know where Oliver is?"

Sienna gave a choked-off sob. "I've called his work phone, and it just rings and rings, then goes to voice mail. I tried his cell—same thing."

"Maybe he's in a meeting with a client? I always turn my cell phone off when I'm with a client. He probably does the same thing. It's rude otherwise."

Sienna gave a sniff that ended in a hiccup. "I was so excited to move here and have a baby." She opened the glove box and took out Gigi's tissues. "I grew up in a town just like this, and I loved it. Mumsy ran the bookstore and Pops taught at the university. I wanted the same thing for our baby." She pulled a tissue from the box and blew loudly. "I guess Oliver doesn't."

Gigi glanced at Sienna again. "Oliver grew up in the city, didn't he?"

Sienna nodded. "I suppose he's just more comfortable there. But he always said he wished he'd had the kind of life I'd had growing up. He never even knew his father! When his mother hit forty, she decided she wanted a baby, and she went to a sperm bank!"

Gigi couldn't imagine growing up not knowing who half your family was. Her father had been a fireman and had died when the roof of a building collapsed on him. Gigi had only been three years old, but growing up, the house had been peppered with his photographs, and the dozens of brothers, cousins and uncles on the Fitzgerald side had kept his memory as alive as if he had been there himself.

Gigi turned toward Sienna. "Maybe now . . . with a baby actually on the way . . ."

"Do you think Oliver will come around?"

"I'm sure he will," Gigi said, crossing her fingers.

* * *

Gigi had just enough time, after taking Sienna home and calming her down, for a cup of iced chai tea on the patio before she had to begin preparations for her Gourmet De-Lite customers' dinners.

Reg hovered around the counter as Gigi prepared the wild mushroom and chicken stir-fry that was on the menu for dinner that evening. She dropped a tiny piece of chicken into his bowl, and then realized she hadn't fed him yet.

"Sorry, buddy." She poured a cup of dry food into his dish and topped it off with a smidge of canned beef stew—doggie version. The vet had made her promise not to over-feed him, although it was tempting when he looked at her with those soulful brown eyes of his. She thought about how she'd almost lost him and decided that just once wouldn't matter and added an extra spoonful of the wet food to his dry mix.

She still couldn't believe that someone would threaten to hurt him. The thought made her shiver despite the warmth of her tiny kitchen. Tomorrow she would show the note to Detective Mertz. The thought made her shiver again. She had to admit he was good-looking, but that was the beginning and end of his attractiveness. He was stiff, pompous and something of an ass!

But then why did she keep thinking about him, a little voice inside her head demanded to know. *I do not!* she argued back, even as she recognized that the little voice was right.

She just hoped Mertz would take her seriously and not laugh. She glanced at Reg and shivered again. Who could have done such a thing? It could have been anyone. Adora had stomped out of the theater, then Emilio and Alice. Winston and Barbie had also left. Any one of them could have slipped the note under her windshield wiper. They knew she was coming. Perhaps they'd written the note earlier and had it at the ready? No matter how she felt about Detective Mertz, she was going to be glad to place the whole matter firmly in his large, square, capable hands.

Gigi wasn't taking any chances. Reg was going to Sienna's house while she was at the police station talking to Detective Mertz. Reg trotted off happily with Sienna, and Gigi watched until they'd gone into the house and closed the door. She was very worried about Sienna, but she would be back soon and would check on her then.

Mertz was behind his desk, a huge pile of papers and files nearly obscuring him from view. He jumped to attention when Gigi was shown into his office. His short, dark blond hair was as neat as always, his suit immaculate, his tie somewhat unimaginative in color and pattern if free of spots.

Gigi could have sworn he clicked his heels as he motioned toward the chair in front of his desk. She took a seat. He sat down, too, his back as ramrod straight as if he were guarding the Tomb of the Unknown Soldier, not sitting in his own office.

Gigi took the threatening note from her purse, unfolded it, and handed it across the desk to Mertz.

He laid it open on the blotter in front of him. His eyebrows shot up as he read.

"Who is Reg?" he asked in alarm.

Gigi cleared her throat. "My dog."

Mertz relaxed slightly. "Oh. A dog."

"He's a very special dog," Gigi said defensively. "Besides, isn't it illegal to send threatening notes like that, even if he is a dog?"

"This came in the mail?"

"Not exactly. Someone left it under the windshield wiper of my car."

Mertz frowned and glanced down at the piece of note-paper again. "What does this mean . . . if you don't stop investigating?"

Gigi felt her face blossom with hot, red color. She'd been afraid he was going to ask about that. She'd spent a good part of the hours between four A.M. and six A.M. trying to come up with a reasonable answer and failing miserably. "It's not investigating, really—"

"What is it then?" Mertz's crystal blue eyes got even icier, if that was possible. Gigi shivered just looking at them.

"Research." Gigi tilted her chin up and looked him straight in the eye.

"Research?" Mertz looked far from convinced. "I thought I'd already mentioned that the police have closed the case?"

"Then why am I getting threatening letters?" Gigi gestured toward the note still open on his desk. "Someone is spooked. Spooked enough to try to stop me." She raised her chin another notch and continued to glare at him.

To her surprise, he nodded agreement. "You're right." Now he was the one looking her straight in the eye. "Someone is running scared." He picked the note up and let it flutter back to his desk. "And I'd like to know why."

"So would I," Gigi said, but she mumbled it under her breath, and Mertz didn't hear.

"But I don't want you"—he pointed a finger at her to emphasize the *you*—"doing any more so-called research."

He looked frighteningly stern, his brows drawn together straight over his ice-chip eyes, mouth set in a grim line. But Gigi sensed something different buried deep underneath—a warmth that all his posturing couldn't completely obscure.

She felt an answering warmth grow in the pit of her stomach, and a tiny smile played around the edges of her mouth.

"Does this mean you're going to reopen the case?" Gigi fiddled with the strap of her handbag.

Mertz pursed his lips and tapped the note with his forefinger. "Not necessarily. But we're going to look into this note." He tapped it again. "Where were you when you found this?"

"At the theater. I'd stopped to deliver everyone's lunch."

"Who is *everyone*?"

Gigi closed her eyes to think. "Well, Adora for one. She's the lead in the play the Woodstone Theater group is performing. Then Emilio was there, too." Gigi hated having to bring up Emilio's name, but Mertz would probably find out anyway. "Also Alice, and Barbie and Winston. Alice and Barbie are in the play, and Winston was there to have lunch with Barbie." Gigi thought for a moment. "Oh, and Sienna, but she doesn't count."

"Why doesn't this Sienna count?" Mertz scowled across the desk at her.

"She's my best friend, and there's no way that—"

"The first thing you learn in police work is to never rule anyone out."

"But she was with me the whole time, except of course when—"

"Yes?"

Gigi shook her head. "No, Sienna couldn't have had anything to do with it." She crossed her arms over her chest definitively. "Do you think this means someone thinks I'm getting close to something?"

"Close to something? Yes," Mertz said. "But what, I'm not sure. Is there anything else you can tell me?"

Gigi hesitated. Should she tell him about Martha's purse? Would that mean he might take this more seriously?

"There's the matter of Martha's, er, purse." Gigi tried not to squirm as she met Mertz's direct gaze.

"What about her purse?"

"Well you never did find it, did you?"

Mertz sighed, took the top handful of file folders off the pile on his desk and began to sort through them. He picked one out and replaced the others. He glanced up at Gigi and then opened the file.

He skimmed the first page and put it to one side, his index finger scanning the lines on the second sheet of paper. "There's nothing here"—he looked up at Gigi again—"about a purse. Nor"—he flipped through several more pages—"is a purse mentioned in the list of contents of the car."

"That would be because it had been stolen." Gigi suddenly realized that Martha had crashed before getting to the police station to make a report about the theft. "It happened while she was at the theater."

"A lot seems to be happening there," Mertz muttered half under his breath as he closed the file and replaced it on the stack at his elbow.

"I think the person who stole her purse wanted to make sure she didn't have her EpiPen. It's not a pen really, but an—" Gigi stopped short when she saw Mertz's expression.

"I know what an EpiPen is." If possible Mertz was sitting even straighter than before. "If that's true, then this is beginning to smack of foul play." He scribbled something on a notepad. "But how do you know Martha carried an EpiPen in her purse?" He looked up suddenly.

Now Gigi was squirming in earnest. She couldn't think of any way to explain what had happened without bringing Mertz's wrath down on her head.

"I happened to find the purse." She looked at him through her lashes to see how he was taking it. Not good. His face had become a dangerous, dusky red color, and his brows were drawn down low over his eyes. Gigi felt sweat trickle down her back even though she was sitting directly in the flow from the air conditioner that was wheezing away in the window.

"When did you find the purse?" He said the words as if there were a period after each one—slow and deliberate— never taking his eyes from Gigi's face.

The trickle of sweat became a torrent, and she wiped her damp palms on her thighs. "It was a couple of days ago actually."

"And you've only now decided to tell us about it?"

Gigi nodded, trying to think up a reason for the delay and failing. She decided to take the offensive. "The police certainly haven't been very interested in Martha's accident until now." She tilted her chin higher.

"That could be because certain members of the public were keeping things to themselves," Mertz said through gritted teeth, although Gigi thought she saw the ghost of a smile pass quickly over his lips before submerging in his frown.

"Well, I did find it. And her EpiPen was in it. I think someone sprayed peanut oil on her food and then took her purse so she wouldn't have the medicine to counteract her allergic reaction." She drew herself up to every single millimeter of her five feet five inches. "I don't think Martha's death was an accident at all."

"You might be right." Mertz scribbled some more notes on his pad, then tossed his pen down on the desk. "Where is this purse of Martha's now?"

"At my house," Gigi admitted weakly.

"And where did you manage to find this purse?" Mertz

leaned forward as if he were extra anxious to hear her answer.

This was the bad part. Gigi squirmed even more. "We found it in Martha's yard. Hidden in some bushes," she said quickly, hoping that if she glossed over it, he would do the same.

"Who is *we*?" The quizzical look on Mertz's face looked relatively benign, but Gigi knew better.

"Sienna and me."

"And just how did you end up being in Martha's yard? I'm assuming Martha was already dead and hadn't invited you for a garden party." Mertz's lips tilted upwards very briefly.

"True." Gigi traced a circle in the carpet with her toe. "Actually, Sienna and I happened to be walking Reg by her house, and he pulled us onto the lawn and began foraging in the bush. Reg is the one who found the purse." Gigi spoke really fast so that all the words ran together. She felt her face getting hotter with each syllable.

"I'm not going to ask you what you were doing walking past Martha's house. I don't want to encourage you to lie to an officer." This time Mertz's smile lasted an entire two seconds before disappearing. Surely a record, Gigi thought.

"I suppose your hands have been all over it?" Mertz gestured toward Gigi's own purse. "And your friend Sabrina's as well?"

"Sienna. Her name is Sienna."

Mertz shrugged. "Do you mind if I keep this?" He lifted the note from his desk and waved it around.

Gigi shook her head.

"I'll need the purse as well." He looked at his watch. "Would three thirty be okay?"

"Three thirty? For what?"

"For me to pick up Ms. Bernhardt's purse from your house." He said the words slowly and patiently, as if for a child.

"Oh. Yes. Of course."

Chapter 17

Gigi's doorbell rang at exactly three thirty P.M. She jumped, even though she knew Mertz was coming. As a matter of fact, she'd washed her face, redone her makeup, put her hair up, taken it down, put it back up again, and changed her clothes twice. She was exhausted.

He looked as tired as she felt and stood visibly drooping on her steps when she yanked open the door. He straightened immediately, and Gigi felt her heartbeat go into overdrive.

"I hope I'm not keeping you," he said, glancing at Gigi's outfit.

She realized she must look as if she were dressed to go out, and she knew her face was as red as the geraniums in the pot next to the door.

"No. Not at all. I was just about to finish dinner prep and then load up the MINI for my deliveries." She pulled the door wider. "Won't you come in?"

He stood awkwardly by the front door, hands clasped behind his back. Gigi wondered if the man ever unwound.

"The purse is in the kitchen." She gestured toward the back of the house. Mertz followed her closely down the hall.

She'd put Martha's purse on a chair by the kitchen table. Mertz cringed when she picked it up.

"What's the matter?"

"We might be able to get some fingerprints off the bag— after we eliminate yours, of course." That last was tinged with the faintest sarcastic edge.

Gigi paused with the bag halfway toward Mertz. Should she put it down or hand it to him?

Mertz reached into the pocket of his sport coat and pulled out a pair of thin latex gloves. He eased them on, and only then did he put out a hand for the purse.

He started to put it down on the table, but Gigi stopped him.

"Let me put some paper towels under that. The bottom of a woman's purse," she said, hoping she didn't sound like she was lecturing, although it seemed that way to her ears, "is extremely dirty. We put them down everywhere, you see." She gestured toward the table and countertops. "In my business I have to keep everything extra clean."

Mertz nodded approvingly and waited while she spread out two sections of paper towels before putting the purse down on the table and opening it.

He reached inside and drew out a cylinder that looked like a pen. "I imagine this is the EpiPen?"

Gigi nodded. "That's what I think the person who stole her purse was after."

Mertz's expression turned grim. He carefully looked through the remaining contents of Martha's purse.

While he searched, Gigi gave him the whole chapter and

verse that she and Sienna had come up with regarding the murder . . . excluding Emilio's name, of course. This was her last chance to convince Mertz that the case merited reopening.

Gigi was gratified to see that Mertz's expression had changed, and he was nodding approval.

"You could be right." He grinned, and this time it lasted long enough for Gigi to be positive that she'd actually seen it. "I just wish you had come to us with your theory and let us do the investigating." He put the EpiPen back in Martha's purse and snapped it shut. "Do you have a plastic bag or something I can put this in?"

"Of course." Gigi grabbed a bag from the fabric sleeve hanging on the corner of her door. It had *Shop and Save* written on it in red print.

Mertz carefully placed the purse in the bag but made no move to leave. He looked around her kitchen and sniffed. "It sure smells good in here."

Gigi thought she heard his stomach growl. "It's tonight's dinner order. Are you hungry? There's plenty."

A look of hesitation blurred his features for a moment, but then he squared his shoulders and straightened his back. "Thanks, but I have to get back." He glanced at his wrist. "I have a meeting."

Gigi felt slightly foolish, and she stuffed her balled hands into her pockets. She felt her shoulders lift defensively as she walked Mertz to the door.

After an awkward good-bye, Gigi pulled open her door and was astonished to see Carlo coming up her front walk, carrying a square, white pizza box with *Al Forno* scrawled across the top in curly black letters. He stopped short when he saw Mertz.

Gigi sensed Mertz stiffen as he contemplated Carlo, his

face as emotionless as usual, except for the faintest flicker of his left eyelid. Carlo, on the other hand, was anything but a blank slate. His face fell so comically that Gigi would have laughed if she hadn't felt so sorry for him.

Carlo thrust the pizza box forward. "I am bringing this to you for your dinner." He made a vague gesture with one hand. "I was thinking that maybe you are tired of cooking for other people and would like someone to cook something for you."

Delicious smells wafted from beneath the lid of the pizza box, and Gigi's mouth began to water. She swore she heard Mertz's stomach growl again, too.

"It's our famous white pizza," Carlo went on. "None of that Pizza Hut stuff," he sniffed disdainfully.

"That's very kind of you, Carlo. Why don't you come in?" Gigi held the door a little wider.

But Carlo shook his head. "I do not want to intrude—that is the correct word, no?" He glanced sideways at Mertz. Probably putting the evil eye on him, Gigi thought, remembering her maternal grandmother and how she tried to cast the evil eye on anything that displeased her.

"I'm just going," Mertz said in a toneless voice, although he made no move to leave.

Carlo stood his ground as well, hugging the pizza box closer to his chest.

At this rate, they'd be standing on the front steps forever, Gigi thought. She had to do something. She put out a hand for the pizza. "Thank you, Carlo, I'll take this inside and keep it for my dinner. Detective Mertz," she turned toward him, "I will call you if anything else occurs to me."

Carlo breathed a deep sigh, and Mertz's stomach grumbled, but they both turned to leave, being careful not to stray too close to each other on the walkway.

Gigi watched them go. She realized that, while she liked Carlo very much and certainly enjoyed his company, Mertz had somehow gotten under her skin.

If she were going to marry again . . . a big *if* . . . she wanted someone reliable this time around. Someone with whom she could imagine raising a family. That all added up to someone like Mertz. It didn't hurt that she found him insanely attractive

She turned, went back inside and closed the door. She realized with a feeling of deep disappointment that her thoughts were in vain. So far, Mertz—and Carlo, too, for that matter—had not made the slightest move to ask her out.

Gigi completed her dinner prep, packed up her Gourmet De-Lite containers, loaded them into the MINI and delivered them. Then Reg wanted his dinner and a walk. It was almost seven thirty P.M. before she was able to check her e-mail.

She tucked several triangles of Carlo's pizza into the oven to warm, consoling herself with the fact that her walk with Reg had surely burned enough calories to earn her an extra piece. She curled up on the sofa with Reg at her feet and the windows wide open. She could smell the faintest hint of lavender from the garden, which mingled with the lingering scent of the basil from the tomato sauce she'd made to top the chicken breasts she'd grilled for her Gourmet De-Lite customers.

She powered up her laptop and bit the point off one of the pieces of pizza. She closed her eyes in rapture and inhaled deeply as the scent of garlic, tangy cheese and pungent rosemary wafted around her. Between them, Carlo and Emilio had raised pizza to an art form.

She was deleting the contents of her spam folder when the thought occurred to her—was there something in the past that had led to Martha's murder?

Gigi took another bite, wiped her fingers, set them on the computer keys and brought up her favorite search engine. Who should she start with? She paused with her hands hovering over the keys. So far, Winston was their odds-on favorite, so she quickly pecked out *Winston Bernhardt* and hit enter. Barely a second later, the magic of the Internet had produced several pages of links. Gigi scanned them quickly. Winston's name turned up on several annual reports as a member of boards, in articles in business magazines and newspapers and in several obituaries for a Winston Bernhardt who had been born in 1902 and died, at the age of ninety-three, in 1995. She clicked on an article from the *Wall Street Journal*. Several clicks later, she had found nothing particularly revealing about Winston Bernhardt and virtually nothing she didn't already know.

Next up, Barbie Bernhardt. Gigi wished she knew Barbie's maiden name, but she couldn't remember anyone ever having mentioned it. No matter—the first article she pulled up was Barbie and Winston's wedding announcement from the *New York Times*. The heading read "Yablonsky-Bernhardt." Gigi settled down to read. Barbie had grown up in Youngstown, Ohio—so much for the slight southern accent that brought to mind miles of Kentucky bluegrass and white horse fences. Barbie was obviously a better actress than they gave her credit for. Most of the announcement was taken up with information about Winston, who at the time had been head of one of New York's biggest investment firms. According to the article in the *Journal*, Winston had resigned shortly after marrying Barbie so they could "enjoy life together."

Barbie's father had worked for a tool and die manufacturer, and her mother had been a housewife. Barbie graduated from Ohio State University with a degree in theater arts. She'd had an extremely minor but recurring role in a short-lived soap opera before grabbing the brass ring and marrying Winston. None of which pointed toward her being the murderer.

Next up, Carlo and Emilio Franchi. Gigi plugged their names into the search engine and waited while a page of links loaded. She scanned them quickly. Several led to Al Forno's Web site, and one or two referenced an Emilio Franchi who had had a very short career with an Italian opera group based in Milan. Nothing there, either.

Alice Slocum didn't rate a single Internet mention, although there were several obituaries for other Alice Slocums, most of whom had been born and died before the turn of the previous century. Gigi skimmed through the references again but still found nothing of interest.

Last but not least—Adora Sands. Gigi scanned the references that came up, reading one or two here and there. Most related to summer theater performances, in which Adora's parts ranged from almost nothing to miniscule. Gigi clicked on a link halfway down the page and began to skim, her pointer hovering over the back arrow key the whole time. Suddenly, she yanked her hand away from the mouse as if she'd been burned and studied the picture of the smiling couple in evening dress.

She had to call Sienna right away.

"I've just made some wonderful iced green tea. Why don't you come over and tell me about it?" Sienna said when she answered.

Gigi didn't need to be asked twice. She powered down her laptop, slipped it into the case and slid her feet back into her sandals. She hated doing it, but she decided she would leave her dishes piled in the sink. Surely the gods of good housekeeping would turn a blind eye just this once.

Reg was waiting by the back door. Gigi clipped on his leash, and they both got into the MINI—Reg beside her, his head hanging out the window.

Gigi tried to quell the excited feeling that was building in her stomach, but she wasn't having much success. She might be wrong, and this new trail might lead them right back to where they'd started, but she really thought it was promising.

Sienna lived in an old fieldstone and half-timbered Tudor-style carriage house that she and Oliver had spent two years converting into a spacious and cozy home. Doors on the four garage bays on the first floor had been replaced by windows and transoms, and the front door was painted a cheery Victorian red.

Gigi banged the brass, pineapple-shaped door knocker and waited.

"Come on in." Sienna pulled the door wide open. Gigi was glad to see that there was some much-needed color in her cheeks.

Gigi followed her through the spacious and airy open-plan first floor and into the kitchen, which was dominated by an island with a limestone top. Sienna picked up a tray set with a pitcher of iced tea, glasses, and a plate of sliced pound cake.

Sienna swung around to face Gigi. "You look very excited."

"So much for my career as a poker player, I guess."

"Let's sit outside." Sienna gestured toward the French doors leading to a flagstone patio.

Gigi was about to follow her when she noticed a man's suit jacket slung over one of the kitchen chairs, and a tie hanging from the pantry doorknob.

"Is Oliver home?"

"Yes," Sienna whispered. "I'll tell you more outside."

Sienna set the tray on a small wrought-iron café table, leaving room for Gigi's laptop. Gigi tried to control her impatience as Sienna fussed with the tea. Finally, glass in hand, she could restrain herself no longer.

She nodded toward the kitchen. "How did Oliver take the news about the baby?"

"He's thrilled." Sienna beamed. "It's all been a misunderstanding." Sienna stirred her tea. "He hasn't been seeing anyone, and he said"—she dashed a hand across her eyes—"he doesn't regret our life here in Woodstone at all. He's just been really stressed about his job."

Gigi raised an eyebrow.

"Seriously," Sienna said. "More and more people have been getting laid off every week, and he and the rest of the staff have been taking on more and more work. He's been staying late trying to get things done and to prove to his bosses that they need him." Sienna stared into her tea. "He didn't want to tell me about it because he didn't want to worry me. Meanwhile, he's been waiting for the other shoe to drop."

"What—?"

Sienna looked up. "He's lost his job. He didn't survive the last round of layoffs."

"Oh no!"

Sienna smiled. "But now that it's over, he can start to move forward. He's thinking about opening up a small firm of his own right here in Woodstone! That way he can be near the baby when it comes." She ran a hand over her still-taut abdomen.

"That's really good news. So, he's excited about the baby?"

"Oh, yes," Sienna glowed. "He's as thrilled as I am. We've already spent hours talking about names and how to fix up the nursery." Sienna tapped Gigi's computer. "Anyway, tell me what you've discovered."

Gigi swiveled the laptop around and turned it on, her hands hovering impatiently over the keys. "I went to the search engine and plugged in *Adora Sands*, and the first thing I came up with was this." She chose a link, hit enter and turned the screen so that they could both see it.

Sienna tilted her glass in the direction of the screen. "So Alice was right—Adora really was on Broadway once. It's hard to believe. No wonder she sometimes gets so impatient with the Woodstone Players."

"I know." Gigi leaned over the screen. "The play sounds very avant-garde." She read the headline out loud. "'Young Playwright Has New Take on McCarthy Era'." She shook her head. "It doesn't sound like my sort of thing."

"Mine, either," Sienna agreed.

Gigi clicked on another bookmarked site. "Cindy Adams, the *New York Post*. Check this out."

Sienna leaned forward and studied the grainy black-and-white picture that figured prominently in the infamous gossip column. "It's Winston and Adora."

"Yes. Coming out of some fancy nightclub on Fifty-Seventh Street."

Sienna peered at the photo again. "With their arms around each other."

Gigi nodded. "It looks like Adora might be the one who broke up Martha's marriage to Winston, not Barbie."

"It does, doesn't it?" Sienna leaned back in her seat and curled her feet under her.

"There's only one problem," Gigi said as she snapped the computer shut. "If that's the case, then Adora should be dead, not Martha."

Chapter 18

Gigi led Reg up the steps to the Book Nook and pushed open the door. She was happy to see Sienna once again behind the counter, her eyes bright and her complexion much rosier than it had been.

She smiled when she saw Gigi. "I was just going to make some tea. Would you like some?"

"Is there any coffee?" Gigi leaned her elbows on the counter.

"You're in luck. I just started a pot."

"Madison?" Sienna called to the spike-haired girl who was shelving a stack of inspirational romances. "Can you watch the register for a few minutes?"

Sienna swooshed out from behind the counter, her bright cotton skirt swirling around her ankles.

Gigi followed her to the coffee corner, where she inhaled the delicious aroma of fresh-brewed coffee. "Smells heavenly." She unclipped Reg's leash, and he sat down next to the sofa, his pink tongue bobbing with each breath.

"It's the Sumatra blend—your favorite," Sienna said as she poured out a mug and handed it to Gigi. She took a second mug, filled it with hot water and added a tea bag to steep.

"Hey there." Alice popped around the corner carrying an armload of colorfully jacketed romance paperbacks. "Two weeks to the wedding, and I'm right on track." She pulled at the waistband of her skirt to show how loose it was. "I've lost all the weight with time to spare." She beamed at Gigi and dumped her stack of books on the sofa. "And wait till you see my dress." Alice put her hands on her hips and wiggled them provocatively.

"I wish all my clients were like you." Gigi took a cautious sip of her steaming coffee. "Too many of them cheat and then blame me when they don't lose as much weight as they'd like."

"Any more news on that deal with Branston Foods?" Sienna stirred agave nectar into her tea to sweeten it. "I keep thinking they're going to change their minds—see what a great thing it could be for them—and come back with an offer."

"No, not yet. I keep hoping, too." Gigi stared into her mug of coffee. She tried not to think about it, but her resources were getting low, and she could really use that deal.

"If it makes you feel any better"—Alice pushed aside the novels she'd dropped onto the sofa and sat down—"Detective Mertz has been asking some questions. I don't know if it will lead to anything, but he's a good detective—one of the best. And"—her eyes twinkled—"he seems to have taken a personal interest in this case." She wiggled her eyebrows at Gigi.

Gigi tried not to look as pleased as she felt. Alice had probably just imagined it.

"Speaking of the case"—Sienna perched on the sofa arm and cradled her mug of tea—"Gigi and I found some information online about Adora, and you were right. She was on Broadway once."

"And only once as far as we can tell." Gigi glanced at Alice and Sienna. "I wonder what happened? All her roles after that seem to have been in summer theater or other amateur productions."

"Maybe she got married? And they moved away from the city? We don't really know much of anything about her at all." Alice began stacking her pile of romance novels. "For all I know, she might have had half a dozen kids between then and now."

"I doubt that." Sienna looked shocked.

Alice shrugged. "You never know."

"Who would know?" Gigi looked from one to the other.

"Winston maybe." Alice started to get up. "I think he's known her longer than any of us."

"And speaking of Winston . . ."

Something about the way Gigi said it made Alice plunk back down on the sofa, the pile of books mounded in her lap.

"What about Winston?" She looked from Sienna to Gigi and back again. "Come on, girls, dish. It's your old friend Alice here." She leaned forward eagerly.

Gigi didn't have the heart to make her wait any longer. "We've discovered who broke up Winston's marriage to Martha."

"Well, who? Tell me."

"Adora."

"No!"

Gigi nodded. "We found a picture and a small item on them in the gossip column in the *New York Post*."

Alice whistled. "No wonder she and Martha never got along. They must have been pretty surprised to see each other again—both moving to the same small town in Connecticut." She absentmindedly ruffled the pages of one of the paperbacks in her lap. "It does kind of make you wonder, though."

"Wonder what?" Gigi and Sienna echoed.

Alice spread her hands wide. "Whether Martha ever got her revenge or not." She grinned. "And if so, how?"

Gigi was surprised to see a car parked in her driveway when she got home. She wasn't expecting anyone and didn't recognize the cream-colored Cadillac that was blocking her way. She pulled the MINI up alongside, got out and went around to the passenger side. She opened the door, and Reg immediately ran, barking, toward the back of the cottage.

Gigi was walking up the path when three people came around the side of the house, a young couple followed by an older woman. The young couple were smartly dressed in sophisticated outfits that suggested they must have come out from the city. The older, blond-haired woman was wearing a flowered shirtwaist dress that screamed "Realtor."

Gigi rushed over to where they were standing and pointing at the front of the house. Her house. Reg got there first and ran back and forth between their legs, wagging his tail.

"*Reg!*" Gigi shouted and whistled.

The other three stopped talking and turned toward her.

"Ah, there you are," the older woman said, coming toward Gigi with her hand outstretched. "I'm Amanda

Parker." She shook Gigi's hand briefly, extracting her own just as soon as they made contact to dig in the Louis Vuitton handbag that dangled from her arm. "My card." She pushed the white square into Gigi's palm.

"What are you doing here?" Gigi said, her heart hammering loudly.

"I'm sorry." The woman patted her perfectly coifed blond hairdo. "Didn't Mr. Simpson tell you we were coming?"

Gigi shook her head and bent down to pet Reg, who was leaning against her leg. He seemed to sense her dismay.

"These young people"—Amanda gestured toward the couple who were both intent on their smartphones—"are interested in buying this charming little cottage."

Gigi's mouth went dry, and her heart hammered even harder. She wanted to scream that they couldn't buy the cottage. It was hers. Or it would be, as soon as she figured out how she was going to pay for it. But instead she smiled, bit her lower lip with her teeth and opened the front door.

Amanda rounded up the couple, who barely looked up from their mobile devices, and herded them through the front door and into the foyer, much like a sheepdog collecting its flock.

Light was slanting through the windows, leaving mellow streaks on the dark wood floor. It was Gigi's favorite time of day in the cottage—late afternoon—when the sun's rays took on a golden bronze hue and the cooling air carried the scent of lavender through the open windows.

She followed the couple and the Realtor into the living room, tagging along like a lost puppy. She was struck anew by how much she loved the place. She'd never felt so at home before, and she wasn't giving it up without a fight. Fortunately, these two didn't look like the cottage type. They'd probably take a spin around and then go look at some place more suitable.

The girl lifted her head briefly from her phone, her thumbs still hovering over the miniature keyboard, and looked around. "It's kind of small."

The young man's head bobbed in agreement. "Kind of small. Yes."

"Nonsense," Amanda swept out an arm to encompass the room. "The space is lovely, and"—she paused for dramatic effect—"you can always bump out the windows and enlarge."

The couple looked around, grunted and then followed Amanda as she led the way to the bedroom, her full flowered skirt swishing from side to side as she walked.

These people couldn't possibly buy the cottage, Gigi thought. They had no feeling for it whatsoever. It would be a crime to ruin the charming bay window in the living room for the sake of a couple of extra feet. What were they going to do with all the space, anyway?

Gigi was glad, as they all trooped into the bedroom, that she made her bed and hung up her clothes every morning. The girl poked her head in the closet and wrinkled her nose. "It's awfully small."

Amanda laughed. "That's how these old places were built. If you want charm, you might have to sacrifice some space." She peeled back the white eyelet curtain at the window and stared out. "Nice view," she said as she let the curtain fall back into place. "Now, if it's size you want, I can show you this new place just outside of town. It used to be a furniture factory, but they've created some of the most amazing spaces out of it. Very avant-garde."

Now that sounded a lot more like this couple's kind of

place. City Girl, as Gigi had come to think of her, grunted again.

"I kind of like this place. What do you think?" She looked over at City Boy, who was still busy texting, his thumbs flying over the keys.

He looked up suddenly, probably sensing that City Girl was staring at him, her lip curling in dissatisfaction.

"What did you say?"

"I like this place." City Girl gave an imperceptible stomp of her foot.

Gigi crossed her fingers. Surely he would say it was too small, too old, too something for his taste.

"Yeah. Me, too."

"Wonderful." Amanda clapped her hands. "That's done, then. Shall we go back to my office and draw up the papers?"

Gigi's heart plummeted to the pit of her stomach. They were actually going to buy her cottage. She looked at Reg, who cocked his head sadly. What would she do? Where would she go?

She'd just have to solve Martha's death, prove that her Gourmet De-Lite food had had nothing to do with it, persuade Branston Foods to reconsider their deal and put a down payment on the cottage herself.

Sure. Nothing to it. Easy as pie.

Gigi usually found contentment in certain menial, repetitive tasks. It was one reason she'd been so drawn to cooking. Chopping, kneading and stirring all brought a measure of calm and comfort, even under the most stressful circumstances.

Except now. She had a stack of newspapers to be tied up for recycling—a boring job that she did while watching television or listening to music. She would usually find, halfway through, that she'd entered a zone of Zen-like tranquility.

Tonight, however, the task seemed merely irksome, a chore and nothing more. Her fingers kept getting tied up in the twine, her knots refused to hold, and all she really wanted to do was throw the whole stack in the garbage. But she believed in recycling. She really did.

The television was tuned to a favorite show, but tonight it didn't hold her attention. She couldn't get City Girl and City Boy out of her mind. The prospect of their living in the cottage—*her cottage*—made her stomach feel as if she were on a ship being tossed around in a storm.

Reg sighed and rolled over on his back, and Gigi reached out to scratch his tummy. She was sitting cross-legged on the floor with a glass of iced green tea within easy reach, a tottering stack of newspapers to her left and a finished stack to her right. She grabbed a handful of sections and carefully aligned their edges. An advertisement for Abigail's caught her eye. The dress in the picture looked like the blue silk one she'd tried on. She sighed. It really had looked good on her.

The section had been left open to an inner page, and Gigi began to unfold it so she could straighten it out. The advertisement was opposite the obituaries, and Martha's name jumped out at her. She read through the notice again, wondering if they would ever discover what had really happened to the poor woman.

She was shaking out the section prior to refolding it correctly when a thought occurred to her. Quickly, she opened the paper and scanned Martha's obituary again.

She dropped the paper and sat for a minute, thinking. She was on to something. Definitely, she was onto something. The seesawing feeling in her stomach settled and changed to prickles of excitement. She just needed to ask a few questions.

But who would have the answers?

Winston, of course!

The big opening night of the Woodstone Players' production of *Truth or Dare* was hot and humid with the rumblings of bad weather in the distance. Sienna and Oliver were picking Gigi up and, despite everything, she was quite excited.

She'd taken extra care with the dinner entrée that night for her Gourmet De-Lite customers since so many of them were in the cast of *Truth or Dare*. She carefully packed poached salmon with yogurt dill sauce and oven roasted green beans in her specially made boxes, spent extra time inking the names on top and even included a short "break a leg" message. She lined the containers up on her kitchen counter—ones for Barbie, Alice, Adora. She thought of everyone else who had somehow been involved with Martha—Carlo, Emilio, Winston. Was one of them really a murderer?

A trickle of sweat crawled slowly down her back, and she shivered. Maybe it was the effects of the weather, but she had a feeling that things were going to come to a head very soon.

Gigi dressed as coolly as possible in a sea green sleeveless cotton dress. The air-conditioning at the Woodstone Theater was notoriously unreliable, but if she actually did get cold, she had a darker green shawl to wrap around her bare shoulders. She glanced at herself in the mirror. Not bad, although she still wished she had been able to afford that sweet little number from Abigail's.

Sienna and Oliver picked her up right on schedule, but still, when they pulled into the parking lot of the Woodstone Theater, many of the spaces were already taken. Oliver offered to drop them at the front door.

"I can walk perfectly well, darling," Sienna said, patting his cheek, but there was no reproach in her voice.

"I know." Oliver turned toward her. "But humor me, okay? I feel like pampering you a bit."

They sat grinning at each other until finally Gigi cleared her throat. She'd noticed Winston's car in the lot and thought this might be the perfect opportunity to talk to him.

Oliver put the car back in gear and moved around toward the back of the theater, finally maneuvering their silver Audi into a spot.

It was still light out, but dark clouds made it seem later than it was. Gigi felt a drop or two of rain, and brushed at her bare arm. They quickly made their way across the parking lot, crunching over bits of gravel and trying to avoid the holes that were notorious for causing twisted ankles.

A woman slid out of a red Volkswagen Beetle just ahead of them, and Gigi recognized Evelyn, the proprietress of Bon Appétit. She had her usual cardigan draped over her shoulders, and her dark gray hair was pulled back into a ribbon at her neck.

She turned briefly and waved to them. "It looks like all of Woodstone is here tonight."

Oliver held the door to the theater open and grinned. "It's showtime, folks."

The lobby was crammed with people, their voices rising and falling like the babble of a fountain.

Gigi looked around for Winston but didn't see him anywhere. She really hoped to talk to him before the performance started. All the pieces of the puzzle swirled around in her head much like the kaleidoscope of colors and prints on the ladies' cotton summer dresses.

The crowd started to shift almost imperceptibly toward the open doors of the theater.

"Shall we go in?" Oliver tucked his arm protectively around Sienna and gently touched Gigi's elbow.

She shook her head. "You go on in. I want to ask Winston something." She craned her neck and looked around the crowded room once again.

Sienna raised her eyebrows questioningly, but Gigi ignored her.

"I'll be fine, really," she said when Oliver and Sienna still didn't move. "I've got my ticket"—she held up her stub—"and I'll join you in a minute."

As they reluctantly joined the crush moving slowly toward their seats, Gigi continued to scan the crowd for Winston. She was betting that he'd be going outside for one last smoke before the performance started.

Gigi was about to give up and join Oliver and Sienna when a side door opened and Winston emerged, cigarette and lighter in hand.

Bingo, she thought. She knew he'd need to light up at least once more before the curtain rose on the first act.

She followed as he slipped out a side door marked *Emergencies Only* and took shelter under the narrow overhang of the roof. A flame flared in the shadows, and Winston's face was briefly illuminated.

The wind had picked up, and it fluttered the ends of Gigi's shawl. She let the door close quietly behind her.

"Winston?"

He turned abruptly, the cigarette halfway to this mouth.

"Ah, it's the Gourmet De-Lite girl." He inhaled a long drag, letting the smoke trickle out his nose. He fished a

packet of cigarettes out of his pocket and held them toward
Gigi. "Smoke?"

"No, thanks."

"Getting a bit of air, then?" He gestured toward the theater with his head. "Awfully stuffy in there." He snickered.
"And it's only going to get worse when they unleash all that
hot air."

"Actually, I wanted to talk to you."

"Really?" He raised his eyebrows and took another
thoughtful puff on his cigarette.

"It's about Martha."

"My dear ex?" He took a last drag, dropped the cigarette
to the ground and snuffed it out with the toe of his shoe.
"You still determined to prove that someone killed her on
purpose?"

Put like that, it did seem rather ambitious of her, Gigi
thought. She nodded briefly.

"I'm sure I can't help you." He smiled even as his features
hardened. "It was merely an act of divine providence."

Well, it certainly was providence for him, Gigi thought,
divine or otherwise.

"Actually, I wanted to talk to you about your affair with
Adora." Gigi let out her breath. She'd summoned up all of
her Italian and Irish courage to come out with that so bluntly.

"My, my, you have been digging. That was eons ago."
Winston fumbled around in his pocket, retrieved the battered pack of cigarettes and shook one loose. "And, I might
add"—he tapped the tip of her nose with his index
finger—"none of your business."

Gigi shrugged. It might have been eons ago, but she felt
it in her bones that it was connected somehow to Martha's
death.

"I found some clippings online about Adora and the

Broadway play she was in." She thought it best not to mention the society column photograph of him with his arm around Adora.

"Yes. I remember that. What was the name of that dreadful bunch of tripe?"

"*The Silent Tongues*," Gigi supplied.

"Hmmm, yes, I think you're right." Winston leaned against the wall, one foot crossed casually over the other, the picture of relaxation—although Gigi could see the muscles in his jaw clenching and unclenching. "It didn't last very long as I recall."

"No, it didn't," Gigi agreed. "Was it really that bad?"

"Oh, yes, my dear." Winston straightened, patted the lapels of his navy blazer and shot the cuffs of his pale pink shirt. "It was a terrible play. With hideous sets, nonexistent direction and dreadful acting." He took a puff of his second cigarette. "Although that doesn't seem to stop half the stuff produced on Broadway these days, so perhaps it wasn't that bad after all."

"Did you ever think it odd that Adora never appeared on Broadway again?"

Winston laughed, and the sound caught in his throat and turned to a raspy cough. "She was an abominable actress. Barely fit for summer stock or amateur productions." He waved a hand toward the barn-turned-theater.

"But you'd think that with her ambition she would have secured at least another part or two."

Winston shrugged. "She was always late for rehearsals, couldn't get along with the rest of the cast, argued with the directors." He leveled a look at Gigi. "Pick one of those, any one. Adora acted offstage as if she had talent onstage. Some things—anything—can be forgiven if a person is good enough, but if you're not"—he shrugged again—"you'd better make yourself as accommodating as possible." He paused for a moment. "And she didn't."

"I was wondering . . ." Gigi held her breath for a second. *Here goes nothing*, she thought. She'd drawn her own conclusions but didn't have any proof. "I was wondering if there wasn't more to it than that."

Winston jerked, and the glowing stub of his cigarette fell from his hand. He looked down at it briefly, before crushing it under his heel. "What do you mean?"

Gigi crossed her fingers behind her back. "I happened to reread Martha's obituary. It mentioned that at one time she'd been a <u>theater</u> critic as well as a restaurant reviewer."

The tension from Winston's face cleared, and he threw back his head and gave a bark of laughter. "You really are good, Little Miss Nancy Drew." He pulled a linen handkerchief from his pocket and dabbed at his mouth. "Yes, Martha did review theater. Under the name of Sarah Bernhardt. Clever, don't you think?" He looked at Gigi. "You do know who Sarah Bernhardt was, don't you?"

Gigi nodded. So that was why she couldn't find anything under Martha's own name.

"You're quite right." Winston leveled a finger playfully at Gigi. "I'd been a bit of a naughty boy with Adora, and Martha found out. Very unfortunate. That shrew who wrote the gossip column for the *New York Post* caught us coming out of La Côte Basque one night." He sniffed. "Had to put it in her column. Martha was furious." He shook his head, then looked up at Gigi. "The columnist fancied me herself, that's why she did it." He shot his cuffs again.

"What happened then?" Gigi asked, although she was pretty certain she already knew the answer.

"Martha panned the production of *Silent Tongues*. Absolutely panned it." His eyes lit up with what looked to Gigi

like admiration. "Of course, she picked on Adora specifically, even though her part in the play was relatively minor
and hardly warranted mentioning. And it certainly wasn't
the cause of the entire play flopping. Frankly, the director
was to blame for that."

"So Martha got her revenge."

Winston smiled. "Yes, I guess you could say that." He
shot his cuffs again and straightened his shirt collar. "Good
old Martha. She certainly did get her revenge. As you have
already noted, that was the beginning and end of Adora's
Broadway career." He started to reach for another cigarette
and then changed his mind. "Adora became known as 'the
Silent Curse.' No one would touch her. No one," he repeated.
"It was merely Hunter Pierce's bad luck that he became
tarred with the same brush, so to speak."

"Isn't Hunter Pierce the director . . . ?" Gigi inclined her
head toward the theater.

Winston nodded and smoke streamed out his nose into
the thick, humid air. "Yes. He's the director of tonight's
little production." He blew out a sigh. "Which is why I don't
have much hope for this evening's performance. Adora can't
act, Hunter can't direct, and I don't even want to think about
the rest of them."

"So, Hunter had every reason to hate Martha as much as
Adora . . ."

"Exactly, my dear." Winston glanced at his watch. "But
surely the curtain on tonight's little drama is about to rise.
Shall we go in?"

Winston pulled open the door for Gigi and motioned for
her to go first. The lights in the lobby were flashing to signal
the start of the play, and Gigi fumbled in her purse for her
ticket stub.

The theater was already dark. The usher took the ticket

from Gigi and shone a pen light on it. "Follow me." She clicked the light off and headed down the aisle.

Gigi apologized profusely as she slid past a half dozen pairs of legs to the empty seat in the middle of the row.

Sienna leaned across Oliver and whispered, "Where were you?"

The curtain began to slowly creak upward, and Gigi mouthed, "Later," before turning her eyes to the stage.

But she wasn't thinking about the play.

She was thinking about how many lives Martha had managed to ruin wielding her nasty pen—all the restaurants that had gone out of business after one of her bad reviews, and people like Adora and Hunter Pierce whose careers were ruined. And Carlo and Emilio, who had so much to fear from Martha's vitriolic writing.

The question was—which of them had hated Martha enough to kill her?

Chapter 19

Gigi was enjoying the play, although she wasn't sure if half of her fascination didn't come from seeing people she knew up on stage. But the first act went quickly, and she was surprised when the curtain rang down on intermission.

"What do you think?" Sienna took her arm as they made their way up the aisle, leaving Oliver behind to mind their wraps and hold their programs.

"I'm rather enjoying it. Adora isn't half as bad as Winston made out."

"Speaking of Winston"—Sienna moved to one side to let a couple of teenagers pass—"what were you two talking about before the play? I thought you were going to miss the opening act."

Gigi glanced around her. "I don't want to tell you here. Let's see if it's raining, and if it isn't, we can step outside."

The lobby was full of people milling around, sipping glasses of chilled white wine. Their faces were flushed—the ancient air-conditioning system wasn't up to the task of coping with so many warm bodies. Women fanned themselves with their programs, and men pressed handkerchiefs to their faces. Gigi and Sienna were headed toward the door when Carlo came up to them.

"Please." He touched each of them lightly. "Let me get you a glass of wine."

"Water for me." Sienna patted her tummy.

"An orange juice maybe?" Carlo glanced over toward where a table covered in white linen had been set up as a bar. "I believe they do have some."

"Wonderful."

They both watched as he insinuated his way through the crowd.

"Okay, tell me, quickly, before he comes back." Sienna glanced toward the bar. "There's quite a line, so I think we have a few minutes."

They leaned their heads together, and Gigi filled her in on her conversation with Winston.

Sienna whistled. "So Martha basically ruined both Hunter Pierce's and Adora's theater careers."

Gigi nodded. "Neither of them ever got another shot at Broadway, according to Winston. Of course, in Adora's case, Winston says that's partly because of her own behavior."

"Still, I imagine Martha's review carried a certain amount of clout. And theater people are so superstitious— just think of all that nonsense about the Scottish play—they probably viewed Adora as bad luck."

"And she wasn't good enough to overcome their prejudices. They could easily just pick someone else."

"I guess that's not what she bargained for when she tried to steal Winston away from Martha."

"Fame and fortune is more like it."

Gigi thought about Ted and the woman who had ruined their marriage. Would she go as far as Martha had to exact her revenge? She didn't think so. Funny, but she just realized that she really didn't care all that much anymore. At first, she couldn't think about anything but Ted, and now she went for weeks without having him cross her mind at all.

Gigi looked across the crowd and noticed Devon Single-ton slouched in a corner, scribbling in a pocket-size note-book. She wondered if he were reviewing the play for the *Woodstone Times*. She hoped his review would be more charitable than some of Martha's had been.

Carlo returned with a glass of white wine for Gigi and juice for Sienna. The girl with the spiky hair who helped Sienna in the Book Nook drifted past on the arm of a young man in a polo shirt with a popped collar and carefully pressed khakis. Gigi watched them go by. She supposed they were proof that opposites did attract.

The lights blinked once, in warning.

"I'll take those." Carlo took their empty glasses and headed toward the bar, which was now strewn with dis-carded plastic tumblers and screwed up napkins.

Gigi turned around, and coming toward her was Detec-tive Mertz. With a young girl on his arm. Gigi looked her over—young and pretty. Maddeningly pretty, with long hair, long legs and a perfect tan. Gigi was suddenly seized with irrational jealousy. There was no reason why Mertz shouldn't bring someone to the play. It was just that she'd hoped . . .

Mertz glanced in Gigi's direction and obviously noticed her staring at them. A strange, startled look crossed his face, and he grabbed the girl's arm and began to steer her in the other direction.

"Isn't that your policeman?" Sienna asked, staring after the couple.

"He's not my policeman. Obviously." Gigi dabbed at her upper lip with her crumpled cocktail napkin.

"Honestly, Gigi, if you played your cards right, I think he very much could be your policeman. Or"—she turned to Gigi and smiled coyly—"is it Carlo you're after? Either way, you have to admit, they're both quite the catch."

"I like Carlo. Very much. But he wouldn't be right for me. I'm ready to settle down, and,"—Gigi glanced at Sienna's belly—"and maybe have a family. Carlo's still a boy."

Sienna pounced. "So it's Mertz you're interested in. I knew it."

She smiled smugly, and Gigi could easily read the look in her eyes. It said, *I haven't known you for this long without being able to read your thoughts.*

Gigi was ready to protest, but fortunately the lights blinked their warning again. "Come on, let's get back to our seats," she said instead as the crowd began to edge toward the theater.

Gigi and Sienna went back to their seats. Something nibbled at the edge of Gigi's mind, but she couldn't put her finger on it. It was an idea that had begun to formulate while watching the first act. Maybe she would be able to track down the elusive figment during the second half.

The curtain rose on a living room scene. Gigi recognized the armoire that Sienna had painted. Adora was wearing the too-tight shorts in this scene, although Gigi thought they looked just a bit looser, so maybe Adora had lost some weight after all. She squinted at the stage. Yes, it looked as if Adora must have shed at least five pounds.

Emilio appeared in the second act as Adora's character's love interest. Gigi wondered if practicing this scene had led to their real-life affair. It certainly lent an air of realism to their performance. She found herself forgetting that these were people she knew and began thinking of them as their onstage alter egos.

Poor Emilio was in a suit and tie, and Gigi could see the sheen of perspiration breaking out on his forehead. The air conditioner had only managed to cool the theater to lukewarm—it must still be beastly hot under the lights.

Thinking about that tickled that elusive thought she'd had earlier. Something to do with the heat perhaps? Certainly something to do with Martha's death. Everything about the theater brought that day back in sharp focus. She tried to forget it and concentrate on the play, but scenes from that afternoon kept flashing like streaks of lightning across her mind.

She remembered arriving with the lunches, and the tension she'd sensed crackling in the air. Then the rain, Barbie and Winston going out to their car, the smell of Martha's wet coat in Gigi's MINI and Martha taking her first bite of the melba toast. She closed her eyes for a moment. Should she have stopped Martha from eating the food? But why? She knew there hadn't been any peanut oil near Martha's lunch.

The thought she'd been chasing suddenly swam into focus, and she sat bolt upright in her seat.

"Are you okay?" Oliver turned toward her, eyebrows raised.

"Yes, fine, sorry. Foot fell asleep."

Gigi thought furiously. It all made sense now—Martha, Emilio and Al Forno, the teenage boy the UPS woman had seen. Like dominoes, everything plunked into place.

Gigi could barely sit still. She had to tell Detective Mertz right away.

Gigi had no idea how the play ended. All of a sudden the audience was on their feet applauding. She jumped up to join them and clapped furiously, as if that would make up for her lack of attention.

"It was wonderful, wasn't it?" Sienna said.

"Oh, yes," Gigi enthused, in spite of not having the least idea of what had taken place in the second half.

"Adora really is quite good," Sienna commented as Adora came forward for her bow. "It's a shame Martha ruined her career the way she did." The clapping and cheering went up a notch, and there were several whistles from the delighted audience.

Winston emerged onstage bearing an enormous bouquet of red roses. He presented the flowers to Adora with a curt nod.

The entire cast came forward again, hands clasped, bowed before the audience, and then the dark red velvet curtain came tumbling down.

The audience shuffled in their seats, retrieving programs and discarded wraps. Gigi was thinking frantically. She had to talk to Winston again to confirm her suspicions. She was positive now that he *had* seen someone outside by her car the day Martha was killed. But first she had to get rid of Sienna and Oliver. Later she would worry about how she would get home. She could always ring for Woodstone's lone taxi—an ancient, dusty van with an even more ancient driver.

"I'll go bring the car around." Oliver pecked Sienna on the cheek and joined the crowd trying to squeeze through the open doors.

Gigi stood frozen for a minute. She had to get away from Sienna. "I'm just going to run to the . . . the ladies' room," she said, fingers crossed that Sienna wouldn't insist on joining her.

"I'll wait here. For once, I don't have to go."

Gigi let out a sigh of relief and quickly made her way through the crowd, head down, thinking furiously. She was rounding the corner toward the restrooms when she ran smack into a hard, masculine chest. She looked up slowly.

"I'm so sorry . . ."

Her words trailed off as she stared up into Carlo's very warm brown eyes.

"My pleasure, *cara*," he said, then blushed lightly under the caramel color of his tan. "Do you need a ride?" he asked hopefully.

"Thanks, but no, I'm going with Oliver and Sienna."

"There is going to be a little party at Al Forno tonight for the cast. Please say you will come," he said, and blushed again.

"I'd love to." Gigi smiled brightly wishing he would let her go. She had to catch Winston before he left. She had probably already missed Detective Mertz and his glamorous young date, but she could always call him later at the station.

"See you soon, then." Carlo gave her shoulder a squeeze and moved away.

Gigi stood for a moment, the crowd parting around her like water flowing around an obstruction in a river. She watched as Carlo disappeared into the crowd.

Carlo! That was it.

She turned around and began to make her way back toward where Sienna was waiting.

"That was fast." Sienna started to move toward the door.

"Wait," Gigi called after her.

Sienna turned around with a quizzical look on her face. "I think Oliver is here. I thought I saw our car." She gestured toward the door.

Gigi shook her head. "Yes, but I ran into Carlo." She felt

terrible lying to Sienna, but there was no other way. "He's offered me a ride." Gigi managed to blush.

"Looks like the universe is trying to tell you something." Sienna gave Gigi a playful tap and winked. "Perhaps you should think about having a good time before you settle down," she called over her shoulder as she began to walk toward the doors.

The crowd was thinning now, with only a few clusters of people left in the lobby. The air conditioner had picked up speed, and Gigi could hear its deep rumble as cool air blasted out of the ducts. She felt the chill tickle the hairs on her arms, and she shivered, pulling her wrap up around her shoulders.

Winston was probably backstage with the cast if he hadn't already left. She had to talk to him right away. If he gave the answer she suspected, then she was right, and she knew who'd killed Martha Bernhardt. Gigi headed toward a door marked *Cast Only*. Just as she reached for the knob, the door swung open.

"Oh," Alice cried as she and Gigi narrowly missed colliding.

"Sorry." Gigi smiled, trying to control her impatience.

"Are you coming to Carlo and Emilio's?"

Gigi nodded. "Yes, but first I want to talk to Winston. Is he still back there?" She inclined her head toward the door.

"I think so. My guess is he's waiting for everyone to leave to close up."

"See you in a bit then." Gigi began to inch toward the door. She was relieved when Alice waved and walked away.

Gigi pushed open the door to the backstage area. It was dimly lit with only one naked bulb hanging suspended from the ceiling. She felt a chill as the door closed behind her with an ominous-sounding *click*.

She stopped and listened carefully but didn't hear anything or anyone—just her own heart beating at twice its normal speed. She took a deep breath and looked around. There were several doors, including two marked *Men's Dressing Room* and *Women's Dressing Room*. She tapped on the door to the women's dressing room and waited. Nothing. She hesitated for a second and then rapped on the men's dressing room door. Nothing there, either.

Someone had finally turned off the air conditioner, and it was hot and close in the narrow corridor. A trickle of sweat slid down her back, and she jumped. What if she ran into the murderer? Everyone had probably left the theater by now. She could scream, and no one would hear. Every horror movie she'd ever watched ran through her head like a lightning-fast filmstrip. She mentally shook herself. She was letting her imagination run away with her.

She heard a faint sound and stopped to listen. Maybe it was Winston getting ready to lock up. She continued down the corridor, which was becoming increasingly dark and shadowy. She heard the noise again, louder this time. It must be Winston, she thought.

Suddenly the light went out, and Gigi was surrounded by black, velvet darkness. She stifled a small cry and felt in front of her with her hands. Nothing. She took a few steps forward, carefully, shuffling her feet along the ground, trying to feel with her toes. The blackness was oppressive. She felt smothered, as if a heavy pillow were pressed against her face, keeping her from breathing.

Her waving hands brushed against something soft. Fabric. Specifically velvet, her exploring fingers told her. She fought her way through the heavy folds, and suddenly there was a pinprick of light.

Gigi continued to bat at the enshrouding drapery until

she was able to push it aside. Blessed light greeted her. She closed her eyes against the sudden glare. When she opened them again she realized she was standing in the theater wings. The light was the ghost light casting a hazy glow over the theater interior.

A movement caught her eye. Coming across the stage was a teenage boy. He was dressed in shorts and a T-shirt and had blond hair—just as the UPS delivery woman had described him.

Gigi stood rooted to the spot as he came closer and closer and closer. She tried to hide in the shadows, but he saw her and smiled—a chilling smile that made her gasp.

"You've guessed, haven't you?" He reached up and pulled off the short blond wig.

Chapter 20

Adora swept the wig from her head, and her own long, blond curls tumbled out. She was still wearing her costume—shorts and a T-shirt—which, combined with the wig, gave her the appearance of a young man—at least from a distance.

"I don't know what you're talking about," Gigi insisted as she tried to quietly back away. If she continued to deny it, perhaps Adora would let her go.

"Don't be silly. I knew that you knew as soon as I saw your face." She tossed the blond wig onto the dark red sofa that was part of the set and ran her hands through her hair, lifting it up off her neck. "You have no idea how hot that wig is."

"I was just looking for Winston." Gigi took another cautious half-inch step backward into the folds of the musty curtain.

"He's gone." Adora turned and looked out over the empty

theater. She turned back toward Gigi. "I told him I'd close up, and he should go on ahead to the party at Al Forno."

"I should go, too." Gigi took a step backward and made a half turn. How was Adora going to keep her there against her will?

"I don't think so," Adora replied, pulling a very nasty-looking pistol from the waistband of her shorts and aiming it in the vicinity of Gigi's heart.

A gun would certainly work to keep me here against my will, Gigi thought. The realization that Adora must have lost some weight crossed her mind. How else would she have fit the pistol into the waist of those too-tight shorts?

Gigi tried to quell her panic. Surely someone would notice she was missing? And Sienna and Oliver would come? Or Carlo? Or, maybe when she didn't show up with Carlo, Sienna would suspect something and call the police? Another irrational thought crossed her mind—that Mertz would have to put a precipitous end to his date with that eye candy he was with. Meanwhile, she knew enough from the books she'd read and movies she'd seen that she'd have to keep Adora talking to buy time.

"Shooting me won't do any good." Gigi was horrified to note that a pleading tone had crept into her voice. "You won't get away with it." Now she sounded like the protagonist of a hideously clichéd movie script. Her legs were ready to buckle at any moment. "Can I sit down?" She gestured toward the sofa where Adora had discarded the wig.

"I suppose so."

She kept her eye on Adora and the gun as she made her trembling way across the stage and sank onto the sofa. "What are you going to do?"

"I'm not doing anything." Adora gestured with the gun, and Gigi flinched. "You are. I know you're counting on all your friends rushing to your rescue. But when they do, they're going to find you dead from a self-inflicted gunshot wound." She held the gun up to her own head as if to demonstrate. "Administered while the balance of your mind was impaired. All caused by the thought that you'd accidentally killed your client, the dear, departed Martha Bernhardt." Adora gave a shrill bark of laughter. "I actually had to say a line like that in a play once." She shook her head. "I've had to work with some dreadful scripts, believe me."

"That must have been difficult." Gigi's glance kept swiveling toward the door, but so far it had remained stubbornly closed.

"You have no idea how difficult!" Adora screeched. "If that bitch Martha hadn't ruined my chances on Broadway . . ." She pointed the gun at Gigi. "It was all her fault. She wanted to get back at me for my affair with Winston." She shook her head. "It wasn't my fault Winston was tired of her." She shrugged. "Anyway, as I was saying, your friends are going to find you've committed suicide. You could no longer stand the burden of guilt knowing you'd accidentally killed poor, dear Martha."

"But I didn't!" Gigi jumped to her feet in protest.

"Sit down," Adora commanded, waving the gun in a wild arc.

"Why now?" Gigi asked as she sank back down onto the sofa. If Adora was going to kill her, she figured she might as well at least satisfy her curiosity. "All that was years ago. What made you—?"

"She was going to do it all over again," Adora snapped. A dreamy look came into her eyes. "She was going to ruin Emilio this time. All because that clumsy waitress spilled some water on her when she went to do her review."

"Maybe she wouldn't have—"

"Yes, she would." Adora spun around and pointed the gun at Gigi. "Martha was like that. Vindictive, mean, nasty . . . and jealous, too. She wanted Emilio for herself." She threw back her head and laughed. "As if Emilio would even look at her! He said it made him sick to pretend—"

"To pretend what?" In spite of herself, Gigi was sitting on the edge of her seat.

Adora gave a contemptuous toss of her head. "That he liked her. He pretended to be in love with her to try to get her to cancel her review and give Al Forno a second chance."

"I'm sure she would have—"

"No." Adora stamped her foot. "She wouldn't. Do you believe it? Even after Emilio had somehow managed to convince her that he loved her . . . she still planned to go ahead with her review." She swiped at a tear of what Gigi supposed was frustration.

Gigi gauged the distance from where she was sitting to the door. What were her chances if she made a run for it? She doubted that Adora was a particularly good shot—if Gigi bobbed and wove, she might have a chance at making it.

All her muscles tightened at the thought of bolting, but she couldn't make herself do it. The idea of being shot— even in some relatively harmless location like an arm or a leg—was enough to paralyze her. She'd have to pray that someone at Al Forno missed her and came looking. Meanwhile, she'd have to keep Adora talking.

"Are you the one who let Reg out of my car that day at the theater and left that threatening note?"

Adora wiped her cheek with the palm of her hand then straightened her shoulders. "I had to do something. You were getting too close."

Gigi got mad all over again at the thought that she could have lost Reg.

"If you weren't so nosy, none of this would be happening."

"You're blaming me?" Gigi's voice rose to a squeaky crescendo.

"I didn't think anyone would recognize me in my costume, but then you managed to put two and two together."

Gigi remembered back to the day of Martha's murder. Adora had run outside in her costume, hoping that anyone who happened to be passing wouldn't recognize her in that garb.

Until Gigi saw her on stage and the light finally went on.

Adora looked at her watch. "It's getting late. Let's get this over with." She gestured toward Gigi with the gun. "I need your fingerprints on here."

"No." Gigi struggled as Adora tried to grab her hand and press it against the handle of the gun.

"Stop squirming," Adora commanded. "Your prints have to be on here just the right way."

Gigi looked up into Adora's eyes and realized it was hopeless. Adora didn't care what she had to do to get her own way. Gigi shivered and glanced toward the door again. No one. No knight in shining armor coming to save her. She'd have to do this herself.

She began to struggle in earnest, but Adora was surprisingly strong and succeeded in twisting Gigi's arm around so that the gun was pointing at her head. She felt the sharp edges of the barrel pressing into her temple and renewed her struggles.

"You're not going to get away with this." Gigi strained to put as much distance between her head and the gun as possible. "Someone else might have seen you that day. They'll figure it out."

"No one else saw me. Just that stupid woman driving the delivery truck."

"Au contraire, my dear." The voice came from somewhere out of the blackness enveloping stage right, and both Gigi and Adora swiveled abruptly in that direction.

Winston stepped from the shadows and stood in front of them, arms crossed over his chest.

Gigi went limp with relief. Surely Winston would be able to do . . . something.

The gun in Adora's hand wavered but still hovered in the vicinity of Gigi's head. Gigi's mind whirled through an entire gigabyte of thoughts in a matter of seconds. If Winston had seen Adora tampering with Martha's food that day, or had even seen her outside at the relevant time, why hadn't he said anything before now?

Winston cocked his head in Gigi's direction. "I'm sure you're wondering why I didn't immediately go running to the police." He shrugged. "Frankly, it was in my best interests not to. Not"—he held up a hand palm facing out—"that I had any idea what you were up to that day." He pointed accusingly at Adora.

Adora snorted. "Darn right it was in your best interests, as you put it. You wouldn't have been able to make the deal for this property if Martha were still alive."

"And you"—Winston pointed at Adora again—"are getting a completely new, state-of-the-art theater, so I don't know what you're complaining about."

"But they'll arrest her when they find out, and you . . ." Gigi trailed off in the face of Winston's expression.

"I know." He paused dramatically. "I'll be an accessory to the crime. My girl, you are truly naïve." He threw his head back and laughed theatrically. "I have no intention of allowing you to ruin my happy little scheme. I couldn't believe my good fortune when Adora decided to take things into her own greedy little hands and get rid of that large, cumbersome obstacle known as Martha. Far be it from me to stand in her way. She took all the risks"—he gestured toward Adora—"and I get all the rewards."

"And so you're throwing me to the wolves?" Adora jumped to her feet. "If I'm going down, so are you." She moved the gun from Gigi's head and Gigi breathed a momentary sigh of relief.

Adora held the pistol at arm's length, braced with both hands and aimed directly at Winston.

"No!" Gigi cried. She waved an arm trying to throw off Adora's aim.

Winston just stood there and watched. "Don't worry," he said with a smirk, "it's not a real gun." He gestured toward the revolver in Adora's hand. "It's a prop."

"This"—his hand disappeared into the folds of his jacket—"is a real gun," and he pulled out a serious-looking pistol. He aimed it casually but steadily at Adora. "What a pity, but this has to be done. You"—he cocked the pistol in Adora's direction—"are going to kill yourself after having murdered our little Gigi here. So sad. You were overcome with remorse and saw no way out but to take your own life."

"You won't get away with this," Gigi stammered, realizing how ridiculous that sounded even as she said it.

Winston took a step toward Adora.

"Don't you come any closer!" Adora brandished the prop gun as if it were real.

"Nonsense, dear, I don't want to put too much trust in my aim." Winston steadied the gun with his left hand and moved his finger to the trigger.

Adora closed her eyes and squeezed the trigger of the prop pistol a second before Winston squeezed his.

The explosion was massive, and Gigi's hands flew to her ears practically of their own accord. It took her several seconds to realize she was screaming and several more to force herself to stop.

Adora's bullet had grazed Winston's arm, tearing through the expensive fabric of his suit jacket and the custom-made shirt beneath. Blood tinged the edges of the fabric a bright red.

"What the bloody hell!" he shouted. "That was supposed to be a prop, not a real gun. Bloody stagehands can't do anything right." He stared at the blood welling up from the deep grove in his left arm. His face was pasty, and prickles of sweat broke out on his forehead.

He lurched forward, and Adora began to scream. "Don't you come any closer, or I'll shoot again." She waved the gun around wildly.

She was equally pale, and Gigi could see the sheen of perspiration on her upper lip.

Winston looked to be in shock, and Adora didn't look much better. Gigi wondered if she could slip away unnoticed and summon help before either of them actually succeeded in shooting the other . . . or her.

Winston tried to aim the gun again, but he swayed violently, grasping at the air for balance. Adora dropped her gun and ran toward him, one arm outstretched. He sagged heavily onto her shoulder.

Somehow Gigi struggled to her feet. Her legs quivered but she managed to put one foot in front of the other. She didn't look back. She didn't want to know if either Adora or Winston were aiming at her.

She ran straight into the folds of the curtain, stifling a sneeze as dust went into her nose and mouth. She couldn't see and batted her arms around uselessly trying to find the opening. The velvet fabric weighed heavily on her arms and molded to her face. She could barely breathe.

Finally, one arm sliced through the opening, and she was able to push the cloying fabric to one side. She plunged through it into shadowy darkness.

She stopped for a minute to get her bearings. As her eyes adjusted, dark, looming shapes came into slow focus. One of the shapes suddenly detached itself from the others and moved toward her. Before she could utter the scream that rose in her throat, arms were thrown around her, and she was held roughly against someone's chest.

"Are you okay?"

Gigi looked up into the blazing blue eyes of Detective Mertz.

"I . . . I . . . think so," she stammered. "How did you . . . what . . . ?"

"Never mind that now. If you go through that door"—he pointed behind him—"it will take you outside. Wait out there for me."

Gigi nodded. "Okay." She noticed his gun was drawn and held loosely, but confidently, in his right hand.

She started to turn away, but he put a hand on her shoulder.

"Oh, and Gigi?"

"Yes?"

"That was my niece I was with tonight."

Gigi couldn't be sure in the gloom, but she thought he was blushing.

"Oh" was all she said before breaking into a big smile.

Several police officers brushed past her as she made her way toward the open door. She thought she heard the sounds of a scuffle, but she didn't linger long enough to find out. She was more than happy to take Mertz's advice and wait outside.

Chapter 21

"Oh, thank goodness," Carlo declared, clapping his hands together, as Gigi pushed open the door to Al Forno. He rushed forward to greet her. "We were so worried." He took both her hands in his and held them for a moment.

Gigi felt a warm glow that started in the pit of her stomach and spread in both directions until she tingled from her head to her toes.

"Come in, come in." Carlo whisked her into the room, his arm tucked protectively through one of hers. "We've been so worried. We heard the sirens and saw the police cars speeding past but had no idea . . . and then when you didn't show up, we . . ."

"Feared the worst," interjected Alice, who was perched on a bar stool nursing a small glass of chardonnay.

"Let me get you something to drink." Carlo turned toward the bar, where Lara was sorting through the day's receipts. "Lara, if you please, pour Gigi a glass of the white port that just came in."

Lara nodded and reached for a bottle on the shelf.

"If you don't mind," Gigi began, "just this once I think I'd actually rather have a whiskey."

"*Dio mio*, it must be really bad." Emilio motioned to Lara. "A whiskey, Lara, please." He turned toward Gigi. "You must tell us what happened, *cara*. Do you know?"

"Let her have something to drink first." Carlo pulled out a stool and motioned for Gigi to sit. Emilio handed him two plates of fried calamari, and he put one in front of Gigi and another on the table where Oliver and Sienna were sitting. "Pizza is coming. Emilio just put it in the oven."

Gigi glanced at Sienna. "Was it you—?"

Sienna nodded. "We ran into Carlo in the parking lot, and when I saw you weren't with him, I suspected you were up to something. So I called the station just in case, and they got hold of Mertz. He insisted on going back to the theater himself."

"Really?" Gigi felt a huge grin erupt across her face.

Sienna nodded.

Gigi looked around. The small group had gathered to celebrate the opening night of *Truth or Dare*. Carlo and Emilio had invited all the shopkeepers on High Street, and she recognized Evelyn from Bon Appétit sitting with an older gentleman clutching an unlit pipe. Yvette from the Silver Lining was at another table, a periwinkle blue pashmina draped around her bare shoulders. Deirdre, the saleswoman from Abigail's, sat across from her sipping a tiny glass of sherry.

All eyes were on Gigi. Gigi could see the concern on their faces.

Emilio spun around suddenly. "And where is our star? Where is Adora? She's not with you?"

Gigi didn't know what to say. "I'm sorry," she began.

Emilio put a hand to his chest. "Something's happened?"

"And where are Winston and Barbie?" Alice said.

"We thought we heard shots, too," Evelyn's husband said around the pipe stem clenched in his teeth.

Gigi opened her mouth, but everyone around her began to talk at once.

Carlo clapped his hands. "Quiet, please, let's hear what Gigi has to say."

Suddenly the room was hushed, save for the faint hum of machinery from the kitchen. All eyes were on Gigi. She took a gulp of her whiskey for courage. She wasn't sure where to begin.

"Were those really shots we heard?" Yvette shivered and pulled her shawl more closely around her shoulders.

"Yes. Adora was trying to shoot me, but she shot Winston instead."

"*Mama mia!*" Emilio exclaimed.

Gigi noticed that Alice had slipped off her stool and was behind the counter helping him cut the pizza. She put a hand on his arm.

"Why was Adora trying to shoot you?" Evelyn peered at Gigi over the tops of her glasses.

"She realized that I'd guessed that she was the one who killed Martha."

"*Mama mia!*" Emilio exclaimed again.

"Gigi has been investigating all along, even though the police gave up on the case long ago," Sienna said.

"I know Martha and Adora had their little arguments, but murder?" Evelyn shuddered.

"It goes back a lot further than their recent arguments,"

Gigi assured her. "They knew each other in New York. Martha was reviewing theater back then as 'Sarah Bernhardt,' and Adora was appearing in her first play."

"Oh dear, was Martha a naughty girl? Did she pan Adora's play?" Evelyn looked around the room.

Gigi nodded. "She did. And not just the play, but Adora's performance specifically."

"Why would she do that?" Yvette held her hands out, palms up. "I didn't think Adora was really so bad."

"No, but Adora was having an affair with Winston. Martha found a very clever way to exact her revenge."

A low murmur went around the room.

"How ever did you figure it out?" Deirdre plucked an olive ring from her slice of pizza and nibbled it.

"It wasn't easy," Gigi admitted. "At first I thought Barbie or Winston was responsible. They seemed to have the most to gain. As a matter of fact"—she paused and took a sip of her whiskey—"Winston did see Adora outside the day Martha was killed, but he chose not to say anything. Her death was actually a windfall for him."

She cradled her glass in her hands. She had decided not to mention her suspicions about Carlo.

"It's still hard to believe something like that would happen here . . . in Woodstone." Alice shuddered and sidled closer to Emilio.

Emilio looked to be in shock, his eyes glassy and slightly out of focus. Gigi watched the way Alice kept her hand protectively on his arm. She had the feeling that Emilio would be over Adora in no time.

"Who's going to take over Adora's part? Or, will the play just shut down, do you think?" Evelyn blotted her mouth with her napkin and began to rummage in her purse. She pulled out a tube of lip balm, uncapped it and smoothed it across her lips.

"I'm her understudy," Alice admitted. Gigi thought she blushed. "I'm ready to take over the role. And, thanks to Gigi's wonderful diet, I think I almost look the part." She blushed again, and Emilio patted her arm absentmindedly.

Evelyn took her napkin from her lap, crumpled it and put it on the table alongside her purse. "When is the big wedding?"

"It's next week. Friday. We got a better deal not having it on the Saturday."

"You're going to look beautiful." Gigi nibbled on a crispy bit of calamari, surprised to discover she was suddenly hungry.

Alice sighed. "I hope so. Did I tell you the groom's mother went out and bought the same dress as mine?"

"No!" Several people exclaimed.

Alice nodded. "Exactly the same. Only hers is a size six, and mine's a size ten."

Gigi felt so bad for Alice. She knew how much it meant to her to look good for her daughter's wedding.

Deirdre snapped her fingers. "First thing Monday morning, meet me at Abigail's—early, before we open to the public. I have just the dress for you. And I am sure I can give you a special discount." She smiled.

Alice brightened. "But what will I do with my other dress? It's not something you would wear just any old day of the week."

Deirdre smiled, a slightly wicked smile. "You can wear it for the rehearsal dinner the night before the wedding. That will put that miserable future mother-in-law in her place once and for all."

The party broke up shortly before midnight. Oliver and Sienna drove Gigi home. She could hear Reg barking as they pulled into the driveway. At least she didn't have to worry about him anymore.

But she did have to worry about finding a new place to live. The cottage looked so snug—white against the dark night with a shaft of moonlight spilling over the front. The lilacs were starting to flower, and the rosebushes were thick with heavy, fragrant blooms. Gigi felt a deep ache settle in her heart. She'd felt more at home in her little cottage than she'd ever felt before. How was she going to give it up?

She waved to Sienna and Oliver and watched as they backed down the driveway. She opened the door, and Reg came flying down the hall, slipping on the spill of mail on the foyer floor. After giving Reg his due, Gigi gathered up the envelopes and took them out to the kitchen.

She ought to have been tired but felt restless instead. The shock of nearly being shot at was starting to set in, and she was surprised to discover that her hands were shaking slightly. She filled the teakettle and put it on the stove to heat, then took a box of Calming Karma tea from the cupboard. Maybe a hot drink would soothe her enough to let her sleep.

As she waited for the water to boil, she flipped through the letters that had been pushed through her mail slot. Three pieces of junk, a postcard from a local tanning parlor and an envelope from Simpson and West. Gigi was tempted to leave the last until morning, but instead slid her finger under the flap and pulled out several pieces of expensive vellum. It probably had something to do with the sale of the cottage. She'd better find out now when they expected her to move out.

She was unfolding the letter when the kettle boiled. She put the letter to one side and made her tea, dipping the tea bag again and again into the hot water until it had become a deep, rich honey color.

She picked up the letter from Simpson and West again and began to read. When she got to the third paragraph her hand jerked, and hot tea spilled onto her arm. Had she really read what she thought she'd read? Maybe she was tired, and her mind was playing tricks on her.

She sat down at the table and smoothed the letter out in front of her. Carefully, tracing the words with her finger, she went back over the contents again. Yes, she had read what she thought she'd read. Her heartbeat ratcheted up several notches until it felt as if it would burst out her ears.

According to the letter from Simpson and West, Martha Bernhardt had left a substantial sum of money to whoever took over the care of her precious dog, Reg. That person happened to be Gigi. And the money just happened to be enough to buy Martha's cottage. She'd have to outbid City Girl and City Boy, but she hadn't gotten the impression that they were so keen they couldn't be bought off.

The cottage was going to be hers. Reg was hers.

She felt a warm glow that had nothing to do with the hot tea she'd been sipping. And everything to do with her wonderful new life in Woodstone.

Gigi's De-Liteful Diet Tips

Presentation is one of the keys to satisfaction. Arrange your meal on attractive plates, set a place at the table and use a linen napkin. Everything is more satisfying when it looks good! If you're brown-bagging it to work, take along a real fork, knife and spoon. Nothing tastes good when eaten with plastic utensils!

Buy good ingredients. Use the money you would have spent on chips, cookies and other snack foods and treat yourself to the best meats and produce you can find. Better to enjoy a sliver of the finest French cheese than to devour an entire frozen cheesecake that tastes like the cardboard wrapping it came in.

Two words: *portion size*! No food is truly off-limits if you are careful about portion size. Eat slowly, pay attention and when you are approaching full . . . stop eating!

If you don't trust yourself when it comes to serving size, consider measuring and/or weighing your food for a period of time.

Serve yourself half of what you think will be a satisfying portion, but promise yourself that you can go back for seconds. Then take only half again as much as you think you want. You might be surprised to find yourself very satisfied after the first helping.

Take your lunch to work or school. It's much easier to create a satisfying but low-calorie lunch if you make it yourself. And you'll avoid the temptation of the usual lunchtime fare of burgers and pizza. And think outside the sandwich box. Leftovers make great lunches, as do soups and salads. You'll also save money. Use your savings to purchase yourself an outfit in your new size and splurge on an attractive insulated lunch bag.

Be prepared. Carry low-calorie snacks in case you are caught waiting for a meal or are suddenly starving. Apples, string cheese, almonds and baby carrots are all great to keep on hand.

······················

Recipes

······················

Shepherd's Pie De-Lite

Shepherd's pie was originally created to use up leftovers and to expand the traditional Sunday roast. It is tasty enough, however, to make in its own right! It can be loaded with fat and calories or lightened up, as this version is. It's perfect for that meal when you're craving comfort food!

1 tablespoon olive oil
1 medium onion, chopped
2 garlic cloves, pressed
1.25 lbs. lean ground turkey
1 cup sliced mushrooms
1 cup frozen peas
Salt and freshly ground pepper to taste
1 10.5-ounce can fat-free turkey gravy
¼ cup ketchup

1 tablespoon Worcestershire sauce
Mashed potatoes (see recipe below)
3 tablespoons grated Parmesan cheese

Heat oven to 350°.

Heat olive oil in sauté pan over medium heat. Add chopped onion and pressed garlic, and cook until soft. Add ground turkey and cook, stirring occasionally, until meat is cooked through. Add sliced mushrooms and cook, stirring, for 1 minute. Stir in frozen peas and add salt and freshly ground black pepper to taste.

Mix turkey gravy, ketchup and Worcestershire sauce and pour over turkey mixture. Mix thoroughly and transfer to a casserole dish. Spread mashed potatoes (see below) evenly on top and sprinkle with grated Parmesan cheese.

Bake until bubbly, approximately 30 minutes.

Makes 6 servings. 376 calories/serving.

Mashed Potatoes

4 to 5 medium-sized potatoes, peeled and cut into
    quarters
Skim or low-fat milk

Place potatoes in saucepan and cover with cold water. Bring to a boil and cook until tender when pierced with a knife. Drain potatoes, add milk as needed and mash. (Quantity of milk will depend on density and age of potatoes.)

Pork Tenderloin Stuffed with Spinach and Feta

*Pork tenderloins, usually packaged in pairs, are very lean,
rivaling even chicken breasts. This stuffing provides enough
for a pair of tenderloins, or around 2.5 pounds of meat.
Both pieces can be filled and cooked, or one can be frozen
for future use. Use 1 tablespoon of oil per tenderloin for
browning.*

1 package pork tenderloin, approximately 2.5 lbs.
1 5-ounce package baby spinach
3 garlic cloves, pressed
1 pinch nutmeg
1 cup crumbled fat-free feta cheese
1–2 tablespoons olive oil
Fat-free cooking spray

Heat oven to 350°.

Spray sauté pan with cooking spray and heat over
medium heat. Add pressed garlic cloves and sauté for a
minute or two, stirring and making sure the garlic doesn't
burn. Add spinach and a pinch of nutmeg and sauté until
spinach is wilted but still bright green, approximately 3
minutes.

Butterfly each tenderloin: Using a very sharp knife, preferably with a long, thin blade, slice almost, but not quite, all
the way through each tenderloin along its length. Lay tenderloin open on cutting board. Place half of the filling along
its length on one side, spreading evenly. Fold tenderloin
pieces together and secure with toothpicks or kitchen twine.
Repeat with second tenderloin.

Heat 1 tablespoon of olive oil in sauté pan over medium to high heat. Brown tenderloin on both sides, approximately 5 minutes per side. (At this point you can remove the first tenderloin, add an additional 1 tablespoon of olive oil and brown second tenderloin, or you can wrap and freeze the second tenderloin for future use.)

If your pan is oven safe, place pan and meat in oven (alternatively, transfer meat to an oven-safe baking pan) and bake for 1 hour or until internal temperature reads 160° on an instant-read thermometer.

Allow meat to sit 5 minutes before slicing into 1-inch slices.

Each tenderloin makes 4 servings, 8 servings total. 349 calories/serving.

SERVING SUGGESTION: Orzo tossed with olive oil, Parmesan cheese, lemon zest and parsley.

Chicken Tortilla Soup

Craving Tex-Mex? This soup will surely satisfy but for far fewer calories and less fat than the typical Tex-Mex meal.

1 medium onion, chopped
2 garlic cloves, pressed
1 tablespoon olive oil
1 lb. skinless, boneless chicken breasts or chicken tenderloins cut into bite-sized pieces.
1 4-ounce can of chopped green chilies
1 15-ounce can diced tomatoes
2 14.5-ounce cans reduced-fat chicken broth

1½ teaspoons chili powder
1 teaspoon ground cumin
4 tablespoons flour
½ cup water
1 15-ounce can black beans, drained and rinsed
1 cup frozen corn

Saute onion and garlic in olive oil until soft and tender, approximately 3 minutes. Add chicken, chilies, tomatoes, chicken broth and spices. Bring to a boil, reduce heat and simmer for 15 minutes.

Mix flour and water to create a "slurry." Add to soup and stir well. Add beans and frozen corn and simmer for 10 minutes more.

If desired, top with low-fat or fat-free sour cream and baked corn tortilla strips: Cut corn tortillas in strips and place on baking sheet. Spray with fat-free cooking spray and bake at 400° until golden brown.

Makes 6 servings. 190 calories/serving.

This soup can also be made using leftover white meat chicken—just cut into bite-sized pieces and add with the beans and corn.

Anytime Veggie Frittata

This frittata is extremely versatile. You can substitute whatever vegetables you have on hand, and it can be made in advance and reheated in the microwave. It's great for breakfast but also makes a wonderful lunch or light dinner.

1 small onion, chopped
1 cup frozen broccoli, cooked al dente
1 cup sliced mushrooms
3 slices Canadian bacon, diced
1 tablespoon olive oil
4 eggs, beaten
Salt and freshly ground pepper to taste
¼ cup low-fat grated cheddar or Parmesan cheese

Heat oven to 350°.

Heat olive oil in oven-safe pan over medium heat. Add onion and sauté until soft, 2 to 3 minutes. Add broccoli, mushrooms and Canadian bacon and sauté briefly, 1 to 2 minutes or until mushrooms begin to turn golden.

Beat eggs with salt and pepper and pour over vegetable mixture in pan, tilting pan to make sure eggs cover entire surface. Cook until bottom begins to set slightly, approximately 1 minute.

Sprinkle with cheese and place pan in oven. Bake until top is puffed and beginning to turn golden, approximately 10 to 15 minutes. Cut into 4 wedges and serve.

Makes 4 servings. 185 calories/serving.